Monkey Jungle Town

by

Dug Popovich & Roland Minez

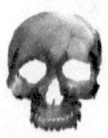

ISBN: 978-0-9961147-2-1
ISBN-10: 0-9961147-2-6
ISBN-13: 978-0-9961147-2-1

To:

Jack, Coop, Cora and Cole.

Roar

Love, Pop

To:

Marie and Julia.

Dream in the Day, Be Dangerous

With Love, Your Father

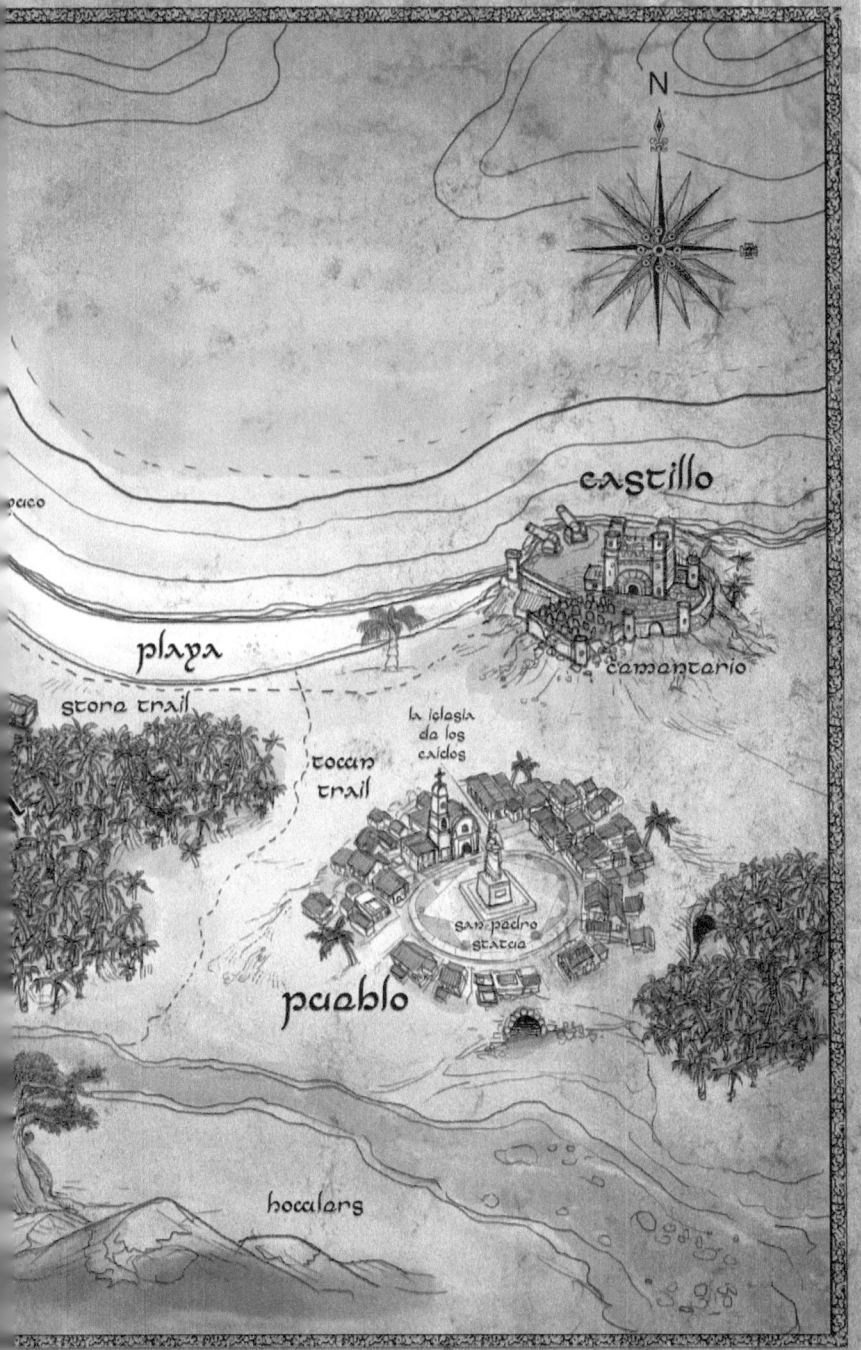

Chapter 1

From above, the beach looked peaceful.

It curved like a cutlass, slicing a sliver of white sand between an endless expanse of blue sea and green jungle. To the east, a Spanish castillo crumbled atop a rocky isthmus. To the west, a jungle mountain rose high into a cloud. In between, a string of simple cabañas dotted the shoreline and a small pueblo hugged the coast. White coral walls and corrugated tin roofs sparkled through incandescent palms. It was simply—as Don Granada said eight years earlier when he first cut through the Interior and saw it—Paradise.

But onshore, a body lay face down in the surf.

The body was tall and athletic like a soldier, but bent and weathered from sun and sea, like an acacia on the high steppe. Its cheeks were hollowed and its ribs showed through its back like a starved horse. It wore shipwrecked shorts and had unruly hair and a long beard, which was ratted and matted with seaweed and salt. It was a wild animal. Part human, part sea.

Waves lapped against it, covering its fingers and toes in wet sand, as if the only thing the Land knew to do with this Sea-thing—was bury it.

Up-beach, a ghost-dog, with one ear and three legs, emerged from a stand of high palms, shimmering like a mirage in the salty air. The mutt seemed to sense the body and trotted directly down the beach towards it, as if it was scheduled to meet it when it arrived but was running late.

When the mutt neared, it slowed and angled in on the body sideways. It slinked its head low like a hyena, prowled closer, and sniffed the body's hand and hair. A wave caught the dog's paw by surprise and it jumped back, then returned, carefully.

After a moment, the mutt looked around and sniffed high air. It looked back up the beach and down, then nuzzled its scarred snout in the body's neck…

And nudged.

Chapter 2

In what was to be the last perfect morning in Monkey Jungle Town for many years, Don Granada sat on his terrace and sipped his café. Waves broke silently on a distant reef, and falcons glided on thermals overhead. Closer in, a newspaper lay on the small mesa in front of him – the first that had arrived in the pueblo in three weeks. Its headline shouted, *Rabies Spreads*, but he eyed a small article at the bottom, that noted:

> Castaway Rescued
>
> Department of Defense officials confirmed that Mexican fisherman rescued a U.S. Army officer off the coast of Tulum Monday. The officer, First Lieutenant Casey "Jinx" Luck, had been adrift in a battered dingy for 87 days. Luck, who was dehydrated but in otherwise sound form, said that his helicopter crashed during a routine training exercise off the coast of Brazil, and everyone else in his platoon burnt to death. They have been categorized; 'Lost at Sea.'

Don Granada leaned back in his chair and scratched his chin.
The currents don't run like that, he thought.
As he did, his daughter, Santa Lucia Granada Braganza, breezed out of the house and onto the terrace. She stopped in front of him and said,
"A body washed ashore."
"Is it burnt?" He quipped, half-jokingly.
"No. It's not burnt. But it has been stabbed. And it is alive."
He cantered his chin and looked directly at her.
Many years later, she would still remember the glint in his eye and the small curl that slowly formed in the corner of his lip, like she'd just told him that a friend he'd lost in the war had returned alive. She realized that she'd seen this look before, and that every time she had, something ended up discovered, conquered, freed or killed shortly after. Tectonic plates shifted, and the world rearranged. She waited until the full weight of the oddity sunk in and he inhaled to reply, then she added:
"Or it was alive. Thirty minutes ago."

Chapter 3

Don Diego Granada Velasquez, they said, was toasted and cursed by outlaws and priests in bars and monasteries on six of the seven continents. At sixty-six years old, he had light eyes, a strong jaw, and a Hemmingway beard. He was six foot and fifteen stone, solid and big-boned, with thick hands, a round, tight grandpa belly, and old-man muscle, built from hunting bonefish and boar.

He was rumored to have spied for the British, snuck into Mecca, mapped the Empty Quarter, scuttled a galleon, slept with a Sultan's wife in Marrakech, survived two plane crashes, saved the Man of the Hole, cultivated the spider orchid, discovered a salt-water snake, found and then lost the Lost City of the Were-Jaguar, thrown Sandinistas from a helicopter, survived the Sand Sea, tackled a suicide bomber, cut a pygmy from a python on the River Congo, delivered a litter of albino leopards near Manu, been shot by a poison-tipped arrow, invented a hookaroon for tropical mahogany, crossed the Tanarú Gap on foot, summited Nanda Devi the day after it was closed to climbers, been slapped by a Maharaja with a white glove, and played, and won, a game of Russian roulette against the Mad Czar to free a Brazilian princess, even though the Mad Czar disappeared in the upper Amazon ten years before Don Granada was even born.

Although many of his older feats from older eras could not be proved, or disproved, it was widely agreed that he had hacked a trail through the Interior and over the mountains, rediscovered the lost pueblo after it had been banished and forgotten during La Campaña Desesperada, cured the sick and scattered survivors of a rare tropical disease, and carved his Ranchero, beach bar and cabañas out of the jungle's ribs.

Immediately after his daughter told him about the body, he got up from the table without finishing his café. He held her arms in his hands for a moment and kissed her forehead, then strode out of the Ranchero and down to the beach to see it for himself.

Chapter 4

Don Granada emerged from a canopy of strangler figs and ficus and stepped onto the beach. Fifty yards ahead, a crowd of townsfolk and tourists stood under a palm and circled the body like a séance. A sunburnt arm stuck out of the onlookers, laying lifeless on the ground.

Don Granada bowled towards the crowd, which parted like a school of fish with the sheer weight of his presence and the force of his respected authority as he neared. When it parted, he saw the town butcher in the epicenter, holding a clever over the survivor, about to kill him.

"Whoa whoa whoa! What're you doing!?"

"Chopping off his wrist." The butcher, Butch, said, holding the clever high.

"Why?"

"So he can't shoot."

Don Granada stopped and froze, befuddled.

"Shoot what?"

"Me. For one," the town blacksmith, Blacky, reasoned. He didn't want to get shot. Who did?

"He works with the Bonesetter," the town merchant, Santiago del Toro, explained, explaining nothing.

"How do you know that?"

Everyone stared. Nobody replied. Sun glistened off the clever.

"How do you know he doesn't?" Santiago countered, narrowing his eyes suspiciously.

"Put that down."

Butch gruffed but lowered his clever, disappointed.

"Back up. Give him some room."

Don Granada nudged the crowd back and stepped forward, casting a merciful shadow over the sunburnt body.

The castaway was in his mid-thirties and well built, tall but weathered, with his shipwrecked shorts and matted hair. His eyes were crusted shut with salt and he didn't move. A six-foot tentacle of kelp clutched an ankle and ran back down the beach to the water, as if the churning, frothing Sea fought to the end to keep him from reaching the beach and escaping.

Escaping what? Don Granada wondered.

"This man," Mulata from the Amazon assessed, "isn't supposed to be alive. The Sea tried to drown him and the Land tried to bury him."

"And he was planning to murder Blacky," Santiago added.

"I told you," Blacky stated, like that proved his point.

"Best we kill him now," Campasino concluded, "like a runt."

"*Mmgh*," Don Granada grunted, neither agreeing or disagreeing, but calculating.

"Cadejo found him." Don Granada's grandson, Tuck, said.

Granada noticed Tuck standing beside him. He smiled proudly and rested his big hand on Tuck's head, then spotted Cadejo, the beach mutt who found him, panting and smiling in the shade of a nearby uvero tree, next to a weathered oar that leaned against the tree's craggy branches and flakey bark.

"He was lashed to that oar," Campasino said.

"Seven years bad luck," a big black Garifuna Mama said, standing with her two kids, "to be lashed to an oar."

"That's ridiculous," Campasino corrected, "It's eight."

Don Granada squatted and checked the castaway's pulse. It pumped blood through the veins. Or something. He rolled the castaway on his side, and there, in the back near the liver, was a two-inch puncture wound like Santa said, clean and partially sealed, but fresh. Probably a few days old. Don Granada checked his pulse again to ensure he was really alive.

"The blade wasn't serrated," Don Granada's old friend, Barboza, said.

Barboza stood outside the circle, and while everyone else gazed in at the castaway, Barboza gazed out, surveilling the sea from which the castaway came, as if looking for the man who stabbed him.

Granada inspected the castaway's fingernails, which were splintered, and his gums, which were bloody.

"Scurvy," Barboza diagnosed.

"Get him some coconut water." Granada ordered.

The town deaf-mute, who everyone simply called Mudo, or mute, because nobody knew his name, because he never told anyone he had one, scurried up a nearby palm with his machete and chopped off a coconut. It thumped ground and Butch hacked it, happy to finally be hacking something.

As he did, Don Granada inspected a piece of orange plastic that was lashed to the castaway's arm. It was thick but semi-transparent, like it'd been torn from a biohazard bag and had faded in the sun. It looked like it was meant to be used as some kind of waterproof sheath or envelope, because he could see a dry piece of paper and what looked like a photograph inside.

"Give me your knife."

Tuck handed his grandfather a small knife with an ocelot bone handle. Don Granada lifted the castaway's forearm and pressed the blade against the plastic to cut it open, but as soon as he did, the castaway's eyes sprung open instead.

OUUUUUU...

The crowd gasped. The castaway's eyes were as azul and watery as the sea. They locked on the first thing they saw, which was Don Granada.

The castaway thrust his arm up and clutched Granada's collar with surprising strength. He pulled Granada close and croaked, just loud enough for him to hear:

"I have to get back."

"Why?" Granada asked.

The castaway's eyes darted around the crowd, dilated and crazed, seeing but not registering. They circled back to Granada and his mouth parted to speak, but nothing came out.

Silence.

Everyone waited. They leaned closer and listened. But the castaway's strength quickly faded. His arm collapsed and eyes closed, then his head rolled like a dead dog's and he blacked back out.

"What'd he say?" Santiago asked.

"Back..." Granada mumbled to himself, thinking.

"What?" Someone asked.

"What?" Granada repeated, looking up to the crowd.

"What'd he say?"

Don Granada gazed at the townsfolk and tourists for a moment, connecting dots and calculating contingencies. He was good at that, he always was, but these dots didn't make much of a clear picture so far. Backwards currents and rabies blood. The Bonesetter. And now a dead castaway – alive. He was missing something. He was missing a lot. He felt like he was about to get ambushed.

He passed Barboza a look on the orbital fringe, then stood and took commanding stock over his charge, like he'd done during The Starving Time, and when Big Mama's twins were born during the blood moon, and when Blacky thought the Eel Whores were trying to shrink his brain like cannibals while it was still inside his skull, and when Bonesetter appeared and Winter disappeared. The townsfolk watched and waited, loving and trusting him like the father he was. Yes, they were his. They were his charge. They needed him and he had to protect them, like he'd always done. He couldn't lie to them.

"Gunner." He lied, "He said his name is Gunner. He said he's a fisherman. And he fell off a boat."

Chapter 5

"Gunner" regained consciousness a week later. The first thing he did was trip and fall. He felt a pain in his foot and realized that he'd stepped on a stone and had been walking, unconsciously, like a sleepwalker, or mummy. He saw that he wore a pair of near sheer linen shorts, but was otherwise naked, and was kneeling in the middle of a dirt road in the middle of the day, clutching his makeshift orange envelope. It was a disorientating and unnerving place to wake up, particularly in underwear.

WOOF!

He looked up and saw a ragged dog sitting in the middle of the road in front of him, watching him. The dog had one ear and three legs and was panting and smiling. Gunner grunted at him. Cadejo growled back.

"Hehya Gunner!" A voice chirped. "Where're ya going, fishin'?"

Gunner tracked back on the voice from his knee, over his shoulder, and saw a padre waddle up and materialize out of a backlit sun, holding a churro.

"He's going to haunt me." Gunner mumbled.

"Who?" Padre asked, chomping on his churro.

Gunner stared up at Padre a second, then his eyes rolled and he swooned.

"Whoa! Whoa! Whoa! Easy fella."

Padre quickly shoved the rest of the churro in his mouth, caught Gunner and eased him to the ground.

"You need a pint or something."

Gunner sat for a moment and gathered his wits. As he did, a thought slowly surfaced from his brainstem and coalesced in his consciousness:

Get up. Get moving.

He shoved his orange envelope in his back pocket, then pressed his hand on the ground and forced himself to stand. Padre helped him to his feet and blood rushed to his brain. His senses sharpened and he studied Padre closer.

Padre was a jolly-looking, rotund friar with fair skin, chubby cheeks, small circular eyes and a slanted haircut that was sweat-plastered to his forehead. He seemed to wheeze slightly through his nose when he spoke, and he wore a brown frock that bulged around his belly. Churro crumbs sparkled on his frock in the sun, and he kept it wrapped around him with a white rope belt that had a spatula holstered in it like a pistol. Aside from the spatula, Gunner thought Padre looked exactly like how he'd imagine a padre to look if he imagined one.

"The bus…" Gunner said. "Is there a bus station here?"

"A bus station…?" Padre mused, mashing his lips to the side and looking around like he'd never seen the town before.

Gunner followed Padre's gaze and saw that Spanish colonial buildings lined the road. The sun beat against their red terracotta roofs and whitewashed coral walls. They had thick wooden doors and shutters, which were once painted in bright indigos, mandarins and corals, but were now faded, whitewashed and sun stained. Stucco flaked off walls, revealing patches of brick and adobe underneath. Weeds sprouted from gutters and through broken tiles and corrugated tin roofs. The place felt sandy, sleepy and forgotten, like a siesta in the sun.

"Where am I?" Gunner asked.

"Hahahaha…"

Padre giggled and his belly jiggled.

"Here, I'll show ya."

Padre led Gunner off the main road and onto Town Trail, which ran between town and the beach, perpendicular to the ocean, through brackish grass and under green palms. Padre leaned back and waddled as he walked. His belly led the way, and Cadejo trotted alongside.

"That's a chacmool stone," Padre said like a tourist guide, pointing to a relic that was overturned in the grass by the trail as they passed it. "The Mayan used it for human sacrifices. They painted the victim blue and cut out their beating hearts with flint. Mayan blue. That's where the color comes from. Then you know what they did?"

"What?"

"Wait!" Padre said, stopping suddenly. "Hear that?"

They froze in the trail and listened. Cadejo perked his ear.

WHOOP, WHOOP, WHOOP…

WHUUUU…

Distant whoops and howls.

"Howlers," Padre whispered, puckering his lips in his fat cheeks like a blowfish and narrowing his beady eyes to hear better.

"What?"

"Monkeys. Howlers. Closer than usual."

Padre listened for a second, then shrugged and continued walking.

"They tossed them down the steps."

"What?"

"The shaman. They ate the beating hearts and tossed the bodies down the temple like corn husks. Without hearts."

"Oh. The Mayan."

"But anyway, Don Granada, he's got this idea we came from monkeys. Like one day a howler just had a human baby or something, and then somehow that baby met another human monkey baby… I don't know."

"Ya, that's actually—"

"—I know, crazy. Nobody believes it, but we pretend to. People are nice here. And one less thing you know? I mean, Don Granada gets an idea in his head and oh man... And the people here just go on believing all sorts of outlandish things. They're not logical. They're dramatic. Megamelodramatic. You know what they'll believe? The most reasonable thing? Na-ah. The most en-ter-tain-ing thing. And the crazier the better."

"Uh huh."

"You died."

"What?"

"When they saved your life, you died. Don Granada, he had you at his house a week after you washed up. They took care of you. His daughter Santa, and Tuck. They're nice. And Mulata. She resurrected you from the dead, with her witchcraft, like, medically."

"Ah."

"What'd you see?"

"When?"

"When you died?"

Gunner pinched the bridge of his nose and laughed slightly to himself. Padre was talking in circles of his own creation. The townsfolk would have understood him perfectly. So Gunner was thoroughly confused.

"You could ask him about the human-monkey-babies. I wouldn't, especially with this Bonesetter and Simian business, but you could. But whatever you do, don't ask him about the treasure."

"The what?"

"The treasure. Captain Kidd's gold."

"Listen," Gunner said. "This is all very… I mean, are you for real?"

"I'll tell you what's not real, the bus station! Because we don't have one. You know you're not talking a lot of sense right now? We should probably get a pint so you can relax. But the boat comes once a day, so I guess we have a boat station. Instead of asking Don Granada about the human-monkey-babies, you should probably ask him about the boat. That would be the most logical thing to do."

Gunner rubbed his hands over his face and head and kept walking. Someone had buzzed his beard and hair, so he felt light and clean. His puncture wound was also stitched and scarring. He was still thin, but looked considerably better than he did when he washed up a week ago.

A minute later, they reached the end of the trail, or the beginning. There, the grass shortened on shore and transitioned to a bone-white beach, which disappeared under a translucent sea. Waves shushed and a seagull squawked.

From the ground, it was difficult to tell that the beach arced in a bay like a crescent moon, but detail emerged and topography rose. To the east, the beach swooped and tapered to boulders that tumbled up an escarpment, to the seawall of the old Spanish Castillo, which was built in and on the plateau to overlook the bay. The seawall was speckled with barnacles and moss, and it crumbled in ruins atop the plateau, so that only a few feet of the fort's ramparts still existed above ground, and only the stone Keep still stood in the middle. The town cemetery also sat on the plateau, within the outpost's ruins, covered in crooked headstones.

To the west, the beach swooped and widened to the base of Jungle Mountain, which rose steeply into a cloud and was covered by a double thick canopy of kapok, mahogany, mamón and strangler figs. Harpía eagles floated on the thermals around it, hunting for mammal meat and diving like seagulls for baby three-toed sloths in the upper canopy. Near the base, in the trees, sat Don Granada's Ranchero, like a watercolor stepped into.

Below this, at the foot of the mountain, where the jungle hit the beach, stood the Valhalla bar. In front of the bar, hotties tanned on the beach and splashed in the sea, near a dock that ran over the ocean. Behind Gunner, from the way he came, was the old pueblo. Onshore to his left, above the grass and under the palms, was the string of cabañas that dotted the shoreline, following the curvature of the bay like the freckles on the mestizo hooker's hip in Sao Paulo.

Gunner didn't know it, but from that very spot, Barboza had once hucked a rock that, incredibly, accidently struck and killed a white-breasted bat falcon that happened to be flying by, which, inexplicably, shot a flash-thought through Don Granada's brain that made him realize that the shaman stone, terracotta tile, crumbled Castillo, crooked headstones, simple cabañas and old growth kapoks formed a stratified history that had built itself on the bones of itself, on tectonic skin, that ebbed and flowed between riches and ruins like the tide, pushing into the jungle and being strangled back by it every time. Before the bat falcon torpedoed into the ground and Barboza had blinked, Don Granada knew that there were priests and pirates, and kingdoms to stand for a thousand years, and kingdoms that did, but eventually, the dreams and visions, sacrifices and gold, conquest and famine, and blood and madness of Kings and Fools and Gods and Men were epochs and eras whisked away in the wind.

To Gunner, it was simply the most perfect place he'd ever seen.

"Behold," Padre said, stopping in the shade of the last palm, pointing his spatula and spreading his palms like he was parting the Red Sea, "Monkey Jungle Town."

"Monkey what?"

Chapter 6

Gunner and Cadejo trekked across the beach and up to the Valhalla beach bar. The bar had a thatched roof, open sides and a wrap-around wooden deck that was shaded by palms and stretched over the sand. Scantily clad surfers, hippies and backpackers tanned outside and lounged within, laughing, drinking and chatting. The energy flowed out of Valhalla like an alluvial plain, and Gunner followed it upstream and in.

Inside, relaxing reggae swam around and through hardwood floors, exposed rafters, and open windows and walls. Drawings, paintings, maps and old photographs of battles, ships, armies and explorers hung on a long bamboo wall behind a thick mahogany bar. Maps of the Siwa Oasis, the Khumba Icefall and the Empty Quarter. Paintings of the Battle of the Little Bighorn and Camarón, the Siege of Acre and William Barret Travis at the Alamo. There was Hercules and the Hydra, Flatter's doomed march in the Sahara, Captain Cook in Tahiti, Simón Bolívar in Boyacá, Francisco Morazán in exile, Dunsterville retreating from Baku by following three lights on the mast of the British frigate, and the last known photograph of Captain Lawrence Oats near the South Pole, which was taken shortly before he said, "I am just going outside, and may be some time." There was also a photograph of a rugged man smoking a corn pipe, with the caption, "That Son of a Bitch Jan Jeffers," and an Indian painting of the loyal horse Chetak, who saved the Maharana after being cut down at the hooves by Man Singh's war elephant, swinging a Mughal sword from his trunk.

Together, the individual images formed a bigger landscape with an underlying theme: reckless adventure and open rebellion. But in all these, Don Granada appeared only once, in an amber photograph taken in the map room at Castillo San Felipe de Barajas, in Cartagena des Indes. In the photo, a regal women held Don Granada's bicep, and Santa stood between him and a man in spectacles, holding Tuck as a toddler.

Don Granada sat at the bar near the photo, drawing. He wore sandals and shorts and his shirt was open, exposing dog tags that hung from his neck above his tan Grandpa beach-belly.

"Excuse me," Gunner said, walking up. "I'm looking for Don

Granada."

Don Granada held up his drawing.

"What do you think? It's Odysseus at Sea."

It was a landscape of a small ship in a large storm on a rough sea. Gunner's right hand cramped when he saw it.

"Did you know, it took Odysseus ten years to get home after the Trojan War?"

"Ya, it's impressive." Gunner replied.

"I know, I wish I drew it."

Don Granada set the landscape down and picked up a bad copy of it on another piece of paper.

"I'm just tracing it."

"Oh. Ya well, that's uh..."

"Dog breath," Don Granada chuckled. "Actually, I did draw it. Twenty years ago. I had a premonition and drew it. I just can't now. It's strange. It's just a...a random skill I've lost. Locked in a cupboard within a cupboard somewhere. So here I sit, an old man tracing old memories."

Don Granada stared at the intricate landscape a moment, then sighed and patted Gunner on the shoulder.

"Well, I'm Diego Granada. Nice to finally talk to ya, consciously."

"Oh, Don Granada? I heard you helped me. Thank you. I owe you—"

"—It's good to see ya on your feet. You look better. A lot better. Last week when we pinched your skin, it stayed up into a ridge. Didn't go back."

Don Granada took Gunner's hand warmly and pinched the skin on his forearm. It ridged up and smoothed back out.

"Excellent. How do you feel?"

"Weak."

"Ya, food and rest. Take it easy. I was lost at sea once for twelve days. Twelve days that felt like a year. We caught a sea snake and ate every last piece of it, even a seagull we found in its stomach, half-digested. Nasty business."

"When I was out, my veins, they didn't..."

Don Granada waited.

"I mean I'm healthy? I'm not...?"

"That's right. You need some food and a pint to dull down and relax, but other than that you're healthy as a gila monster. You got some spit in your gut I'll tell ya, 'cause that would've killed most men. Twice."

Gunner half-smiled politely, and a new reggae song started playing and soothing the bar.

"Ah! My girl and mys' song!"

"Your wife's?"

A shadow passed over Don Granada's face as he glanced at the amber photograph of Cartagena, but quickly turned back and smiled again.

"No, my beer's."

He reached over the bar and dunked his hand in a bucket of half-melted ice.

"Dang," he said, pulling his arm out empty handed and nodding to an empty bottle on the counter, "looks like that was the last one. We ran out of alcohol for the first time ever, just last night. No beer, nothing. We're running low on meat too. Simian, he... Well anyway, you just missed it. But my daughter's going for more. She should get some for tonight."

He shook ice off his arm, scratched his wet fingers through his thick beard and nodded to some bottles on the shelf behind the bar. They didn't have any liquid in them, but each was filled with roots and a dead snake.

"She can also make gifiti. If it comes to that."

The bottles and their contents looked like body parts in a medieval lab.

"I heard there's a boat I can catch?" Gunner said, not planning to be here to try it.

"That's right. Comes every evening and leaves every morning. The captain is a salty son of a bitch. Usually takes a swing at someone then passes out drunk around here. But he's always up the next day, ready to captain. It'll be here this afternoon. You can leave on it tomorrow if you like."

"That's the soonest I can go?"

"What's the rush?"

Gunner looked around a second, then back at Don Granada.

"I gotta get back in thirty days, or they'll cancel my phone."

Granada eyed him and he grinned, obviously kidding.

"There's a woman and a wedding involved."

"Ah... There usually is. Your wedding?"

"No. But my woman."

Don Granada grinned knowingly, then stood and patted him on the shoulder. "Well, tomorrow's the soonest you can leave. That still gives you twenty-nine days. In the meantime, have a beer tonight and relax. I got a cabaña for you."

He started walking out, and Gunner followed.

"Getting that phone reactivated though, is a pain in the ass."

Chapter 7

Gunner followed Don Granada onto the beach. His bare feet dug through the sunbaked sand awkwardly while Granada's sandals slide through it effortlessly. Gunner hopped to a shadow cast by a cayuco to cool them for a moment in the shade.

The cayuco's wooden hull curved out of the beach and its keel arced skyward. Three girls tanned next to it. The sun shimmered off their sunscreened skin. Young and hot. Breasts and bikinis. Tequila, Coco and Sail.

The girls eyed Gunner, and he suddenly remembered he was only wearing sheer linen shorts.

"Holaaa," Tequila purred.

"Heh."

White teeth and glossy lips.

"Wanna borrow my flats?" Coco teased, arching a long, tan leg at him and pointing pink toes at his crotch. Her flat dangled off her toes and sparkled with silver sequins. "I don't need them. I only have three days to live."

"Jur not dyeen bitch," Tequila shot.

"I'm not crazy. I have Lupus!"

"Can ju even die from that?"

"All the work I do, and on my last-wish vacation, THIS is what I have to deal with?"

"Work?" Sail jumped in. "You don't even have a job."

"Ya, cause my therapist said I should quit, since I'm DYING!"

"Mall modeling's not a job," Sail stated.

"Ju know I love ju," Tequila said.

"I love you too," Coco replied sweetly.

"Jur sexy hot. But jur not dyeen."

Gunner chuckled, then hot-stepped on to catch Don Granada down the beach. Coco started to call after him, but stopped and pouted.

Granada led Gunner off the beach and under the palms to a cabaña. It appeared to doze in the shade. It rested five feet off the ground on pylons, above short Bermuda grass, and it had a thatched roof and wooden deck, which was made of dense mahogany planks that smelled freshly cut. A hammock and a Swahili plantation chair, which was inlaid with camel bone, lounged on the deck. Palms rustled gently in the wind overhead, and a kingfisher sang.

"Nice," Gunner said.

"Ya," Don Granada replied, eyeing the Spanish Keep that peeked out of the graveyard in the distance, "everyone likes it here."

They walked up the stairs and onto the deck. Don Granada nodded to the oar Gunner washed ashore with, which lay off to the side.

"You know the story about Odysseus and his oar, in the Odyssey?"

"No."

"Well, in it, some guy tells Odysseus to take an oar from his ship and walk inland, until he comes to a place where nobody knows what an oar is. A place where they mistake it for a winnowing fan. Then, when you walk so far inland that nobody knows what an oar is, then and only then, you'll find peace. You'll be done with the sea, and your journey will end."

Gunner smiled softly.

"What's a winnowing fan?"

"Hell I don't know. Looks like an oar I guess."

They laughed.

"Listen, you've been through a lot. Stay as long as you like. This is just a beach, and here you're just a fisherman. Who fell off a boat."

"A fisherman?"

"Ya. A fisherman. If you want to leave tomorrow, great, but if you want to stay and rest a while… well, think about it. Maybe that'd be good for ya. Maybe what you want to go back to, you shouldn't go back to."

Gunner nodded. Granada gripped his shoulder and smiled, then shuffled down the cabaña's steps.

"I'll have my grandson bring some clothes, and a fishing net," he said over his shoulder as he walked off.

When he faded from sight, Gunner looked at his oar. It looked like a dry whale bone on dry land. It'd been with him a long time, or what felt like a long time, like an old friend. He picked it up and hucked it as far as he could.

It tomahawked through the sky and crashed through some distant bushes. He then fell back in the hammock, put his feet up and wiggled his toes.

"Dry land…" He whispered. "Paradise."

He took a deep breath and exhaled slowly, then watched a white puffy cloud drift across the blue sky like a jellyfish. Everything was quiet and peaceful. Tranquil.

Perfect.

Something was wrong. He felt...

Safe.

Which made the hairs prick up on the back of his neck.

Chapter 8

The Bonesetter, they called him, followed Polito down an overgrown leopard trail in the deep jungle.

Polito was short for polio in bastardized swamp-slang. Polito didn't have polio, but they called him that because he was the runt of the runt, born with a stunted alligator arm like his crippled upbringing. He was up-brought by whores in the swamp shanties on the jungle-fringe, in humidity, sex-stank and mosquitos. Whores who smelled like dried eel and were run through by toothless fishermen with flakey fish scales stuck in their pubic hairs. Growing up, Polito had jumped between shacks on rickety stilts above mollusk shells in the mangroves, surviving on the cast-offs of these cast-offs like a blue crab with a missing claw, and on whatever detritus he could scavenge from the tide, which brought and left things in the stilt roots and dank peat when it receded. Algae, amoebas…Himself. Even a rusty conquistador helmet, once. Fisher-fights in slap shacks over brackish pussy and warm beer. Intertidal swamp-suck had ebbed and flowed over him his entire life, but he'd swallowed and survived it all, so he was stunted and wiry, but armored with antibodies and tough as a caiman.

They hacked branches and vines with machetes like explorers, while mahogany and guanacaste trees towered overhead, eating the light from the world. Sweat beaded on their neck and stuck their shirts to their chests.

After a hard hour, Polito finally pulled up and stopped, then turned to Bonesetter and whispered:

"Okay. He's around the corner."

Bonesetter nodded with sharp, eager eyes.

"Now you promise me, you won't tell Cazador that I trapped him for you, and didn't kill him?"

"No no, come on, let's go."

"No you won't promise me, or no you won't tell Caz?"

"Yes I won't not tell Caz."

"What?"

"Come on."

"And," Polito added, blocking his path in one last shot at sensibility, which he didn't even believe in much, because the world had never been sensible to him, "you gotta work quick, because if he calls his amigos—"

"—Well then, lets hurry."

Polito hesitated, but Bonesetter walked around him.

There, on the other side of a buttress trunk, was a big black howler, snared at the wrist in a trap. The snare was made from a six-foot-long steel cable, which was latched to a climbing liana. The steel had scraped the black hair off the howler's forearm and cut into his wrist when he struggled, rubbing it pink and raw. The howler, however, didn't seem defeated by it. Instead, his big black eyes were like human eyes; calculating.

Bonesetter smiled.

He smiled and won.

Bonesetter was tall and fit, clean-cut and attractive. He had short hair and a jock-face like a college athlete. Before, in Cartagena and the Lesser Antilles, he dove for conch, and did it so well that he became a champion free-diver, until he blacked out too many times from diving too deep too long and not being able to stop. He never could stop. That was his problem. He had everything, lost it all, and wanted it back.

"Whoa," Bonesetter said, "he's big."

"Ya," Polito replied, "Cazador thinks they're getting bigger."

"Who, the howlers?"

"No, your balls."

"That's not possible."

Polito shrugged, pretty sure they were still talking about the howlers and not his balls. Bonesetter squatted, smiled and wagged a carrot at the howler. The howler straightened and stared back, not smiling. The hair around his neck bristled, amplifying his size further.

"They're impressive up close." Polito said, inching back.

"Stop talking about my balls. We got a job to do."

"He's gonna eat your balls, 'cause I don't think they eat carrots."

"Shhh…If you show fear, they can sense it."

The howler lowered his head, flared his mane and bowed his neck to strike. Bonesetter inched closer, just out of range of the cable, then the howler tightened his black face, coned his lips and howled—a deep, guttural, jet-wash growl.

HAUUUUUUUU…

"Hooooly COW!" Bonesetter yelled, laughing and covering his ears with the carrot. "Hahahaha! That fear thing is BULLSHIT!"

But Polito was afraid, and he didn't fear much, because he'd always, up until this point, survived worse. He put his good hand on the butt of the revolver in his peasant-rope waistband and looked around. Trees on trees. Green on green. Shadow on shadow. Sliced light, layered light, speckled light… All trees and light. All greens and slashes. And hallucinogens, released by the trees. This was their world, the trees. Amoebas, pathogens and pollen. Biological warfare in a chemical war-zone.

He strained his eyes to splice the static, which flipped in his cornea and scrambled his thoughts. Gigantic emergents framed the jungle up, while tiny ants and bacteria tore it down. Leaves growing into sky overhead. Roots worming through soil underfoot. Trees as big above ground as they were below. Harpía eagles snatching sloths in their talons as they clung to branches. Blood bats and strangler figs. Clicking, choking, hunting, hiding. Dangles and deception. Alliance and betrayal. Predators and prey. One and the same, cannibalizing each other to survive. *Why is the chameleon camouflaged?*

Because everything here is here to eat.

"Hurry up."

"I need a blood sample."

Bonesetter opened a black doctor's bag and rooted through it. Something flickered in the canopy above. Something crashed through branches behind.

"They know we're—"

"—Shhh. I'm trying to concentrate."

"We're too far."

Polito glanced over his shoulder, back the way they came. Bonesetter extracted a syringe from his bag and turned to the howler.

WHOOOT!

Suddenly, the howler bared fang and lunged. Bonesetter flinched and fell off his heels and onto his ass as the howler's chain snapped taut and ripped him back. His sharp, white monkey canines snapped shut on empty air above Bonesetter's crotch. The syringe hit the forest floor and the howler spun, grabbed his cable with his furry black fingers and yanked, trying to rip it from the vine. Bonesetter sprung to his feet and dove for the syringe, but the howler whipped his fifth limb, his prehensile tail, and snatched it in its curl.

Bonesetter and the howler squared off and stared, ready to spring. Slowly, Bonesetter recoiled into a squat. The howler flicked his tail like a cat and flashed the sharp syringe in it.

"RAH!"

Suddenly, Bonesetter yelled, jumped and tackled the big howler. They screeched, fought and rolled on the ground like cartoon characters, entangling in the chain.

"Idiot!" Polito yelled, skinning his gun. "Get outta there!"

"RAGHH!"

Bonesetter growled, rolled atop the howler and choked him, digging his hands into his fur and fighting to keep his grip around the beast's powerful neck, like a tree trunk made of muscle. As he did, the howler raised the syringe in his tail above Bonesetter's back.

Polito aimed at the howler, but it was too entangled with Bonesetter for a safe shot. The howler lashed his tail down like a scorpion and plunged the syringe deep into Bonesetter's back.

"AHHH!"

Bonesetter screamed and arched, losing his grip on the howler's neck. He thrashed behind to rip out the syringe out of his spine while the howler twisted to attack.

BANG! BANG! BANG!

Polito blasted the cable on the vine, splitting it in half. The howler hooted and leapt, then realized he was free and monkey-sprung back. In a single, fluid motion, he bounced up a nearby branch, dragging the cable behind him from his bloody wrist.

Bonesetter lay on his stomach with the syringe sticking out his spine.

"You're right," he groaned, "I don't think they eat carrots. I should've tried an apple."

"I should've shot you both."

SWOOSH.

Branches rattled and shook overhead. Howlers were gathering in the high canopy - the alpha howler's amigos.

Polito spun around, looking up.

Black masses encircled.

"Get up." He whispered.

"DAMMIT!" Bonesetter yelled. "I was trying to HELP him!"

"We gotta go."

Alpha sat still on the branch a few feet away, staring at them silently, eerily, with those human, calculating eyes. Eyes that reached back to the first man. To the cosmos. *I am the Alpha and the Omega, the Beginning, and the End.*

Another howler swung from a vine behind, creeping closer.

"Now."

Then, Alpha coned his mouth, extended his jaw and—

—*HAUUUUUUUU…*

HUH HUH HUH HUH…

And the jungle erupted with deafening howls. From all sides; above, around, and seemingly within.

Bonesetter scrambled to his feet and grabbed his machete.

ACHHH!

Suddenly, Alpha leapt from the branch, hit the ground and monkey-sprung at them as his army crashed down through the canopy behind him.

Polito spun in every direction and fired blindly.

BANG! BANG! BANG! BANG!

"RUN!"

Chapter 9

Gunner slept and swayed peacefully in the hammock as the sun set. His leg dangled over the side and a walking stick crept up his arm. Cadejo snored on the deck under him, palms rustled above, a gecko clicked, and the ocean rolled softly in the distance. It was peaceful—evening peaceful—after the diurnals had stopped hunting and before the nocturnals began.

CHINK!

Gunner bolted up and patted his hip. He looked panicked and felt lost, then realized a barefoot beach kid stared at him wide-eyed on the deck a few feet away, standing over a crate of guava juice.

"Sorry, mister," Tuck said.

Gunner looked around, remembered where he was and regained his bearings, then exhaled and relaxed.

"Ya, don't worry about it, kid."

Tuck tossed some sandals and clothes on the deck at Gunner's feet like he was feeding a lion and afraid to get too close. Even after being battered and beat by the sea, Gunner was a tall man with a strong frame.

"Thanks."

Cadejo jumped up and licked Tuck, who laughed and scratched his ear. When he did, something rustled in the bush behind them. Cadejo popped back down and went sharp. His ear perked and his scruff rose. Tuck drew his knife.

They stared over the deck and into the bush, listening, waiting.

Nothing.

Gunner grabbed the sandals.

"You know you can hurt yourself with that," he said, putting the sandals on. "Look, here, hold it like this."

He stood and adjusted Tuck's grip on the knife.

"You like it here?" Gunner asked.

"Sure. I guess. I mean, I got my... friends. And my dad takes me fishing."

"Anyone here sick?"

"Whatta ya mean?"

"You know, sick."

Tuck stared at him, waiting for a better explanation.

"Enlarged veins, muscles… unusual strength, swollen heart…"

"That doesn't sound sick."

"It is."

Tuck shook his head, no. As he did, two chubby girls trucked by the cabaña on Shore Trail, vamped-up for Valhalla. Barb and Pat.

"And DON'T mention chocolate syrup," Barb said as they passed. "You mentioned that waaaay too early last time, and look where that got us."

Pat pursed her lips and nodded in agreement.

Gunner smirked and followed their flow to Valhalla. White Christmas lights sparkled around it. Music waved from within and a group of happy hippies flowed toward it from the beach like moths, smiling and laughing.

"Is it true you fell off a boat?" Tuck asked.

"Huh?"

"Did you fall off a boat?"

"Ya."

"So you're a fishermen?"

"No." Gunner turned back and looked at him. "I'm a bosun."

"What's that? Like a liar?"

Gunner chuckled.

"No. It means I'm a boatswain, a crewman. On a merchant ship. Good with marlinspike, you know? Knots and rigs."

Tuck shrugged, then looked back at the happy people walking to Valhalla.

"Some girls were asking about you."

"Ya?"

"Ya. They want to know if you're coming tonight."

Gunner nodded at Valhalla.

"Ya, so I can leave. I'm gonna talk to that captain about that boat."

Chapter 10

As Gunner dressed for Valhalla, Don Granada and Barboza played dominos inside. They sat at the table they always sat at, their table, off to the side by an open wooden window. A large banana leaf peaked through the widow and a keel-billed toucan sat on the windowsill beside them, looking in like a third player as the bar filled with people around them. With smiles and energy. With youth.

Barboza didn't look young and he didn't smile. He snarled, and looked like he'd just walked in from a bush battle in the nineteenth century. He wore an open tunic, a holster sash with a revolver, dusty bush boots, and short, khaki, Afrikaner shorts. He had a big, round head, a thick handlebar mustache and scarred, grizzled shins. A row of slightly rusty medals paraded across his chest, and a Tibetan ghost dagger stuck out of his waistband. He looked ridiculous. But he didn't play grabass and nobody fucked with him, because he was a veteran of every war that ever was.

"Neptune churned him up and spit him out," Barboza spat, handing a nut to the toucan, who leaned over the table from the windowsill and pinched it in his colorful beak. "And God knows what happened before that. But he sure as shit never fished, or worked on no boat, and I'm not convinced there's any wedding or a woman neither."

"There's always a woman," Don Granada replied.

"So some shooter washes up with a stab wound and scurvy, and needs to get back in thirty days to ruin a wedding? Come on. Bullcrap. Something else's going on."

"He could have combat sensory overload," Granada diagnosed. "Hypersensitivity from intense life events, which can transition to anxiety when you leave the war if you can't dull-down."

"Dull-down? Where'd you get a psychology book from, Sigmund?"

"I just made that up. But he probably has some combat fatigue. Possible hallucinations… Hell, the starving and scurvy alone can give you that."

"Why don't you just say he's got Human, huh? Cause that's what happens to us. We fight, get our asses kicked, get our hearts broken, pain and disappointment… Some people get back up and some don't. That's all. If a caveman got chased by a sabercat he was just happy to make it back to his cave. Now, hell, he's gotta talk to someone about his *feelings* in a *safe space* and how much the big bad tiger upset him. No shit! IT'S A SABERCAT! It better scare you. If it doesn't, something's wrong with ya. We go crazy because we don't want to be crazy, but we're supposed to be crazy. That's how we're made. If we didn't have holes in our souls we wouldn't have drive, and if we didn't have drive we wouldn't survive. Look it even rhymes. There's some fucken psychology for you Sigmund. We've gotten soft. I'll show you what hard is."

"He's at least got clinical PTSD," Granada assessed.

"Stop making shit up."

"Post-Traumatic Stress Disorder."

"Bullshit."

"You got it too."

"Bullshit."

"Twice. PTSD on top of PTSD. And that's a minor problem for you."

"You know how to avoid the Post Traumatic Disease?" Barboza asked, pointing a domino at his old friend. "Find more trauma! If you never leave the trauma, you can't get the post-trauma syndrome."

Barboza slapped the domino down on the table and gave Granada a ridiculous big-eyed look.

"Lord."

"Look," Barboza continued, "ya so great, we got an outsider here who didn't bring his own guitar and vegetarian spatula with him, that's refreshing, but this meat-eater… He's either one of three things."

"What?"

"He's either what he says he is, a rig and deck guy. A regular Joe…"

Granada smirked. *Ya right.*

"…Or you're right, he's connected to that helo and soldier they rescued. Ya, maybe, but if so, that raises a whole 'nother set of preguntas, like who stabbed him? Where are the others? And what's the government hiding? The Government's always hiding something, and everyone knows 'routine training mission' is code for bullshit. If that's the case then he's all jacked up. He's more spun around his monkey brain than the hairy hippies. He may never get his balls back and heh, no fault of his own, because whatever happened to him out there… coming in like that, after eighty-something days on blue-water, ya that's worth a toast, but I don't trust him."

"That's what I'm saying."

"That you don't trust him?"

"No, that he's all jacked up."

"Oh." Barboza said, "I wasn't listening. I couldn't hear you over my P-T-S-D."

"What's three?" Don Granada asked.

"Three what?"

"Your third… hypothesis."

"Oh ya, the correct one."

"What?"

"That he's a spy. Working with Bonesetter. For Simian."

Chapter 11

Gunner strolled up the beach and entered Valhalla.

Inside, a hip crowd partied. Hotties danced, drank and laughed in skirts and glitter, board shorts and sandals. Energy and heat flowed with the music and rolled like waves, because there was no other place in the universe, only the Here and Now.

He scanned the room and his eyes fell like gravity on the fiery bartender. Tanktop, tall and toned. Santa Granada.

"Last one!" Don Granada's daughter called.

She poured a strip of whiskey on the bar and lit it afire. Sail, Surfer, Coco, Coy, Bikini, Bumster, Frat Boy, Trust Fund, Tequila, and Yummy Chad flinched back and laughed. Santa poured the rest of the whiskey in shot glasses and slid them through the blaze. They caught fire as they passed. The group grabbed and pounded them, swallowing the flames like dragons.

Tequila slapped her empty shot glass on the bar, poured salt on the back of her hand and grabbed the last two shots.

"What're you doing?" Coco asked.

"I'm a buzz-saw baby, and chicos me chocan."

Tequila threw Coco a cocky Cuban smirk, then winked, turned and strode directly at Gunner with the shots. She was a hot-blooded Havana hurricane, and she came at him like a runway model. She slid through the crowd and her heels clicked across the dancefloor. Her hair bounced, her lips shone and her bohemian batwing blouse trailed behind her. She catwalked to close, but suddenly, Fat Pat threw a wild dance move and accidently hip-checked her. She stumbled in her heels and the shots spilled over her wrists.

"Aye vaca!" She cursed.

"Sorry." Pat snarled, wrinkling her nose. As she did, her eyes drifted up to Gunner and expanded excitedly.

"That's not even a dance move!" Tequila scolded, "Esta es salsa!"

"Yaaa…" Pat agreed, looking back at Tequila.

"URGH!"

Tequila huffed and wiped her wet hands on Pat's dress like a bath towel, then rolled her eyes and hip-turned to Gunner, bumping Pat out of the way as she did.

"Well, that was jur one chot," she told him, "because they're outta booze."

She flashed the back of her salty hand and licked it.

"Ju can't swallow, but ju can still lick."

"You're supposed to lick first," Gunner replied, "then swallow."

"Ayyyye Papi… That suuucks. It's sooo… hard."

He smirked and looked away, back at Santa. Santa had dark, chestnut hair, cut in a short, side swept bob that accented her arched eyebrows, high cheekbones and sleek chin. It shined, sun-streaked, and contrasted beautifully against her amber eyes and snow white smile. She had fair skin from high latitudes, which she got from her father's ancestors, who were Viking raiders, and thin hairs on her lower back, which she got from her mother's family, who were Portuguese royalty. She was more Nordic than the cocoa Latinas or bronze beach girls, and she moved with more authority and crisp intent, like a winter warrior. She looked flawless.

"Cheese a single mother." Tequila interrupted.

"Huh?"

"Where's jur linen chorts?"

"My what?"

She looked at his crotch and cocked an accusatory eyebrow. Gunner frowned.

"Ju coming to Coco's fiesta?"

"Who's Coco?"

"Coco-nut. My friend ju met today on the beach, the one who wanted to loan ju her flats. Chee says cheese dyeen."

"She's—"

"—Cheese not. But chee told everyone that, tinking che'd leave on the boat before anyone actually saw her die, but then the boat got cancelled. Oh it's so great, so now cheese stuck with her lie. Chee didn't think about that. Chee never thought the boat'd be cancelled. So we're having a big party for her and putting her on the spot. A 'living wake'."

"A funeral doesn't sound like a lot of fun."

"Ohhhohohoho… Ju wanna see her squirm?"

"Well…"

"It's an End of the World thing, 'cause then, cheese either going to have to really die, or when cheese still alive after, chill have to admit cheese faking it and that chee has some really deep insecurities. It's therapy. We're helping her."

"What if she's really dying?" Gunner asked.

Tequila frowned and glanced over her shoulder.

Gunner followed her eyes. Across the bar, Coco put her hand on Surfer's chest, leaned into him and laughed flirtatiously. Her smile glowed and her eyes sparkled. She pinched the thin strap of her slip back up on her shoulder and stole a side glance at them.

"Ya," Gunner admitted, "she doesn't look that sick."

"Chee is," Tequila laughed, spinning her finger around her temple.

Gunner grinned.

"See ju at the funeral. In forty eight hours."

Tequila squeezed his bicep, then hip-turned and sashayed away, feeling his eyes on her ass.

"Gunner!"

Gunner looked left and saw Don Granada and Barboza sitting at their side table across the bar, next to the toucan. Granada flagged him over.

"You know how to get his head right, don't you?" Barboza leaned forward and said as Gunner started through the crowd towards them. "If you're right and he's not faking this castaway cover story."

"A castaway cover story?" Don Granada asked. "He's not a spy, but even if he was, what kind of spy pretends to be a castaway?"

"You see? You see how good it is? Nobody would ever suspect that."

"Because nobody would ever use it!"

"Listen, if you wanna get his head right," Barboza continued, "get him back in the fight."

Suddenly, Barboza pulled a pineapple grenade out of his pocket.

"Jesus! When'd you start carrying that around?"

"I'm gonna set it on the table and pull the pin."

"Put that—"

"—BOOM! Ten seconds of instant clarity. Nothing clears your mind like a hand grenade."

"Ya, then what? You're gonna blow up my bar?"

Barboza scowled.

"Calm down cowboy. Give him some space. To disappear, work back. Untangle whatever happened to him out there. This is a good place for that. Stick with the fishing story."

"Fishing?" Barboza scoffed, pocketing the grenade as Gunner

neared. "Ho ho ho I hate to news-flash you cabron but this guy… He ain't ever fished and he ain't ever gonna fish again. He's too far gone to come back. Normal isn't normal for him. War is. I seen it, you seen it, you know. You wanna help him? Just let him do what he does best, and get the hell out of the way."

Gunner walked up to the table and nodded.

"Or use him," Barboza added as Gunner stood over them.

"We're used enough," Granada concluded.

"Who?" Gunner asked.

"Warriors," Granada clarified.

"Moving," Barboza quizzed, shifting gears.

"What?" Gunner asked.

"Moving," Barboza repeated, setting his empty beer on the table, leaning back, crossing his arms over his chest and looking at Gunner suspiciously.

Gunner stared, confused.

"Firing," Granada answered for him, darting Barboza a look.

"Fine," Barboza continued, "Sandinistas roll in here hot. They're blocking the entrance and windows. How do you escape?"

"What is this," Granada interjected, "Some kind of test?"

"Quiet."

"He wants you to say that there's usually an exit in the—"

"—Stop answering for him! You want me to pull it out?"

Granada leaned back, raised his hands and surrendered. Gunner raised his eyebrows, amused.

"The answer's the kitchen," Barboza grumbled, "There's usually an exit in the kitchen."

Barboza tilted his head and twirled his mustache, thinking.

"All right, next question." He pointed and continued, "You're a soldier on patrol, passing through a Zeta village. There's landmines in the village but you don't know where. How do you get past?"

"Grab a couple villagers," Santa said, suddenly striding up with a tray of sodas, "Make them your guides and walk them in front of you."

"Hahaha…!" Granada laughed at Barboza, proud of his daughter. "See…Now she's tactical!"

"Screw it," Barboza said, eyeing some twenty-year-olds dancing in bikini tops, "Let's get some tail."

"So what are you guys, old soldiers or something?" Gunner asked, smirking and sitting with them.

"Ha! Old men!" Santa laughed, setting the sodas down.

"Mghmm…"

"Ahhh, Papa…" She said, hugging him. "Old, great men."

"I'll kick anyone's ass in here," Granada declared.

"Colombian neckkk-tie," Barboza added, slicing his hand across his neck.

"Ya, well," Santa hedged, "they've also heard a few too many war stories in this crossroads over the years."

"Epic stories," Barboza confirmed. "Great battles."

"Headhunters and kings," Granada added. "Fortunes made, and lost."

"Betrayal, seduction…sedition," Barboza said, brandishing his ghost dagger.

"Revenge," Granada stated.

"MURDER!" Barboza yelled, *THUNKING* the dagger into the table and spooking the toucan, who flew off.

"Heh!?" Granada said, holding an open palm to the dagger and eyeing Barboza incredulously.

"Ah sorry, I was talking about the saint."

"Ah, ya, well…" Granada conceded, nodding thoughtfully. "Simón Pedro. He was crucified upside down."

"Colonel Flatter's retreat across the Sahara," Barboza continued.

"The Sergeant who became a God in the Himalayas." Don Granada said, raising a definitive finger.

"Yes…" Barboza acknowledged, staring off in thought. "Ah! The slave mines of Hanuman, the Monkey King."

"There was no such thing."

"I saw it with my own eyes!"

"*PHUFF*," Granada snorted, waving his hand dismissively.

"See?" Santa said to Gunner. "Crazy old men."

"We're the rear guard," Barboza explained, "stationed at this outpost now. For humanity. For the end of days."

"Aye aye," Granada said, raising his bottle to toast. "To the best of man."

"And the worst."

"Amen."

The four toasted and drank. After, Barboza smacked his tongue like he'd just swallowed gas and scowled at his soda.

"Sorry," Santa apologized, "We're out of beer."

"I got more bad news," Granada added. "The boat didn't come

today."

"What?" Gunner asked.

"Ya, it didn't come. Which is why we're outta beer. Partly. Sometimes it happens. But don't worry, it'll come tomorrow. Probably. Just stay another day. Recover. Talk to some girls. That still gives you twenty eight days. Not so bad."

"What about the road?" Gunner asked. "Where does that go?"

"The road…" Barboza snorted.

"Nowhere," Granada replied. "The road turns into a trail, which turns into jungle."

"And the jungle turns into a mire," Barboza added, "which turns into death."

"Serious road," Gunner noted.

"Serious jungle," Granada said. "It's like walking into quicksand. The only reasonable way out's over the water."

"But you can do it?"

"Well, ya. But it takes months, if you survive, and there's only two people here who could make it now and guide you, aside from Barboza and myself, and no way in hell I'm doing that again. Mudo, and Simian's got someone, a scout, in town at the Cantina. I heard he can probably make it. If you're desperate."

Barboza shot Granada a look. Granada held his stare silently as Gunner's eyes drifted up and he mapped the contingency in his head like a constellation of stars. After a moment, Santa ran her hand through her father's thick, salty hair and kissed his broad forehead, then smiled at Gunner and slid back to the bar.

"I heard a story myself here," Gunner contributed, "or part of one."

Barboza grabbed the dagger to wiggle it from the wood.

"Something about a treasure."

Barboza froze, the knife still stuck.

Silence.

Don Granada and Barboza glanced at each other.

"What?" Gunner asked.

"Aghhh…" Barboza gruffed.

"No, what?"

Barboza left the knife in the table, leaned back and crossed his arms.

"Tell me."

"I'm getting a soda." Don Granada said, getting up and

following his daughter to the bar with his full soda.

Gunner looked back at Barboza expectantly.

"Simian didn't tell you?"

"Who?"

Barboza studied his reaction with narrow, suspicious eyes, as if debating whether or not to believe him.

"Ever heard of the pirate, William Kidd?"

"The one who—"

"—Legend has it that about three hundred years ago—and by the way, a journeyman once told me that you should think about history as if it happened yesterday, and the future as if it will happen tomorrow, especially when committing to something—so yesterday, got it? Ya, so yesterday, when this place was overrun by monkeys, with their Monkey God, and they went in the houses and cavorted with the women, Captain Kidd attacked a merchant ship in the British West Indies. A ship with two hundred sacks of gold coins. Aztec coins. He took the gold and fled, obviously."

Barboza leaned forward, yanked the dagger from the table and wiped the blade on his shorts. He then took a long, dramatic moment to feel how sharp the tip was with his thumb, even though he already knew how sharp it was.

"When word got back to Kingston that Kidd got the gold," he continued, "the British sent a man-of-war after him. Kidd heard the ship was hunting him, so he took four pirates and went ashore and buried the treasure. But only Kidd and three pirates returned. They left the fourth pirate, this buccaneer named Caravaggio, to guard the treasure, and set sail again. But a couple days later, the crew mutinied. They marooned Kidd and two of the pirates who he buried the treasure with on an island. The third pirate and the crew took the boat and went back for the treasure, of course."

"Did they find it?"

"Nobody knows. Nobody ever saw them again."

"What happened to them?"

"A hurricane. Headhunters. How would I know?"

"Headhunters?" Gunner frowned.

"Ahh, but Kidd got it worse. You know what happened to him?"

Barboza paused for dramatic effect until Gunner finally complied and shrugged.

"What?"

"The Brits found him. On the island. And when they did, the other two were… eaten."

"Eaten?"

"Ya, nothing but bones. You can't make this stuff up. All three got sick and fought. Got monster strong. Metastasized. Until worm larvae popped out their ears."

Barboza's eyes drifted away, carried off by the thought.

"And?"

"And…" Barboza said, his old-soul eyes sludging back and refocusing on Gunner, "…the worms ate their brain, so they ate their shoes, then they ate each other."

"Like zombies?" Gunner snickered.

"Worms bored through their brain," Barboza stated flatly, staring dead frozen at him as if that explained it. After a long, melodramatic moment, he blinked theatrically and continued:

"Anyway… Kidd was rotten. His brain was cored like an apple. He didn't care where the treasure was, if he could even remember. He was useless, and dangerous. So the Brits sentenced him to 'Death by Strangulation' and walked him down Execution Dock to do Marshal's dance. Ever heard of that?"

"Ya, it was—"

"—In London, on the Thames. The dock went past the lowest low tide, so the Admiralty still had jurisdiction over sea crimes committed and could use maritime law against pirates. Anyway, they paraded him, this pirate par excellence, to the dock, but they didn't let him stop at a pub for an ale on the way, like tradition. It was tradition. You got a pint. They had to do it, but didn't, because he'd gotten too strong and unruly. They just hung him, with a short rope to make it worse. That's the Marshal's dance part. The short rope makes your feet kick and dance while you choke out, because it doesn't snap your neck. But the hangman's rope broke, so they had to string him up and hang him again. That killed him, the second time. They left him hanging there until three tides washed over his head, then they put him in a cage like a canary and gibbetted him above the River Thames. They hung him there, on display, for forty years. Forty years. Tough sons of a bitches, the Brits—back then. After a year he was a ragged pile of bones in clothes, and crows had pecked his skull clean."

Barboza gazed out the window, as if Kidd's cage hung in the shadows just outside.

"And on grey days in England, boys looked up at Kidd in his cage, hanging there by an iron hook, and thought, '*A pirate. A real pirate, from the West Indies…*' A boy's will is the wind's will, and the thoughts of youth are long, long thoughts. That's Longfellow."

Gunner smiled slightly.

"And you know what Kidd's last words were to those boys, swirling around Execution Dock before the Admiralty hung him, the second time?"

"What?"

"Fucken savages."

Gunner laughed, certain Barboza had made that last part up, at least. Barboza smiled proudly at himself, like he'd made the last part up, at least. Then, after a moment, he leaned over the table and lowered his voice, like he was on Kidd's crew, plotting mutiny in the galley.

"But guess what?"

"This is the most ludicrous sea story I've ever—"

"—Guess where Kidd buried the treasure?"

"I have no idea."

Barboza darted a quick look to each side and returned his gaze with a wilder look in his eyes.

"Here," he said, *TAP, TAP,* tapping the dagger on the table. "Ya, here. Somewhere around here, somewhere near where we're sitting right now. Two hundred sacks of Aztec gold."

Barboza looked around, as if the treasure might be in the bar.

"How do they know that?"

"'Cause that's what everyone's always said!" Barboza snapped. "That… and the worms. Ya see, in the jungle out there, just right out there, is the only place—in this world or the next—where you can get Monkey Jungle Worm."

Gunner studied him suspiciously.

"And Kidd had it. That's a fact. It's in the ledgers. In Newgate Prison. He had Monkey Jungle Worm."

Barboza looked around to see who may have heard him talking about the treasure. But after a few seconds he waved the dagger in riddance.

"Ah, but it's bullshit. It's just a legend. A good story. Pirates, headhunters, zombies? I mean, come on. Nobody ever believed it. I mean only one guy was ever looking for Captain Kidd's gold around here. Winter. And everyone thought he was crazy."

Barboza shook his head.

"Until…"

He stared off until Gunner finally capitulated and replied.

"Until what?"

"Until last year. When Winter disappeared."

Barboza glanced over his shoulder and leaned in like a conspirator.

"Most people think Winter just ran off, abandoned his family. But no way."

"Why not?"

"'Cause I know him. And the morning he disappeared, he got up early and made pancakes for his son."

"Ya but that could mean—"

"—It doesn't. And here's the thing. A couple weeks later, your buddy the builder, Simian, he starts buying the town, the cemetery, the coast… everything. Everything but this place and the rest of Don Granada's land. With guess what?"

Gunner eyed him suspiciously.

"With gold." Barboza tapped the dagger against Gunner's chest. "Cabron."

Gunner laughed.

"So? He's got some gold."

"He never had any."

"Gold coins?"

"Nah, he melted them down or something."

Gunner looked at him sympathetically.

"You know what I think?" Barboza continued. "I think Winter found the treasure, then one of Simian's thugs killed him and took the coins."

"But if this builder—"

"—Simian. You know."

"If he knew where the rest of the treasure was—"

"—Exactly. He wouldn't be mining the cemetery and trying to get Don Granada's land."

"So wait. Hang on. Back up. This local guy, Winter, he's looking for Captain Kidd's treasure—"

"—For years. For his wife."

"Then one day he disappears, and Simian has some gold a few weeks later?"

"Uh huh, ya."

"And then he starts looking for the rest?"

"Yep. All of a sudden Winter disappears and now Simian's looking for gold, although he says he isn't. He says he's helping the town, developing it, protecting it from howlers. He really believes that, but it's bullcrap. He's possessed. Gold fever. He goes from building the town to digging it up. Brings in some mercenaries like you. What do you know about them?"

"What're you talking about?"

Barboza studied him.

"But if Winter found the treasure," Gunner asked, ignoring him, "and had some gold coins as proof, why would this guy…Why would anyone kill him without finding out where the rest of the treasure was first?"

"Exactly. That makes it a crime of passion. Which doesn't make sense. Doesn't fit the… narrative."

Barboza looked off and twirled his thick handlebar mustache, thinking, trying to make it all fit, like a puzzle.

"Where's Winter?" Gunner asked.

"Tuck thinks he's coming back, but…"

"They never found a body?"

"Nope. Winter had this, like, bangle. Everyone always thought that either Winter would turn up or that bangle. That some hippie would come in and try to pawn it for a beer. It was from Cartagena, you know, unique and valuable. A pit viper, eating its own tail."

"What'd the police say?" Gunner asked, crossing his arms skeptically on his chest. "Where are they in all this?"

"Winter was La Policia."

Barboza gave him a hard, definitive look, then chugged his soda, still staring at him.

"So anyway," Barboza concluded, "this gold, it's a curse on Granada, who's a good man, cause Simian wants his land, because he thinks the treasure's buried here, maybe in the jungle. The old man is telling him to go to hell because he doesn't care about the gold. He's happy. Or. The law's dead. God's dead. And Winter, well here's the thing about him…"

A heavy darkness descended over Barboza's face.

"What?"

"Winter, was… *is* Santa's husband. The boy's father."

Gunner narrowed his eyes.

"There's history here. In all this. In every person you pass on the street and see in this bar there's a story. Lifelines, transects reaching back. Someone they love, hate. An ancestor who killed someone, if they didn't themselves. How far back do you have to go to find a murderer in your line? A prostitute? We're flawed genes with conflicting motives colliding on force vectors. But anyway, Tuck. He's been having a bit of a…hard time… making friends."

Gunner nodded slightly.

"He doesn't have any. Friends. He's told everyone his dad's found the treasure and gone off to sell it, but he studies his map and writes notes in his journal, then runs off, disappears, looking for him."

Gunner crossed his arms, leaned back and digested the tale like a bloody ribeye. He guessed that at least fifty percent of that sea story was bullshit, if not more. He just didn't know which fifty percent.

Barboza leaned across the table and pointed the dagger at him.

"So don't you ever goddamn hurt him."

Chapter 12

Gunner stood on the beach, leaning against the cayuco's wooden hull and holding a soda. Cadejo lay in the sand next to him and Sail shifted seductively in front, dancing barefoot to the hum of bossa nova coming from a group of bumsters lounging around a distant bonfire on the beach. Silverfish light from a full moon flickered off the sea and her skin.

Sail was hippie wild. Tan and toned, with perky tits and sixty's hips. She had sandy hair that wisped when she walked, or laughed, and sea-green eyes that sparkled like sunlight through palms. She was a natural beach beauty who radiated a champagne aura.

She smiled flirtatiously and danced close like a cobra, then unbuttoned his shirt, stuck her nose behind his ear and inhaled.

"You smell like the sea," she whispered in his ear.

"You smell like suntan lotion," he replied, smiling wryly and reaching for her hip. She retreated, teasing him.

She knew he wanted to leave town, but she wasn't letting him go without a fight. There wasn't any sport in that, and she'd read somewhere that men are most happy when they're chasing something they can't quiet catch. Her skirt flipped up, flashing panty. He stared directly, unapologetically.

"So what happened out there?" She asked, "Where'd you come from?"

"I fell off a boat."

"Fishing?"

"No. I work on a merchant ship. *The Orion.* A rig broke in a storm and knifed me in the back. And I went over."

"Uh huh. And what're ya doing now? What's your... big plan?"

"Nothing. Just trying to get on that boat and get back. Leave here. Get home. That's all."

"Why? What's so important back home?"

"I don't know. A girlfriend, my job. I mean, it's not like you can just quit your job and go live in a tropical paradise without any income or anything, right?"

She laughed. In one way, he was right—the big city didn't let you escape. Everyone was free to get up from their cubicles and walk out whenever they wanted, and many wanted to, but how many did?

Nobody. Hardly nobody. In another way though, he was wrong—because the jungle provided, if you fed yourself to it.

"What girlfriend?" She hissed.

"Cindy. The one getting married in twenty-eight days. To an accountant."

"Ahh, I thought we were talking about your girlfriend."

He chuckled at that, he couldn't help it.

"So, a handsome accountant or a rugged, rebel sailor, hmmm…"

"I never said he was handsome."

"You know what's handsome about him, don't you?" She asked.

"What?"

"He comes home every night. And looks at her."

Gunner scoffed.

"Well, you better hurry back and ruin that wedding. In the meantime, you can have a bottle of whiskey at Coco's wake and relax. Blow out your mind. Coco-nut's really boxed herself in a corner this time. But me, I don't care if the boat ever comes. Because I'm never leaving."

"Is it like this every night?"

"Every night is one night, making it all nights and forever."

"Flippin' hippie," he teased.

She laughed and serpentined back into him. She pressed her nails into his chest and dragged them down his obliques, until they snaked around his lower back and hit his puncture wound, where the rig jabbed him. Or somebody stabbed him.

"Oh. Does that… hurt?"

He wince-smiled, trying not to.

She inched her nails back over the wound and pressed gently. He knotted his jaw and took it, so she pressed her hips and lips into him.

"I can't," he said, stopping her.

"Why? Your girlfriend? Cindy?"

"No," he smirked, "you're not hot enough."

"Hahahahaa…" She giggled.

Because everyone knew that was bullshit.

Chapter 13

Santa walked barefoot up Mountain Trail, carrying her flats. Her skirt flowed around her legs and brushed white orchids and orange birds of paradise that grew wild over the clay path. Cicadas chirped, geckos clicked and a candle flickered in Tuck's window in the Ranchero ahead, on the hill above Valhalla, in banana trees and heliconia, overlooking the crescent bay.

She left the trail and walked into the yard to the front porch, with its stone-framed entrance and thick wooden doors. When she did, a large shadow strode across the trail behind her.

She didn't notice, and entered the house. She dropped her sandals on coral stone and locked the door behind her. Inside was a great room with a leather couch, cocoa rug, old family portraits, large rosewood windows and French doors that opened to the mahogany deck and sea, where Don Granada took his café in the morning and read the paper when the boat captain remembered it. A rustic Enfield rifle hung above a stone fireplace, and a large family table bridged the great room and the kitchen. Splashes of turquoise and red annatto dye accented whitewashed wood, giving warmth to the earthen stone.

Her father, Don Granada, dozed in a leather chair near the fireplace. A book entitled *La Leyenda de la Ciudad Perdida* lay atop his belly. She smiled, grabbed a caribou blanket from the couch, but from another world, and lay it over him.

She checked on Tuck in his room and kissed his forehead, then entered her room, stripped her tank top, and tossed it on the bed. Drapes drifted from a breeze that came through an open window, and the moon painted her skin silver. She removed a locket from her neck and opened it. Inside was a picture of her, Tuck and Winter, together. She smiled at first, then her face tightened and she set it on the nightstand. When she did, something scurried outside.

She drew a thin boning knife from her waistband and slid to the window.

Outside, a few cumulous clouds drifted low over the bay. Beneath them, the jungle sloped down to Valhalla and the beach. Palms rustled, but, other than that, it was quiet.

Normal.

Nothing.

I'm going crazy, she thought.

She reached through the window and lifted a large heliconia leaf. Underneath, four white bats hung upside down along the mid-rib, clumped together like the puffy clouds above. Someone giggled in the distance. She lowered the leaf and looked back to the beach. She saw Sail lead Gunner by the hand to his cabaña.

She started to shut the pale green shutters, but decided to leave them open.

Chapter 14

The next morning, the sun cut across Gunner's eyes and scratch marks raked his chest. His eyes blinked open and he rose up on an elbow. Sail slept beside him. The morning sun shined through the mosquito net that hung over the cabaña's entrance, casting a checkered shadow over her naked hip and round ass.

"Damn," he awed, in the light of day.

He got up, pulled his shorts on, pushed the mosquito net aside and stepped onto the deck, into the sun. As soon as he did, he squinted and tripped.

"Gah..."

Cadejo slept in the entrance like a speedbump. The dog kept his head perfectly still, but rolled a lazy eye up at him. For such a small town, Gunner thought, it sure was hard to be left alone.

"Heya Gunner!"

He looked up and saw Padre reclining against a palm in front of his cabaña. Padre's feet stuck straight out on the green grass, exposing sandals and pale shins, and his belly formed a surprisingly symmetrical circle in his brown robe. He looked like a brown panda.

"You hungry? I'm hungry."

"What?"

"I'm feeling a bit peckish. But I got this!" He held up a bottle. "I borrowed one of Simian's fiiiine beverages."

Gunner eyed the bottle.

"I thought priests didn't steal."

"It's not stealing if you're stealing it back."

"Hmm..." Gunner wondered. "What're you drinking?"

"A cerveza."

"It's nine in the morning."

"Ya, you slept late."

Gunner frowned. As he did, Cadejo hobbled down the stairs to Padre, wagging his chewed and tattered tail.

"Goooood boy... Guuuud boy..." Padre cooed, scratching his stump. "This dog, boy... He's a legend. Came out of the In-ter-i-or with Don Granada. But three legs, man. I don't know. How many more fights can you have in you after that?"

"That mutt's following me around."

"Ya, he's protecting you. You're his spirit human."

"His what?"

"Nice net."

Padre tipped his beer at a fishing net hanging from his deck. Gunner gave up on chasing the previous conversation and reluctantly followed Padre into another one. It was almost impossible not to.

"Ya. Don Granada sent it over. But I don't know how to use it. I'm not a fisherman."

"Ya, nobody believes that."

"I work on a merchant ship."

"Nobody believes that either."

Gunner shook his head.

"Not a lot of entertainment around here, is there?"

Padre stared with his beady eyes, like he had no idea what Gunner meant and was waiting for him to explain. After a moment, Gunner simply frowned again.

"Going to town?" Padre asked.

Gunner frowned further.

"Great!" Padre said, getting up. "I'll show you where Scout hangs out."

Chapter 15

Padre led Gunner down Town Trail, from the beach to town. Cadejo hopped alongside effortlessly on three legs and a ghost leg.

"What'd Don Granada say about the treasure?" Padre asked as they strode. "What's Simian going to do?"

"I thought you told me not to ask him about that?"

"I did. What'd he say about the deadline? Is he serious?"

"What deadline? He didn't mention anything about a deadline."

"Oh man, he didn't?"

Padre's eyes were big and beady again.

"Simian says that if Don Granada doesn't sell him his land by the day after tomorrow…"

"What?" Gunner asked, reluctantly.

"He's gonna kill 'em."

Gunner scowled, but glanced at Padre sideways, wondering if he was serious. He didn't care about their problem, but he couldn't help wonder what kind of place he was in if someone was really going to openly announce that they planned to kill someone two days from now, and do it. Padre, however, waddled ahead, smiling goofily and moving on, having already seemingly forgotten about the conversation. And the premeditated murder.

A few minutes later, they stepped off Town Trail and onto the main road, which was mixed dirt and cobblestone and led past the colonial houses and adobe shops to a cobblestone plaza at the center of town. A large stone statue of Simón Pedro, or Saint Peter, stood proudly in the middle of the plaza, facing the town church, which was christened; La Iglesia de los Caídos–The Church of the Fallen.

The church was the biggest structure in town aside from the ruins of the Spanish Castillo. It was an impressive monolith of white stucco and stone that suggested the locals had once invested the majority of their thin surplus income in it, probably at great personal expense for considerable time. Its walls were a meter thick to keep evil spirits out, and a bell-tower rose three stories into the air, above the flat, airy canopies and merciful shade of nearby acacia and guanacaste trees.

Nobody knew how old the church was, like a Miskito grandmother, but Hernán Cortés reportedly laid the cornerstone of the first foundation on the grave of a Mayan king nearly five hundred years ago. Just twenty years ago, however, during the last plague, when half the pueblo died and the other half began praying to the old Santería and monkey gods again, the townsfolk sealed off and abandoned the church. Those who survived—and were still alive twenty years later, like Prospector and Butch—never spoke of it again, like a dark family secret. If children or tourists asked why they'd sealed up such a beautiful church, the young townsfolk shrugged because they didn't know, and the old townsfolk furrowed their brows and dropped their heads, or fell into a dark stupor and walked away with part of their day ruined. Not even Don Granada, who arrived twelve years after they'd sealed the church, was sure why they had abandoned it, or could ever convince them to re-open it.

Still, the plaza remained the gravitational center of town and. In the evenings, kids played fútbol in the open space and townsfolk sat on the stone steps at Saint Peter's feet. They strolled, held hands, ate topogigios, played dominos, discussed politics, and entertained themselves with wild and impossible stories about Captain Kidd's gold and the Interior.

The sun blazed on Gunner and Padre as they strolled down the road, toward the plaza. The light reflected off the bleached buildings and corrugated tin roofs in sharp, blinding rays, but it dulled to flat, soothing browns and greens on the dirt and vegetation that filled the cracks in the town like grout.

They passed Mulata from the Amazon, sitting on the Tack shop porch in the shade, flipping tarot cards with henna hands. She flipped the Hanged Man, the Sun, the Hermit, the Tower, Justice, Judgement…Then she spied Gunner and stopped. She flipped the last card slowly as he passed:

Death.

They moved on, like ghosts to her, to the Cantina.

The Cantina was a two-story building made of mixed blocks and eroded plaster. It had a covered wooden terrace, large shuttered windows and a sign on the wall near the front door that read, "No Guns. No Gambling."

They entered and saw Gambler, Awol, Intel, Cazador and Scout sitting at a circular poker table, gambling. With guns. Gambler, the gunslinger, rolled a card over his fingers, whipped it from one hand to the next and flipped it over:

A two of hearts.

Like Mulata, he looked up from the card and eyed Gunner.

"The hole." He mumbled to himself.

He tucked the two of hearts in his back pocket and drew another card for himself: the ace of spades. He grinned and slipped the black ace in his vest.

The Cantina was large, bright and airy. It had hardwood floors made from Spanish cedar, which had been salvaged from the deck of an old galleon that had once wrecked on the reef off-coast. It had white slat shudders on the front, side and back walls; a stone staircase that ascended to an open second-story loft; exposed brick arches over the doorway and windows; and high ceiling fans that pushed a gentle breeze through the space. The poker table sat in the middle of the room by some other wooden tables and chairs near the windows, and a long mahogany bar stretched along the right wall. Shelves lined the wall behind the bar, in front of a large mirror that reflected back on the customers and the space behind them. Liquor bottles lined the shelves, and crates of beer chunked up under them. Burlap sacks of pineapples, bananas and coconuts were also stacked by a large cabinet under the stairs, and old photographs of Cuba hung slightly askew around the room.

Someone had once put some thought and design into the room. But that must have been many years ago, because stucco flaked off the walls, exposing white stone and red brick underneath; colorful mosaic tiles that trimmed the fascia on the steps were broken and chipped; a wrought iron handrail that ran up the steps was timeless but rusty; red paint faded on the back wall, contrasting against the green bananas and yellow pineapples; and sun, storms, and tremblers had pressed, pushed and pulled the floors, walls and rafters over time, so that they now ran slightly askew and didn't quiet align. The Cantina was frozen in time in urban decay.

Gunner stepped to the bar. A fat barman dozed upright on the crates behind it, by a backdoor that led to a kitchen. Butch stood in the corner nearby, in a bloody smock, filling a metal jug from a large tin container. Butch's glazed blue, cataract eyes tracked up on the sound of Gunner's sandals scratching sand on the hardwood floor.

"I'm looking for the... Scout." Gunner said. "Heard he knows how to cross the Interior."

Barman's eyes slothed open. He stared a moment, then dragged his eyes over Gunner's shoulder to the poker table behind him. Gunner followed his gaze in the mirror, then turned on the table.

Barman nodded to a thirty-something-year-old rough-rider with a long mustache and slouch hat, pinned up on one side. Scout was chewing on an unlit cigar and had a rifle slung over the back of his chair.

Scout met Barman's eyes and nodded. He folded his cards, slammed a shot and stood to come over, but Awol handed him a deck of cards and stopped him. Awol shook his head at Barman, and Scout shrugged and sat back down.

"Scout's not here," Barman stated indifferently.

Gunner checked the table again.

"Come on, Scout," Awol said, "deal some violence!"

Scout chewed his cigar and dealt the cards. Awol took his with a cocky smirk. Gambler read them in his expression.

"Fine," Gunner conceded. It wasn't worth the fight. It wasn't worth getting mixed up with that crew. The boat was coming that afternoon anyway, and overland was just a contingency plan and curiosity. "How 'bout a doctor? You got a doctor in this town?"

Barman nodded over Gunner's other shoulder to the door. Bonesetter stood square in the doorway. He had just entered, and was holding his black doctor's bag and a machete. He was sweat-stained, disheveled and dirty, and his left hand was wrapped in thick, bloody gauze.

"Where you been?" Awol asked.

"Working." Bonesetter replied.

"What happened?" Gambler queried, spotting his hand.

"Nothing."

"Where's Polito?" Cazador asked.

Bonesetter shrugged silently, then strode past them to the cabinet on the other side of the room. He opened it and removed a staple gun, staples and pliers.

"That blood on your machete?" Intel asked.

"Mmgh," Bonesetter grunted indistinguishably and began arranging the tools in his bag.

"It's pronounced *ma-che-tay*," Cazador corrected, throwing chips in the pot, "like chotgun."

"Shotgun?" Awol said.

"Ya, chotgun."

"You know how to pronounce 'cabron'?" Awol asked.

"Ya," Cazador smirked. "A-wall."

"Fuck," Awol growled under his breath, having his own

punchline used against him.

"What's the worst hand in poker?" Gambler asked.

This time, Intel smirked, knowing Gambler was screwing with them.

"He's bluffing," Scout stated, unnecessarily.

"No shit," Awol replied.

"Chit," Cazador corrected. "No chit."

"He knows what the worst hand in poker is," Scout added.

"Ya, I said no shit."

"It's a seven and a two," Cazador explained anyway.

"Heh," Scout whispered, tapping Awol's arm.

Awol ignored him and studied Gambler to be sure he really was bluffing like he'd said.

"Heh," Scout repeated, tapping him harder and leaning in.

"What?" Awol growled, annoyed.

"It isn't gay to order a monkey lala, is it?"

Awol glared at him.

"All in," Gambler suddenly declared, setting his cards down and pushing all his chips into the pot.

Awol focused back on the pot.

"Shit," Awol mumbled. Gambler had snuck his hand by him before he had a chance to read him.

"Chit," Cazador corrected.

Awol threw him a dirty look sideways, then narrowed his eyes and settled in to finally study Gambler without being interrupted. The others let him, but Gambler simply smirked cocky, which could have met anything, knowing Gambler. Given this, instead of playing off Gambler's cards, Awol glanced at his own cards and decided to play off his own hand: a king in his hand and one on the river. Two kings. Strong. Almost a guaranteed win. Only a pair of aces could beat him, or an Act of God. Or himself.

"He's not bluffing," Cazador said, changing his assessment completely.

Awol grabbed his chip towers and started to shove them forward to call Gambler's bluff, then he measured Gambler one last time and hesitated. They locked eyes and stared. Excitement flashed in the corner of Gambler's eye.

"Fine," Awol growled, "I fold."

He pulled his chips back and slapped his cards down, frustrated to orphan two kings. Gambler flipped his over. A seven and a two.

King high, on the river. A bluff, with the worst hand in poker.

"Ahhh COCK!" Awol snapped and slapped the table, making the chips jump. "That cost me a song."

Intel, Cazador and Scout laughed. Gambler smirked and raked in the pot. It almost wasn't even fun taking their money. Actually, ya it was.

"'Ain't no medicina in this pueblo, stranger," Awol said, turning his attention from the poker table back to the bar.

He and Gunner locked eyes.

One second.

Two.

CLACK!

Suddenly, Santa burst into the Cantina and strode up to the bar.

"He owes us a hundred cases of beer!" She shot, "And the whiskey!"

Barman shrugged and nodded to the poker table. She saw the mercenaries and spotted Bonesetter in the cabinet behind them.

"Where's Tuck?"

Barman shrugged lazily.

She nodded a quick hello to Gunner and turned on the table.

"Guys!" She said, striding up, fearless.

"Damn she's smoken," Gambler muttered.

Bonesetter glared at Gambler and eased towards the table behind them.

"Your boss owes us—"

"—If your Dad," Awol interrupted, "doesn't get off that land in forty-eight hours—"

"—It's our land!"

"Not in forty-eight hours."

"Bullshit!"

"Whoa!" Scout said.

"Are you on your menstrual?" Awol asked, "Don't come in no house of cards on your menstrual."

"It's bad luck," Cazador explained.

"Heh, listen," Gambler interjected calmly as he stacked his chips in front of him. "Just relax. Let's all just take a deep breath and think, okay. Take a step back. First off, is Simian offering you a good deal?"

"It's a threat! Not a deal!"

"And not just the money. He can get running water out there, secure the perimeter—"

"—Perimeter?"

CLACK!

Butch's clever fell from his waistband and clanked on the floor beneath him. Everyone snapped to the noise, except Gambler, who watched everyone watching it. As they did, Bonesetter slid up in front of her.

"Heh, heh, hang on," Bonesetter said, trying to sooth her. "It's gonna be cheque, Santa. Todo cheque. I'll take care of this. I'll deal with these... lechers." He continued, glancing at the guys at the poker table behind him, "And Simian—"

"—He's a thief."

"You don't have to worry about the specifics. I'll get the beer, and the grain. I always take care of you, don't I?"

Santa's eyes narrowed suspiciously. Bonesetter inched closer, like frost. He lowered his voice further and touched her arm tenderly.

"Listen, these guys, they think I'm..." He glanced over his shoulder again. "Anyway, I'm going to watch over you. I'll fix this. I'm going to put this all back together again. Make it whole and perfect, like before. Just like before. That's why I came."

"He's gonna fence the jungle, that my Dad—"

"—I KNOW what your dad says about me, but I'm a DOCTOR now!"

"What?"

Bonesetter took a deep breath and calmed himself. After a moment he smiled again and rubbed her arms.

"Look, heh. I'm trying. I'm really trying, that's all. I know, I mean I'm not perfect, but I, I became a doctor, I... Look..."

He dug in his shirt and fished out a necklace. It was the locket she set on the nightstand the night before.

"I'm wearing your locket to remind me to protect you, always."

"What? How'd you get that?" She jerked out of his grip. "Stay the hell away from me and my family, you creep."

"I'm not a FREAK!"

"Heh," Gunner said calmly, suddenly stepping between them. "Heh, you uh, you got something in your back."

Gunner gently pressed Bonesetter's shoulder and turned him to the side. The syringe still dangled out of his back. With that, the others spotted it. Gambler looked suspicious, Intel looked intrigued, and Awol shook his head, annoyed.

Bonesetter's eyes darted from Santa to Gunner, distracted from his fixation and agitated, but after a second, he focused on Gunner, followed his lead and made a half turn.

Gunner put one hand on his shoulder and grabbed the syringe with the other. As he did, he carefully fingered the clasp on Santa's necklace, which was resting on Bonesetter's spine. He yanked the syringe out and unclasped the necklace simultaneously, then patted Bonesetter on the shoulder, turned him back and pocketed the necklace discreetly.

"And uh," Gunner said, lowering his voice and leaning in discretely, "your fly's down."

Bonesetter darted an alarmed look down, which alerted the others. His fly was ripped open and pink underwear showed through.

Scout snickered and Awol grinned.

"I, I…"

Bonesetter's eyes bounced around the room, seeing everybody seeing him. Cazador swallowed a laugh and Santa shook her head slowly, looking at him like he was pathetic.

"Looks like your panty line's showen, Valentino," Awol mocked.

"You!"

Bonesetter pointed at Awol angrily with his bloody hand, but his fly opened further as he did. He rushed his hand down to zip it up, but struggled to get it with it wrapped in gauze.

While Bonesetter was distracted, Gunner turned and walked out of the bar. Santa pivoted and followed him.

"Wait!" Bonesetter called, turning and stepping towards her with his hands working his crotch.

GRRRRRRRR….

Cadejo growled and coiled between him and Santa and the exit, head low, eyes red and hair raised. Bonesetter immediately halted. Cadejo's muzzle wrinkled and his fangs drooled, showing black spots on bloody red gum.

Bonesetter tried to step around him.

RUFF!

Cadejo barked and snarled louder.

"DAMN!" Bonesetter cursed, retreating.

Intel patted Bonesetter on the shoulder and walked passed, right by Cadejo to the door.

"Where ya going?" Awol called after Intel from the table. "To see the eel whores in the swamp shanties?"

"To work," Intel replied, and left.

Cazador followed him out, snickering at Bonesetter as he passed.

The door clacked shut and the echo faded, leaving them trapped in the room with themselves and their schemes. Bonesetter stared at the door—covering his crotch and grinding his teeth—and seethed:

"Who the hell was that?"

Chapter 16

Gunner strode down Town Trail to the beach. Cadejo trotted in front and Santa paced behind, struggling to catch up.

"Wait," she called.

He walked on, ignoring her, so she jogged up beside him.

"Thank you."

"Mghm," he grunted.

Tuck skipped up alongside.

"Tuck!" she said, grabbing his hand. "Where've you been? I told you not to play around here."

"That was wonderful," Butch said, suddenly striding up.

"What happened?" Santiago asked, jogging up with Mudo, Santiago, Prospector and Undertaker.

"He, he... I... I don't know," Butch recounted as they trekked. "He stood up to the bonesetter."

"I KNEW it!" Campasino proclaimed, appearing alongside.

"You can't see anything," Prospector told Butch.

"I saw it with my own eyes," Butch said.

"That's what worries me."

Suddenly, a large banana leaf smacked Butch in the face and knocked him off the trail. He threw his arms up to shuck it off and rejoin the group.

"Nobody fight da Boonsetta," Big Mama said in a slow Caribbean drawl.

Gunner tried to march on and ignore them, but half the town had suddenly appeared from seemingly nowhere, so he snuck a glance back and saw Santa, Tuck, Butch, Big Mama, Campasino, Santiago, Prospector, Undertaker and Mudo hovering behind like horse flies. He did a double take on Mudo because he looked like a shipwrecked bellhop or colonial soldier. He was about twenty-three and skinny, with tan skin and windswept hair, and he wore a red felt jacket with gold buttons and lapels. The jacket was foreign and somewhat regal, but was scuffed on the cuffs and collar. It looked hot and heavy, and he wore it open without a shirt underneath, with shorts, a machete and flip-flops.

"He did." Santa confirmed. "He stopped him."

"He wasn't afraid?" Santiago asked.

"No," Butch said, catching back up to the group. "He must be trained. Like army."

"He's a soldier!" someone proclaimed.

"An Army Ranger?"

"You can save us!" Prospector suddenly declared, lurching forward, "Simian, he's digging up our ancestors—"

"—He took the grain—"

"—There's no meat—"

"—And he's going for Don Granada's place," Santiago added. "He owns everything else. In forty-eight hours, he's going to..." Santiago paused, it was too terrible to say. "He wants the treasure!"

Gunner walked faster, trying to outpace them and their problem. This problem. Some guy threatening to kill Don Granada with his goons. It had nothing to do with him, but kept boomeranging back to him. Hell, he'd just washed up in the middle of it. He had his own problems.

"Listen," Prospector reasoned, advancing to the front of the group and striding up alongside Gunner, "you can help people."

"You can save my store," Santiago added.

"You can save the town!" Campasino escalated.

Mudo banged on Butch's arm and gestured.

"What's Mudo saying?" Santiago asked.

"That we have to help him," Butch interpreted.

"Wait..." Santiago said, slowing. "Help Gunner? Against Simian? And his hitmen? Whoa, heh now, I know he's a Ranger and all, but we can't just—"

"—I'm going to talk to Simian RIGHT NOW!" Prospector proclaimed, inspired. "Sir! SIR!"

Suddenly, Gunner planted and pivoted.

"STOP!"

The group braked and bumped into each other like cartoon characters. They jumbled up and settled around him. He looked them over. They stared back. They watched and waited, waiting for his big response and declaration that he'd help.

"Listen, you guys are blowing this waaay out of proportion. His fly was down, that's all. How does that mean I'm, 'Trained like army?' I couldn't even run the length of this beach right now. And even if I was, this isn't my problem. There's a war or something and you want a warrior, so you think that's me, just because I showed up in the middle of it and you want it to be me, because you need it to be me because maybe there's nobody else, but it's not. I'm just a deckhand. A sailor. An ordinary guy that's getting on that boat and leaving tomorrow, that's all. I got my own problems. Hell, I'm a pacifist! I don't even know... I mean what do you want me to do? Like get a gun? Who the hell do you think I am?"

The group watched with open mouths like baby birds. After a moment, Prospector ventured:

"A Ranger?"

"No! Ugh. Look... I'm sorry, but I can't help you."

He stared at them directly to punctuate the point, but they simply stared back, not accepting it. Eventually, he grunted and waved his hand, then turned and powered on. They stood frozen and watched him go.

"I told you he's not a Ranger," Butch said when he left, turning on Prospector and smacking his arm. "He's Delta Force!"

Chapter 17

Gunner strode off the trail and onto the beach, leaving the others behind like brides at the altar. Only Tuck jogged after him.

"Heh mister…" Tuck said, catching up and striding alongside, "Do you have a gun?"

"Ah, kid…."

"Well, do ya?"

Gunner marched on, determined to get on that boat as soon as he could. At least half the town was at least half-crazy—that was clear—and he didn't need any part of some local blood feud, especially when the whole town was involved and that crew looked like real shooters.

"It's just that my dad and mom… And grandpa…" Tuck continued, "He fought falconers in the Empty Quarter. But he's old. And these guys, the bonesetter and his friends, I mean… you know… they're dangerous and…"

Jesus, he's still talking.

"And my dad's not here."

"Aghhh…" Gunner groaned.

He remembered what Barboza had said about Tuck's dad, Winter Lorca. How he was missing, and how Tuck was still running around looking for him. Reluctantly, he slowed his forward inertia and eased to a stop in the middle of the beach. He looked down and shook his head.

"All right, listen, kid… That guy, the bonesetter, and his… friends. You don't need to be scared of them."

"I'm not scared."

"Well actually, maybe you do."

Tuck's eyes widened.

"I mean…"

He grunted and looked around, searching for helpful words on the stark beach.

"Well, I'll tell you what's worse, how 'bout that?"

"What?"

"Shaytan. The devil."

Tuck's eyes widened further.

"Ya see, when the devil comes to you, he always looks good. He never looks bad. He looks like a friend, a mentor, a women, even a priest sometimes. So you never know he's the devil. These guys, they look bad. Real bad. All those tattoos and guns. So obviously they're not the devil. Well, they may be working for the devil, and the devil's in them for sure, but I mean, anyway…. The devil always looks good."

Tuck stared with big, disbelieving eyes, half-confused and half-scared. Gunner's mind ran off with his own thought, like a dog chasing a squirrel into the bush. At first he stared directly at Tuck, then began to stare through him, into the past, like he was looking into a well, waiting to hear a pebble splash.

"So you never know he's the devil…" Gunner repeated.

A ghost walked through Tuck. A chill ran through his spine. He stood frozen and petrified. Slowly, Gunner returned. He refocused and noticed that Tuck was more scared now than he had been before he tried to de-scare him. Gunner frowned and straightened.

"Damn. Hmgh. Alright, well, just… you know."

Tuck waited. He didn't know. He didn't know what the hell the castaway was talking about.

Gunner scratched the back of his neck and looked around the beach, uncomfortable.

"What?" Tuck asked.

"Ah you know. I'm here."

"What's that mean?"

"It means if anyone scares you, I'll fix it."

"You promise?"

"Of course. As long as I'm here."

He'd be gone by tomorrow. He stared at Tuck a second, then grinned and grunted definitively. He patted Tuck on the shoulder, turned and strode on, ending it.

"So wait," Tuck said as he walk off, "you have a gun, right?"

Chapter 18

To the east, Cazador sat on an old Spanish canon, in the Castillo on the plateau that overlooked the bay, watching Tuck watching Gunner vector off down the distant beach.

Cazador had thick, wild hair, a long, Latino mustache, and a scruffy face. A howler fang hung from his neck and a hunting bola hung over his shoulder. The bola was made of braided leather cord and orange osage balls. He looked like an Argentinian gaucho—all wood and suede and spit, and gut and gun and earth.

He loved animals but hunted howlers, because he was good at it and knew it had to be done, that's all. He didn't think too deep or worry too much about it, or anything. He just did his work and moved on, which was fine with him.

He believed, however, in all sorts of fantastical things, and claimed to have seen many of them in his travels, like chupacabras, La Llorona and howlers of unusual size. He swore, for example, to have found a dead vaca once that didn't have a tongue in its mouth or blood in its veins.

He also swore to have seen La Sucia. He stumbled on her squatting by a rumbling río one night, washing her clothes in the moonlight. Her hair was long and her naked ass was wide, just like the old abuelos said. But when she turned, her face was the face of a horse's skull. She sprang and lunged at him, and he didn't even pretend to have fought her. Instead, he readily admitted that he ran like a coward as fast as he could, because she was the most terrifying creature he'd ever seen.

Women were his greatest enemy. He enjoyed silent and desolate places that they avoided and abhorred like a jealous mistress, like the campo and high plains, because these sanctums felt limitless and Godly to him, even though he wasn't a religious man. He would wander the earth like an outlaw forever if he could, but he loved women too much, so the small of their backs and the curve of their hips tricked him back into pueblos and outposts on the civilized fringe. He came with dust on his boots and a guilty grin on his face, smelling like chaparral and sage. Grown women frequently giggled together when he passed, although they said they didn't, and he shocked them at a statistically improbable rate when he touched them, like he was ionized by heat lightning. Women both hated this unruly power in him and wanted it in them. They wanted to suck and swallow it like a thunderclap into their stomach, to snatch and sire it, but it was nearly impossible to steal and saddle wildness like this, by definition, so he came and went and walked out on them, every time, leaving them flushed and fevered.

He feasted and laughed with many women, but never said the same one's name twice and never once mentioned any sort of lasting female relationship. Because of this, Gambler knew there was one. Gambler, whose fate paralleled Cazador's more than the others and intersected with his at a life event, believed that Cazador had a home, and instead of travelling alone, he travelled with the presence of some kind of Wife-like-Mother-Goddess, because, Gambler reasoned, to wander so far for so long he had to be wandering from something—at some fixed place, like a point of reference in the stars. Something so strong and furious at an embryonic epicenter that it scared him. Thus, Gambler imagined that Cazador's home was in a village in Argentina, by a river, and that his Wife-like-Mother-Goddess waited for him there patiently, because both she and Cazador knew that someday even the free few have to come home, dragging their laughing lawlessness with them like a hyena with misaligned eyes. And, when he did, she would do what no other women could and devour him whole.

On the ground near Cazador's feet by the canon, six cane corso puppies played. They were about four months old, all big paws and loose skin, hardly puppies anymore. Three tans, two brindles and the largest alpha—a silk-grey muscular male that Cazador named War Dog.

In the graveyard nearby, two dirty gravediggers stood waist deep in a grave, shoveling. One hucked a pile of dirt, and leaned on his shovel to rest.

"I have a question," the gravedigger said.

Cazador pivoted on the cannon and looked at them.

"Why would they put the graveyard, inside the fort?"

Cazador chuckled.

"You sure there's tunnels here?" the other gravedigger added, wrinkling his nose and kicking the dirt beneath his feet. Cazador pointed his finger in the air and said:

"This, was a Spanish castillo."

The gravediggers gazed at him blankly.

"The tunnels run underground," Cazador explained, "to the town. And the tombs."

The gravediggers kept staring, with sweaty, wretched faces

"That's where..." Cazador started to elaborate, "Agh. Forget it. Keep churching. Jur job's to dig, not think. Y after this, jur getting back on the wall."

Another thought dawned on the first gravedigger, and his face lit up.

"And why we rebuilding a fort, that's been destroyed for thirty-three thousand years?"

Cazador chuckled again.

In the middle of the fort, inside the stone Keep, Simian sat at a desk. He was short and stocky and dressed in a flashy shirt and gold chains.

The inside of the Keep had been remodeled into a construction office. Maps and blueprints covered old frescos on stone walls. There was a mock-up of a modern resort where the fort and graveyard sat, with the words *Paradise, Coming Soon* arcing across it. Next to the mock-up was a blueprint of a tall guard tower, with razor-wire and a machine gun turret drawn into it.

Like the frescos, parts of the mock-ups and blueprints had been overlaid by another layer, of topographical maps. This created three sedimentary layers of history and man-plans. One large topo covered an entire wall. It demarcated the coast, fort and town, and stretched around Jungle Mountain and out to an arroyo, labeled *Quebrada Quemada*. Every structure in town was neatly delineated with sharp, straight lines that were much sharper and straighter than they were in reality, including the cabañas, Valhalla and the Ranchero. But the wilds around and beyond these areas were colored green or brown, curved by topo lines and simply labeled *Maleza* or *Selva*.

A blue hash line, labeled *Frontera*, had been drawn further out, around the Ranchero, out to the arroyo and through the swamp shanties, which were drawn at disjointed angles with more crisscrossed lines than straight ones. Guard towers were etched at sensible intervals along this blue line, and some small red X's were drawn within it, mostly in the cemetery and immediate areas around town. There were no X's on Don Granada's land.

Prospector sat at the desk across from Simian, on three boxes of whiskey, wearing his pick-axe in a holster and gripping a floppy straw hat in dirty field fingers. He was weathered and bony, but he puffed his chest out proudly, emboldened by Gunner's arrival and his victory in the Cantina.

Bonesetter, Awol, Gambler and Intel lingered in the stone hollow further back. Bonesetter gripped bloody gauze in his hand. Intel ripped a strip of olive-green duct tape off a roll, which was attached to his hip like a gaffer, and offered it to Bonesetter, smiling. Bonesetter took it and wrapped it around the gauze to secure it better.

"You see," Prospector said, "I mean, it's just, it's just that, that this is our cemetery."

Simian gazed past Prospector's shoulder, out a window and across the bay at Don Granada's bar sparkling on the distant coast.

"What if someone was digging up your grandparents?"

Simian kept staring and didn't respond.

"You're going to release ghosts. They'll wander around. Their souls—"

"—How much booze they got?" Simian asked.

"Pardon?" Prospector asked.

Simian looked past him to Awol behind him.

"How much?"

"None," Awol replied.

"We got it all?"

"Ya."

"Good."

After a moment, Simian looked back at Prospector and smiled.

"Ah… well, like I said," Prospector continued, "this is our cemetery. The town's, you see, our ancestor's, and it's just that, well my wife and I… we buried a son here."

"Awright, I'll look into it." Simian stated.

Prospector stared at him, waiting for more details. What the hell was Simian going to look into? Himself? It began and ended with him. Simian didn't elaborate, and a long, quiet moment passed.

"Jesuz! You're bustin' my bawlz here." Simian said.

Prospector fidgeted, unsure what to do. Simian smiled like a chimpanzee to help, which didn't. Prospector glanced around and noticed that Intel had gotten up and was standing over and behind him like a prison guard, smiling softly. Prospector wrung his straw hat in his hands, and Intel placed his heavy hand on his shoulder. Slowly, Prospector stood. Intel smiled encouragingly, patted him on the shoulder and guided him towards the door.

"Oh heh heh," Simian added as Prospector exited, "watcha name, compadre?"

"Don't worry," Intel interjected, "I know it."

Prospector glanced at Intel nervously. He did, in part, because Intel was a force. A force of calm, confident strength. He was a solid fifty-year-old man with thick arms, a buzzed head and round cheeks. He was built like a fullback, but taller, and was handsome like a bull. He usually wore field kit: nylon pants and short-sleeved, collared shirts. He never carried a gun, like he didn't need one, but always had a pen in his breast pocket and a roll of olive green duct tape latched to his belt.

Intel smiled warmly at Prospector, pressed his hand on Prospector's back and eased him out the door and down the steps, clacking the door shut behind him.

"So ya never seen this guy befawr?" Simian asked.

"No. Never," Bonesetter answered, holding his wounded hand.

Simian looked at Intel for more intel.

"He washed ashore eight days ago," Intel said.

"Washed a'shore?"

"He washed up on the beach, literally. He says he's a deckhand, who fell off a boat. But Don Granada—"

"—Granaada!? DONG Granaada!?"

"Ya, Don Granada says he's a fisherman. But nobody believes that."

"Watta they think?"

"That he's a soldier. Delta Force."

Simian's eyes narrowed. He rubbed his chin with his small hands, thinking.

"Delta Force, huh?"

"He was unconscious at Granada's place for a week," Intel continued. "Woke up yesterday, and turned up at the Cantina today, asking for Scout and a doctor."

"Scout? Why?"

Intel shrugged.

"So he like waat," Simian asked, "pops up like a bawbber? Awtta nowhere?"

"About."

"And just like that," Simian said, turning to Bonesetter, "this fisherman's been awake a day, and he humiliates you?"

"Humiliates?" Bonesetter asked.

Awol chuckled.

"Fuck you," Bonesetter shot.

"Fuck you," Awol shot back.

"You shouldn't be experimenten on those howlers neither," Gambler interjected, rolling a playing card across his knuckles, "without killing 'em. Ask Caz. And you think that dog forgot what happened to his leg?"

Bonesetter grinned.

"How tawl iz he?" Simian asked.

"What?" Awol asked.

"How tawl iz he?"

"Who?"

"This stranger," Simian replied. "The fisherman."

"Tall, I guess," Bonesetter replied. "I mean—"

"—Does this postpone the deadline?" Gambler interrupted.

"You tell me huh?" Simian snapped. "No it doesn't postpone the flippin' deadline but it'z illogical, unplanned and I don' like it. Everyting's going fine. We gotta plan. We're executin' it. We're helping the town, then BAM! Right before ejaculation this jokka bawbs up awtta nowhere for a cawk-block? Who's he working fawr? Did ya ever think about that? Huh? Huh?"

"He—" Bonesetter says.

"—He'z a SPY! For GRANAADA!"

The shout echoed off the stone walls and hung in the air.

"What do you want us to do, boss?" Gambler asked.

"Watta ya think I wantcha ta do? You wanna see if he's a fighter? Fight 'em. See wat he does. He poked ya in the eye, poke him back!"

Bonesetter grinned, pleased with the order. He popped up and tromped out the door. Gambler tapped the playing card against his head and followed Bonesetter out with Awol. Intel, however, stopped at the door on the way out and looked back at Simian, waiting for orders.

Simian looked at him a second, then nodded once, silently.

Intel nodded back and followed his associates out.

Chapter 19

Gunner woke from a siesta to a presence.

He was reclining in a wooden chair on the backshore, under the uvero tree, near where Don Granada first saw him. His bare feet rested in the sand and two whiskey glasses sat on a small table next to him. They were dusty and bone-dry, and a rattlesnake rattle lay in one like a crime scene. Distant waves washed, a seagull squawked, and Mulata from the Amazon towered over him, backlit by the sun.

"Pick a card." She said.

She fanned a stack of tarot cards out in front of him. He cracked his eyes open, cantered his face into her shadow so he could see her better and focused. After a second, he straightened in his chair and pulled one.

"The sun," She mused. "Hm."

He waited.

"The boy, Tuck."

"Ya?"

"Many years from now, after he's crossed the Interior, and that's not just a word to him anymore, the only memory he'll have of his father… is eating plantain chips with him on the couch."

"Uhhh…"

She bent over and leaned forward, inches from his face. She rested her henna hands on his cheeks and rubbed her thumbs across his cheekbones, studying the supernovas in his Aegean eyes. She was exotic and wild like a leopard, with cocoa skin, silk hair, rings on every finger and a loose, sheer top that flowed and flashed body chains and flesh.

She slid her lips to his earlobe and whispered:

"If he lives."

He watched, transfixed.

She ran her fingers through his hair to his neck and slowly massaged behind his ears.

"Shhhhh…." She cooed.

He woke into a dream. She was so surreal and interesting in his half-sleep phase-state that he surrendered and followed her to see where she would go. He stopped fighting and resisting, and accepted that everything at that moment was perfect the way it was, because it was, even the imperfect things. He dropped want and fear, and the yolk of trying to control everything everywhere all the time. The world was as was, in the moment, without judgement or concept, and like this there was peace. He fell into that space and was suddenly back on the water. He saw shark gum, a turtle shell, a Carib born with fish scales under his wrist, and a manta ray flying underwater that was so big that a community of small coral reef fish swam with it like an underwater island in the open ocean, darting across its black back, far from where they were supposed to be.

"Interesting," she whispered.

She smiled, intrigued, then snatched the sun card back from his hand. She looked him over once more, as if trying to decide what to make of him but not knowing. Suddenly, she simply turned and left as quickly as she came, hip-swaying away like a mirage.

Gunner sniffed the air after she left, smelling her.

She smelled like creosote in the desert before a monsoon.

"Boy, you should have seen how she used to vex men!" Padre hooted, suddenly waddling up from behind and breaking the spell. "Like voodoo! And dogs would howl from blocks away, not knowing why. That's what they say anyway. The gypsies."

He plopped in a chair next to Gunner.

"But you gotta be even more careful with her now," Padre continued. "'Cause she'll get in your head and play around a while. Re-arrange things. Hide some memories in one place, desires in another. And you know what's the most dangerous part?"

"What?" Gunner asked, not wanting to, but unable to resist.

Padre looked around, then leaned over his armrest and whispered, "You'll like it."

Gunner looked back in the direction she'd gone, but she'd already disappeared. There was only beach and the hypnotic ebb and flow of the waves WISHHHISHing and WASHHHHHing ashore. On the high shore, however, he noticed Mudo, shaving the cayuco. He'd salvaged it from the sand and raised it up on coconut tree logs. A box of tools lay by it.

"Ya know the Greeks," Padre said, picking up Gunner's empty whiskey glass and smelling the rattle in it, "they believed that once ya died and entered Hades, ya could either drink from the river Mnemosyne and remember everything from your life, or drink from the river Lethee and forget it all. If ya drank from one river you remembered everything. If ya drank from the other, ya forgot it all and were reincarnated."

Gunner waited for Padre to make his point, but he just sat there.

"What?" Gunner finally asked.

"Which river do ya wanna drink from?"

"So I'm dead?"

"Are you alive?"

Gunner chuckled. Of course he was alive. But Padre stared serious and waited, without blinking his small black eyes on his big round face, expecting an answer.

"Of course."

"How do you know?"

Gunner chuckled again, but less lightly.

"Because. This. The sun. The heat on my skin. The sand in my toes. Her. Well, maybe she's a bad example. But pain. That's real. Sure as shit that's real. And you. You know I'm alive, so we share a… collective consciousness."

"Ya, but what if *I'm* not alive?"

"Then we're hosed."

Padre chuckled.

"You know," Gunner said, "everyone here thinks I'm the strange one, the strang-er, but what if you're all crazy—you, her, that loon Bar-bozo, all of you—and I'm actually the sane one?"

"Whaddaya mean?"

"I mean you've all been in your crazy-town so long that you can't see how far you've drifted."

"But then we'd never know you're sane, because we're all crazy."

"Ya. That's my point."

"What?"

"That you're crazy. And don't know it."

Padre furrowed his brow and stared at Gunner, seriously considering the thought.

"Naaaaah!" He finally laughed. "That's EXACTLY what a crazy person would think! And if you're the only sane person in an insane asylum, then you're the crazy one!"

"What?"

"Ya, you had it bad out there," Padre concluded, "to believe something like that. Maybe hit your head or something. You should talk to someone about that."

"Talk to who, like a padre?"

"God just wants us to be happy, that's all. Here…"

Padre extracted a bundle and unwrapped it to reveal a moldy block.

"Eat this. It's cheese, cave-aged twenty years. I'm a cook and a gourmand. Made it myself."

Gunner hesitated, but Padre pumped it in his face. Reluctantly, Gunner broke off a morsel and set it in his mouth. And gagged.

Uufff! Uufff! Uufff…!

"Order us a kebab. If ya help the town—"

"—I can't do that," Gunner choked.

"Why not? I'm hungry."

"No, I mean, I can't help… Wait. Aren't you eating this?"

"That?" Padre asked, looking at the cheese block. "Heavens no. That tastes wretched. It's twenty years old!"

Gunner stared flatly at him.

"It has mold on it," Padre added.

Gunner spit and picked a flake off his lip.

"If ya decide to help the town—"

"—That. I can't do that. I'm just a guy. Who's leaving tomorrow. I don't even believe in violence. I'm a pacifist. And why does everybody, I mean, how come nobody thinks that maybe, just maybe, the simplest explanation could be the right one? You know, an Occam's razor thing? That I'm just a deckhand, who fell off a boat?"

Padre stared, expressionless.

"Even if I could help, which I can't, why would I?"

"For redemption." Padre proclaimed.

Gunner stared back. Nobody in this crazy-ass town listened to a word he said.

"But ya better hurry," Padre added, jabbing a finger discretely towards heaven like God wouldn't see, "'cause if ya don't, Don Granada will die."

Gunner spit.

"Ya can't change who ya are, Gunner."

"My name's not even Gunner to begin with! And even if I was the killer everyone wants me to be, don't you think we should try to change and improve ourselves, I mean like, being a friar and all?"

"Sure," Padre said, "give it a shot."

Gunner frowned.

"Ya know what Mulata says is the best part?" Padre said, taking the rattle from the whiskey glass and shaking it at him like a snake.

"The rattle. It still has some venom in it, like a good woman."

"You know a lot about women huh?"

Padre's lips puckered and his beady eyes widened.

"Makes ya see the devil."

Chapter 20

Bonesetter stood barefoot in a bathroom, staring at himself in a mirror next to an open window. His black doctor's bag, a half-eaten sandwich, a frayed photo, pliers, staples, a needle and a red ring box sprawled on the counter next to him. A Hawaiian sling with a barbed spear also leaned against the sink, and his shoes scattered on the wooden floor.

He pulled the duct tape and bloody gauze off his hand. The gauze ripped some of the dried blood and half-healed skin off the raw wound with it as it came, causing him to grind his teeth in pain. Two holes punched through his hand, wide enough for a speck of light to shine through. Fangs.

He shook his hand off and picked up the frayed photo. The word *Family* was scrawled on the back. He stared at it and nodded with conviction, then bit his sandwich and set a staple across the first hole on the back of his hand as he chewed. He grabbed his pliers and pinched the staple shut over the wound. As soon as he did, his eyes sprung wide in pain. He gagged on his sandwich and choked back a silent scream.

Surprised, he took a second to compose himself and level-off his breathing, then set another staple over the second hole, inhaled and stapled it shut. After, he pushed the needle through the puffy skin around the holes and threaded thick fishing line back and forth over them in a haphazard pattern, smiling through the pain as he went. When he finished, Frankenstein stitches zigzagged across the back of his hand.

He grinned proudly at his sloppy, questionable work, and accidently knocked the pliers into the sink. They clanked around the bowl. He cringed and glanced along the length of his shoulder to the door, instinctively trying to catch the noise and keep it from escaping with his hand. As the silence returned, blood dripped from his wound into the bowl.

He quickly cleaned up his mess, threw everything back in his bag and shoved the rest of the sandwich in his mouth. He squatted, opened the cabinet beneath the sink and wedged the ring box between the slip-nut on the drain pipe and the wall. He shut the cabinet, picked up his shoes and grabbed the barbed spear, then opened the bathroom door and stepped out of the bathroom - and into the great room in Don Granada's ranchero.

In the middle of the room, Tuck kneeled on the floor, studying a green topo map. Tuck leaned forward and circled an area out in the bush, far from town, labeled *Quebrada Quemada*, and made a notation in his leather journal.

Bonesetter watched, smiling softly.

Tuck picked up a soda and struggled to twist off the cap. Bonesetter stepped forward to help, but caught himself and stopped. He stared a moment and frowned, then retreated back into the bathroom. He shut the door quietly behind him, tiptoed to the open window on his bare feet, and climbed out.

Chapter 21

As Bonesetter slipped out of the Ranchero, Barboza stood at the end of the dock, staring stern over his handlebar mustache at the sea. He wore his war boots and tattered shorts, which exposed his knobby knees, and held a shortwave radio at his side. The microphone's cable curled past his scarred shins and dangled on the dock by his boots like a severed snake.

Don Granada walked up the dock and stopped next to him. They stared silently over the sea. It was flat and spotless, past the reef and all the way to the horizon, at the curvature of the earth. A seagull drifted in the distance, and the ocean lapped against a piling nearby. After a long moment, Barboza said:

"The boat didn't come."

Slowly, Don Granada nodded.

"The radio?"

"No. Nothing. Static. Silence."

"Strange."

"Yes."

"So two weeks," Don Granada summarized, "and no boat. And no radio."

"And one castaway." Barboza added. He turned and looked directly at Granada.

"Something's wrong, Diego."

Don Granada didn't reply.

"The stranger knows something. I don't know what, but he was out there, and he's the last to come in. Of all of us. Of everyone here. Even the tourists. He's the last person to come to town. And he's hiding something that he's not saying."

"Everybody's hiding something," Don Granada replied.

They held their gaze a moment, then looked back over the ocean, beyond the continental shelf from which the castaway came.

"It's like the Sand Sea," Barboza noted.

"Ya? How so?"

"When we made the run for the oasis, in Siwa, hiding in the old Nazi minefield... I had this feeling, like I do now."

"That there's something out there?"

"Ya. Surrounding us. Slowly choking us..."

Don Granada looked back over the ocean and into the past, considering the thought. But he didn't have to consider it long because he already knew, instinctively; Barboza was right. Something was wrong.

"It's always been out there," Don Granada conceded, "circling like a shark in the sea. But ya, it's close now. Closer than it's ever been."

Chapter 22

After resting on the beach, Gunner strolled back towards his cabaña. Surfer transected him half-way, wearing board-shorts and carrying a surfboard, heading to the point break off Jungle Mountain, which was dangerous to surf alone. He nodded to Gunner as he passed, then stopped suddenly and turned back.

"Heh Gunner…"

"Ya?"

"Did you hear?"

"What?"

"The boat didn't come."

"What?"

"Ya, no, not today brah. Maybe mañana."

"Really?"

"Ya."

"Shit."

Gunner nodded and considered the thought.

"Heh, when was the last time the boat came, exactly?"

"I dunno. About two weeks ago or something?"

"Really? Two weeks?"

"Ya. Something like that."

"And it's supposed to come every day?"

"Mostly. Ya. Every day."

Gunner looked over the ocean. Two weeks was a lot different than one day, or two. Ya, something was wrong.

"Oh heh," Surfer said, starting to leave, "if you run into Coco, tell her I went to town to like… look for beer."

Gunner chuckled.

"Crazy chicks," Surfer explained. "They're wild, but…"

"You pay."

"Yep." Surfer agreed.

"Still," Gunner noted, "sometimes it's worth it."

"Sometimes you don't have a choice."

They shared a knowing laugh and continued their separate ways.

When Gunner approached his cabaña, his saw Santa, Tuck and Butch standing in front of it. But Tuck looked like he was about to cry.

"What's wrong?"

Gunner followed their eyes to the cabaña. There, about five feet up, Cadejo was pinned to the wall. The Hawaiian spear was stuck in his eye, through his head, into the wood. He hung against the wall like a gutted goat.

Dead.

Murdered.

Gunner stopped flat.

Nobody moved. They stood in solemn disbelief—shocked, sad and angry.

After a moment, Gunner climbed the deck, gently lifted Cadejo and twisted out the lance. Cadejo's head rolled and his body slumped in Gunner's arms.

Gunner cradled him off the deck and set him in the middle of the grass in front of everyone.

"This isn't right." Tuck sniffled, white-knuckling his knife, "I'm gonna... I should..."

Tuck turned on Gunner.

"What are ya gonna do?"

Everyone looked at Gunner and waited. He stared back like a stone. The palms rustled.

"Hahaha..."

Suddenly, Awol strut up behind them, laughing cocky. Gambler followed and leaned against a palm, rolling playing cards over his knuckles, and Bonesetter orbited further back, grinning like a ghoul with twitchy energy. Lacerations ripped down Bonesetter's neck and left forearm, above his stitched hand, looking a lot like he'd just been mauled by a dog. A dog fighting for his life.

Gambler flipped a playing card over in his hand; the six of clubs.

"The hole," He said.

He smirked, slid it in his back pocket and flipped over another card for himself; the ace of clubs.

"Two aces," he grinned.

While Gambler and Bonesetter positioned themselves to flank Gunner for a fight, Awol kept advancing and got in Gunner's face like a boxer. Butch stepped back out of the potential blast radius, but Santa and Tuck held their ground in it.

"Ya..." Awol said, staring into Gunner's eyes, "whatcha gonna do, stranger?"

Gunner didn't respond.

Awol stripped his shirt and tossed it aside. He was big, muscled and tattooed, like an MMA fighter who'd spent a few years AWOL in Thailand, training, drinking and fucking. Muay Thai, whiskey and go-go girls. He had a pretty-boy mohawk like a futbolista, and a thick beard like a Spartan, which was trimmed on the sides and long on the chin. He cut a powerful, intimidating figure.

"When we catch the man who did this…" Awol smirked.

Bonesetter paced behind him and grinned sheepishly, picking gravel from his arm.

"You just can't stop, can you?" Santa snapped at him, stepping forward and yanking Tuck away.

"Heh!" Bonesetter called. "Waaait."

But she ignored him and walked off. Gambler watched Bonesetter watching her.

"Don't worry mom," Awol taunted as she went, "the kid can hang out with us anytime."

"Listen, friend," Gunner said, getting back in Awol's face, "her husband's missing, her kid's looking for him, her father's losing his everything, she's trying to run this bar and keep this place together and you… you gentlemen, are trying to… buy their land. Why don't you… back off a little, huh?"

Awol snarl-smiled and inched closer.

"Give me the spear," he whispered, dropping the smile.

Gunner looked down and noticed that he gripped the Hawaiian spear that he'd removed from Cadejo's head like a weapon.

"Now. Ghandi."

They glared, danger close. Bonesetter stopped pacing. Gambler stopped flipping cards. Awol's jaw hardened and Gunner's grip tightened.

One second.

Two—

—CRACK!

Awol head-butted him.

Gunner's head ricocheted back. He flipped the spear in his hand during the recoil to strike but froze before he sprung back. Blood dripped from his nose.

Awol stepped at him again and waited for Gunner to attack. Slowly, Gunner straightened and drew a deep breath, then leveled his eyes and stared at Awol again.

One—

—CRACK!

Awol head-butted him again. He stumbled. Awol lunged forward and shoved him to a knee. Gunner caught himself to spring back but stopped just as—

—*WHUMP!*

Awol kicked him in the face, blasting him back into the dirt.

WHUMP!

"RAGHH!"

Suddenly, Barboza Comanche-yelled out of nowhere and charged to help, but Bonesetter simply stuck out a leg and tripped him, and he thumped flat onto his face, hitting the ground like a bag of bones. His old bones didn't bounce, but he shambled up and continued charging. Gambler stepped forward, collared him and pinned him to a palm with his forearm in his neck.

"Calm down war hero," Gambler advised.

WHUMP!

Awol kicked Gunner again on the ground.

WHUMP! WHUMP!

Gunner rolled against Cadejo. His grip loosened on the spear and it rolled out of his hand and into the dirt.

"This is ridiculous," Awol complained, lording over him, "Come on! Get up! Get up and FIGHT!"

Gunner peeled an eye open and squinted up, but didn't move. Didn't fight.

"It's fun," Awol encouraged.

But Gunner just closed his eye and grimaced.

"That old dog had more fight than you."

WHUMP!

Bonesetter stepped up and kicked Gunner in the chest. The air *umph*-ed from his body and he groaned.

And took it.

He took it. He just lay on the ground and took it. Butch watched, with a confused and hurt look on his face, while Barboza shook his head slowly and scowled, still pinned against the palm by Gambler's forearm.

It was over.

He was done.

He lay on the ground, pressed up against Cadejo's corpse. Neutralized. Impotent. Harmless.

"Well that was disappointing," Awol muttered.

Awol tossed his hands up, exasperated, then he shook his head and walked off. As he passed Butch, he punched him square in the face without breaking stride. Butch dropped to his knees and covered his cataract eyes in pain.

Chapter 23

Gunner retreated from the fight to the ocean. He stormed passed a palm and jabbed the Hawaiian spear deep into its trunk without breaking stride.

"Boy it looked like that hurt!" Padre remarked, following him. "First he kicked ya on one side like this, then ya turned the other cheek like in the Bible or something and he kicked you on the other side like that!"

Gunner ripped off his shirt and hucked it in Padre's face, thundering ahead. Padre bungled it off as he waddled. Gunner wiped blood from his nose, glanced at it on his fingers and smeared it across his abs.

"Boy, if you're done with violence, she's not done with you!"

"Ain't my fight holy man."

"No kidding. He kicked your ass!"

Gunner strode directly into the ocean and dove into a wave. Padre stopped at the waterline and held up Gunner's shirt, offering it back helpfully. But Gunner wasn't looking back. He was surging ahead. Padre shrugged and watched him swim out.

A minute later, Gunner surfaced past the breakers, fifty yards from shore. He looked back on the bay, at Jungle Mountain and Valhalla, and at the cabañas, beach, Castillo, and tips of the town peeking through the trees. The church's bell-tower rose above them, and the setting sun reflected off it.

The sea was calm past the breakers. It washed the blood from his stomach, which floated away like ink from an octopus. Colorful clown fish swam through it. He wiped salt water from his face and slicked back his hair, then lay back and floated, gazing at the sun-splattered sky.

His jaw hurt.

Fuck his jaw hurt.

Chapter 24

An hour later, Gunner relaxed on the beach with the hotties and hippies. They lounged around a bonfire and flickered in the firelight, listening to reggae music and passing a thick joint from hand to hand. They laughed, smiled and chatted about the liquor, which had first dwindled and now run dry.

"So how much alcohol does Simian have?" Surfer asked.

"Plenty jah," Bumster stated. "If this place ran out of booze, it wouldn't be, This Place, you know?"

"That's not how it's made," Burner explained. "I've been here for yeeeears. You gotta wipe the hard drive man, get off the grid."

"I knooow," Surfer continued, trying not to lose his patience, "but how much?"

"How much what bro?" Bumster asked.

Surfer dropped his head and held it in his hands.

"All of it," Protestor answered. "Simian's got it all."

"Then let's go steal it," Surfer pitched, darting back up to them. "Screw Simian. We need alcohol for Coco's party."

"Ha!" Trust Fund mocked. "They'll shoot you in the back. Or front. Probably both. The deserter, or that hunter…"

"I'm not doing it," Protestor declared.

"Don't worry soul surfer," Bumster said, "The boat'll bring more beer."

"Ya, and when's that?"

"Ya know… The boaaaat."

Surfer shook his head, amazed at Bumster and Burners' circular inaction. He looked past them to Gunner and shook his head, exasperated. Gunner smirked knowingly and nodded. He got it.

As he did, Sail straddled him from behind. She slid her hands under his loose shirt and ran her coral nails up his obliques to his broad swimmer's chest. She gently raked them across it, then flung her hair out of the way and kissed his neck.

As she played with him, he reached in his pocket, extracted the locket that he'd taken from Bonesetter, and opened it. Sand fell out and a water-warped picture of Santa and Tuck smiled back from within. A third person had been in the picture, a man, but Bonesetter had ripped off his head.

Chapter 25

The next morning, Intel rode a beach cruiser down a long dirt road. Palms shaded the road from above, and invasive plants grew and stretched into it from the darker jungle on either side, drinking the light-food that breached the canopy and escaped the ravenous leaf-mouths above.

Intel hummed and peddled leisurely. His age, stature, thick forearms and quiet confidence hulked the bike's frame, which clanked periodically under his weight on the uneven surface.

Gradually, the jungle strangled the road—like it did everything else—and it narrowed to a lane, then a jaguar trail. When it became thin enough that he couldn't pedal easily anymore, he dismounted by the trunk of a Spanish lime. At the foot of the tree, at a fork in the jungle, someone had built a small shrine. The shrine was framed by vines that had been interwoven when wet around rocks. At the base was a burnt candle and some coins. Atop was a painting of the Virgin Mary with a skull face. And in the center was a picture of a man in spectacles; Winter Lorca.

Intel leaned his bike against the shrine and hiked on, further into the jungle.

The trail coiled under the canopy, between towering trunks, past white orchids and red heliconia. It shifted slightly underfoot on clay soil, following a clear brook to a large ceiba, which the Maya believe connect the living world to the dead. There, a red, hand-painted sign was nailed to a tree, which read: "Ningún Mal Puede Penetrar Aquí" - "No Evil Can Penetrate Here." Twenty feet up the old ceiba, a sweat-den lay in the tree's lowest branches, like a baby in its mother's arms.

The den was built unevenly with warped planks, into and around the tree, like it grew and bent with the tree over time to the point that the two eventually adapted to each other and became one. But that alignment couldn't last, because the tree kept growing while the den didn't, until someday when the tree would grow through it and swallow it into itself like a memory. The den was simple and rustic, with a deck, single room and thatched palm roof that wrapped halfway around the trunk. Epiphytes grew on the roof above, and vines hung from the deck below. A makeshift net-hammock stretched between the deck and the trunk, and a pan of psilocybin mushrooms dried in the sun on a nearby branch.

Intel stopped below the tree and looked up.

When he did, Gambler exited the sweat-den and stepped onto the deck. He was shirtless and barefoot and his jeans were unbuttoned. He ran his hand through disheveled hair, scratched his fuzzy chest and looked down at Intel. *What kind of bullshit*, Intel thought, *does he think he found this time?*

"War, women and whiskey," Gambler proclaimed for no discernable reason, "fuck."

Dam, Intel thought, *that's actually profound.*

Gambler grinned like a conqueror, flung his holster over his shoulder and stepped to the ladder to climb down.

As he did, Mulata emerged from the smoky lair behind him. She sauntered onto the deck in panties and Gambler's shirt, which was unbuttoned and hung loose, flashing the perfect under-arc of her mocha tits. She held a joint and leaned her elbows on an anteater skin that draped over a railing. She crossed an ankle behind a long, lithe leg, and a thin belly chain dangled and sparkled below her flat stomach, hanging from her sinuous hips.

"Morning," Intel greeted.

"Morning."

He stared and admired her directly, and she let him—not as a predator who would devour her, but as a fatherly bull who would fuck and shelter her. But they both knew she didn't get fucked, and didn't need shelter.

"You know," Intel said, "there's one thing nobody can tell me. That I don't know."

"What?"

"Where you live."

"I don't live here."

"I know."

She smiled like a cat.

"I come here for the medicine," she purred, "for the tamarind, psilocybin, cocao, cat's claw... these things, they find me. I collect them."

"What? Weeds?"

"No. Visions."

He smiled softly.

"What finds you?" she asked.

He cocked his head slightly like a dog, unsure what she meant.

"We fight for things we can't have, and get things we don't even fight for," she explained. "Collect things, that gravitate towards us effortlessly. Each of us, have something that gravitates towards us, and something that pushes away, like a magnet. Money, men, misery… violence."

His smile grew.

"Secrets," she decreed, "you collect secrets. You never set out to, but here you are. And look at you. They just came to you, one after the other, downhill. Tumbling over and atop each other like an avalanche. It wasn't even hard. Everyone's got something like this, that isn't hard for them. And now you have a lifetime of stolen secrets, hidden in you like jars on the shelf. A jar of seduction. Betrayal. Murder…"

"I've been hearing secrets for thirty years," he countered, "and believe me, there's some things in this world, you don't want to hear."

This time, she smiled.

"You're like this tree," she said. "It's over two hundred years old. It's seen everything, but can say nothing."

"I can say plenty."

"And when you do, it stings. Like a scorpion."

I wouldn't be surprised, he thought, *if she just suddenly turned into a leopard.*

"Here's another secret for you," she added. "The monkeys…"

He waited.

"They're sick."

She put the joint to her full lips and inhaled, then parted them and let the smoke waft up. He waited for her to elaborate, but she didn't, and he'd heard enough secrets to know she wouldn't.

"But there's places in the jungle," she said, looking out, "even deeper than this."

"Where?" he asked, knowing she wanted him to, knowing it was a compliance test. That's how she worked. Hooking men, then pulling them in, deeper and deeper. Like most men, he was either unable or unwilling to resist following her where she wanted to go. Most men would say they could resist her but just didn't want to, but what, he wondered, was really the difference at that point?

"In your mind," she said.

He knew she was trying to worm into his own mind to seduce

and steal the secrets he'd seduced and stolen from others. And he knew he could resist her if she was really trying, like in a smoky boteco one night over drinks, but he still wondered what mussurana methods she'd use to do it, and how delicate the fall would feel, which was the only crack she needed to begin. She was like water, searching for a way, and his eyes drifted back to her hips. She'd already begun.

Gambler reached the ground before she could play with his head any more—a thick and tempting target. Gambler walked barefoot over duff on the jungle floor, over leaves that were leaching into the soil and decaying into nutrients that the cannibal roots of some of the same trees they fell from sucked back skyward, recycling nutrients like a dog eating a stillborn, in a place without winter.

"How'd you find me?" Gambler asked as he approached.

But Intel just grinned and hugged him.

"Simian wants a meet," Intel said, "since the deadline's tomorrow."

Chapter 26

Gambler cut across the corner of the town plaza to a guanacaste tree on the far side. Bonesetter's black doctor's bag sat alone on the ground near the tree's trunk, next to one of its elephant ear seed pods.

Nobody was there, so Gambler squatted over the bag. As he did, something rustled in the bushes nearby. He glanced at the sound, then quickly opened the bag and rooted through it, past a flask, stethoscope, nail gun, speculum, a bloody bandage—

"—What the hell?"

He pulled out a stone. An ordinary stone, slightly bigger than an acorn. His stone.

"That cocksucking son-of-a—"

—*CRUNCH, CRUNCH...*

Gambler quickly stood, kicked the bag aside and slyly pocketed the stone in a single fluid motion as Bonesetter crunched out of the bushes, eating a banana and zipping up his fly.

"Gimme that," Bonesetter mumbled with a full mouth, pointing his banana at his bag.

Gambler, however, ignored him. He simply turned and walked away, across the plaza and past the Saint Peter statue towards Simian and Scout on the other side.

Simian and Scout stared up at La Iglesia de los Caídos. Scout chewed on a cigar, and Simian wore a red Hawaiian shirt with dancing luau girls on it. It was unbuttoned halfway, and chest hair and gold chains flashed out from underneath.

Mudo and several skinny laborers in shipwrecked clothes thunked the church's thick walls with heavy sledgehammers. Intel and a few soldados in khaki uniforms watched lazily nearby, sitting on a short wall in the shade under a flowering malinche tree, named after Cortez's Azteca mistress. Intel had his green duct tape roll and gnawed on a tortilla. A gaunt laborer stared at the tortilla like a zombie while another swung his sledgehammer into the church like a mummy.

THUNK.

Cazador ambled across the plaza and up to Intel with his bola slung over his shoulder. *Intel will know something*, Cazador thought, *because Intel knows everything.*

"Where's Polito?" Cazador asked.

"I don't know," Intel replied.

"What?"

"I don't know."

Cazador stopped and stared, amazed.

"Ju haven't seen Polito, or heard anything?"

"No."

"Nothing?"

"No. Nothing."

Yep, Cazador concluded, *he knows even more than I feared, because the only time Intel said he didn't know anything was when he knew too much. Something is definitely wrong.*

Just then, Big Mama waddled by, between the sledgers and soldados with a colorful pagne wrapped around her waist and a bucket of bananas balanced on her head. Her two kids zigzagged and dallied behind. She watched the laborers pound the church, then turned on Cazador and Intel and waved a fat finger at them as she passed.

"Barüti labugún Satanasi Hama lumáfianu sielugiñe turóbuli ubouagun, Gama lumoun málühali sun turóbuli le agumuchagua." She scolded.

"Garifuna?" Cazador asked.

"Ya." Intel replied.

"What chee say?"

"I don't know. I only know a few words."

"What?"

"Ka mini lubéi lebegi asalbaruni."

"What's that mean?"

"How much is the ransom."

After Big Mama passed, Undertaker slinked up, tall and skinny and hunched on his crooked spine and slanted, chicken-bone shoulders.

Intel stood and hugged him, and Undertaker whispered something in his ear. Intel listened, then nodded and patted Undertaker on the shoulders with both hands. Undertaker nodded once, then turned and slinked away like the reaper.

In front of the church, Simian studied the bell-tower. A backhoe claw rose high behind the workers and coiled by the church's bell-tower like a scorpion.

"Think it'll break in one blow?" Simian asked.

Gambler and Scout stood next to him and watched, but didn't reply.

The claw reared back and paused, then thrust forward and crashed into the bell-tower. Instead of breaking it, however, it didn't budge, and the claw ricocheted back and broke. The claw burst off its iron pins and the heavy bucket broke off the boom. It fell two stories towards Mudo. Mudo didn't see it coming, but Campasino did. Campasino's eyes widened and he dove. He shoved Mudo out of the way just as the claw whisked passed Mudo's head, caught Campasino's arm and hammered it to the ground.

"AHHHHH!" Campasino yelled.

He squirmed on the ground, pinned to the earth next to the claw, which was bigger than he was and four times as heavy. His elbow vanished under it without a sliver of space between the bucket and ground.

"Damn," Simian muttered.

Mudo and the other laborers rushed to lift the claw off Campasino, but it didn't budge.

"This is bad," Simian added. "This is willy bad. I mean, where am I gonna get anotta backhoe from? Huh?"

Scout shrugged. How the hell would he know?

"If they don't get that claw off soon," Bonesetter said, striding up with his doctor's bag, "I'll have to amputate."

"Whadya kill the dawg for?" Simian shot.

"I—"

"—I like dawgs. My sansei had one."

"But you—"

"—I told ya to poke him in the eye, not kill a dawg! Boy you escalated alright, Jezuz! Sometimes ya scare me."

"We—" Bonesetter said.

"—WE DO WAAT I TELL WE TO DO! Ya got that?"

"Sure. Boss."

A moment later, Intel, Cazador and Awol leisured over and joined Simian, Scout, Bonesetter and Gambler in front of the church. They huddled up for their planning meeting in the plaza while Campasino groaned on the ground under the iron claw behind them.

"So lemme get this straight." Simian asked as Mudo and the laborers struggled to lift the claw off Campasino, "This schlep, the stranger, he humiliates you, then letz you crush him? He just let you beat him up?"

"Well..." Bonesetter replied.

"And hez sayen hez a fisherman, who fell off a mwerchant ship, wit a knife wound?"

"Well that part, ya, I mean, he says he's a deckhand but—"

"—And he washes ashore, wit scurvy?"

"Ya."

"Can ya get scurvy in a few days?"

Awol looked at Dr. Bonesetter for the answer, but Dr. Bonesetter just shrugged.

"Maybe he hit his head on the oar," Awol speculated, nonsensically.

"What awr?" Simian asked.

"The one he washed ashore with."

"He fell off a merchant ship, wit an awr?"

"Ya."

Simian stared at them a second, then shook his head.

"Do merchant ships have awrs?"

Bonesetter and Awol stared, dumbfounded.

"What is dis, the fifteenth century!?"

"Well," Bonesetter ventured, "in the lifeboat—"

"—That's my point!"

They didn't get his point.

"He was in a raft! For a long time!"

They still didn't get his point.

"The scurvy, awr... He's LYIN'! Come on! Jesuz guyz!"

Simian tossed his arms up and stomped off. It was too much. They were just too much sometimes.

"But if he's really a fighter," Gambler mused, "why refuse to fight?"

"It doesn't make sense," Simian said, charging back to the group. "Who is he and where'd he come from? He's not just anotta hippie."

"Are you kidding?" Awol said, grooming up his futbalista mohawk with his hands. "We just kicked his ass. Toes up. He didn't even take a swing. He's a nobody. A drifter."

"Hez werking for GRANAADA!"

"He's not a threat," Awol countered, bravely, or dumbly, "He's partying with the hippies right now."

"The hippiez dicking around wit their pawt pawlitics on the beach? Thinking they know how the world workz? On the beach!

They're cannon fodda, but him…I don't like it. I'm smart enough ta know there's some'en we don't know. I mean tink about dat, we're about to close this deal, and all of a sudden some stranga' washes up outta nowhere?"

"So how do you want to proceed," Gambler asked, "with this outlier in play?"

Simian paced and scratched his chin with his short fingers.

"The longer we wait," Awol commented, "the smaller Don Granada thinks we are."

"The gold's gotta be up there," Bonesetter said. "Let's just kill him like we threatened and take it!"

"Like a clam jumper?" Simian asked. "Like a criminal delinquent?"

"Ya."

"Why kill him when we can extort if from him legally? Jesuz ya gotta lot ta learn. I'm trying to help him! When someone needs help ya gotta help 'em."

"Heeeelp…" Campasino pleaded behind them.

Simian glanced at Campasino, annoyed.

"We gotta check the tombs," Intel said.

"Please…" Campasino pleaded, raising his free hand towards them.

"Will somebody—"

"—I got this," Bonesetter said.

Bonesetter reached in his bag and extracted a small, Civil War coping saw. The sun splashed off the blade into Campasino's eye. He squinted and covered his eyes with his unstuck arm.

"Alright, listen!" Simian declared. "Here's the plan. The deadline's tamawra. Time ta escalate, so we don't havta kill him. Implement phase two."

Simian turned to Awol.

"Get mwore soldiers. And double their raationz."

"Aye aye Boss."

Simian turned to Scout.

"Go find out where this deckhand came from."

"How?" Scout asked, "There's no boat."

"Go over land."

"What, through the Interior?"

"Ya. We need a long game."

"I'd need Caz and twenty men for that."

"You can't have him. But take Polito. Wherever the hell he is. Where the hell is he anyway? Find him and go. And tell him I'm docking his pay. And come back with mwore soldados! If ya live."

"Crap," Scout swore.

"And you," Simian said, jabbing his finger into Bonesetter's chest, "hold this monk's feet to the fiya, and run him outta town. Wit my CAAWK!"

The mercenaries dispersed to implement phase two, and Simian turned back to the broken claw and laborers. Half were frantically trying to dig Campasino's arm out. The other half were struggling to use a pole as a lever to lift it off. Surprisingly, Campasino didn't look like he was in that much pain anymore, but his arm disappeared flat under the bucket and his face was shock white.

"Awright, amigos. Break's over!" Simian announced, stepping forward and clapping his hands at them. "Get his arm out from under my claw and get it back on the rig!"

The laborers stared at him, confused. As they did, Bonesetter strode at Campasino with his coping saw.

Chapter 27

Scout strode to the guanacaste tree on the other side of the plaza, then grabbed a leather saddlebag, squatted and began placing red dynamite sticks in it. Dynamite was like duct tape for him—he used it for everything—and although he didn't know how, he was certain it would help him cross the Interior and live.

"You're gonna die," Awol said, strutting up behind him.

Scout rolled his cigar in his mouth a half turn and stood.

"You can't cross the Interior without an aero-plane. Or that retard mute."

Scout tipped the front of his slouch hat up, squinted his range eyes and looked south, across the plaza and over the buildings to the distant cordilleras in the green Interior.

"Maybe with Cazador," Awol continued, "but fuck Cazador." Awol grinned and cracked his knuckles like he was about to fight. "I'm here in peace."

"Ha!" Scout laughed involuntarily.

"Alright, that's bullshit. But I'm not here to hurt you."

Scout pulled his cigar out and spit through his mustache.

"I don't want to hurt you," Awol added, "but I swear to God, if you tell anyone I'm here when you're out there, before you die, I'll crush your fucken eel whore's skull."

Scout looked Awol directly in the eye. Awol didn't know it, but his fucken eel whore was coming with him. So fuck Awol.

"Well then..." Scout replied, "You better hope I fucken die."

As Scout and Awol measured their dicks, Bonesetter breezed down the road and away from the plaza, carrying his doctor's bag and coping saw. Blood dripped off the saw's teeth, into the dust.

Gambler strode down the street behind him, gripping the stone he found in Bonesetter's bag. He closed the distance, pocketed the stone and grabbed Bonesetter's arm from behind.

"I don't know what hand you're playing," Gambler said, stopping him, "but I'm watching you."

"If you get shot," Bonesetter fired back, "I ain't sewing you up."

"Ya, cause you did such a crack job on yourself, Doc."

"Suck it," Bonesetter said, pointing the saw at him.

Bonesetter yanked out of Gambler's grip and strutted on.

Chapter 28

Gunner leaned against a tree at the edge of a field as the sun set, watching Santa and Tuck trying to catch a grasshopper in the long grass. Tuck jumped after it and Santa trailed, laughing. Gunner smiled slightly, then shoved his shoulder off the trunk and strolled across the field towards them.

"Oh heh! Hi!" Santa pipped when he walked up, tucking a wisp of hair behind her ear. "How are you?"

He smiled, then saw Tequila over Santa's shoulder in the distance, striding towards them from the far side of the field. Santa followed his eyes and spotted her.

"Sorry to interrupt," Gunner interrupted. "I just wanted to give this back to you, before I leave tomorrow."

He handed her the locket.

"Ah!" She beamed, touching it to her heart, "Thank you."

"Ya."

"Here!" Tuck said, popping up with a root.

"That's it!"

She took the root and brushed it off, then peeled the skin off with her thin boning knife and cut it into three chunks. She popped one in her mouth and handed Tuck and Gunner the other two. Gunner chewed it and his face soured.

"Ughhh!"

"Don't chew it!" she laughed. "It's ginger!"

"Jesus..." Gunner gagged, "What's it for?"

"Gifiti!" Tuck proclaimed, nodding to a bottle in the grass, "We're making it for you. To get your strength back. Dad loves it. He says it makes him strong. Well, one glass. He says one glass makes you strong, two makes you weak, and three makes you..."

"Invincible," Santa said.

"I bet."

"Can we make some for him for when he gets back?"

Santa's smile sunk and a sadness washed over her face, which she turned and hid from Tuck. Gunner saw and frowned. Quickly, he took the bottle and stepped in front of her to screen Tuck's view.

"Lemme see."

He held the bottle up to the light and studied it. Wormwood, guaco, zarzaparilla, pulp, spices and a green palm pit viper floated inside. The snake curled around the roots like the voodoo bottles on Don Granada's shelf in Valhalla, but the bottle was now filled with amber liquid and fermented, which made the snake look even more like a formaldehyde sample forgotten in a university basement—or in Doctor Frankenstein's lab. Its scales were florescent green, its lipless mouth was curled in a traitorous smile, and its eyes were yellow. They looked the same dead as they did alive.

"It's strong," Santa said, quick-wiping a tear from her eye, taking the bottle and uncorking it, "but with the snake, you can never tell how strong. The dosages and efficacy vary, so there's only one way to find out."

"How?" Gunner asked.

"Try it."

She stuck her boning knife in the bottle, stabbed the snake's head and pulled it out. She pressed her thumb on the rubbery roof of the serpent's mouth, and a drop of liquid beaded on its fangs like icicles.

"Venom."

She tapped the fangs against the bottle and the venom dripped in. She shoved the green palm pit viper's head back in the bottle and dropped the ginger in. Then she corked it, shook it and handed it to him.

"Gifiti for the locket."

"Thanks," he replied, turning it in his hands. "I guess."

"Memories for memories," she mused. "Ghosts for ghosts."

He looked up and they stared at each other a moment, understanding each other, because they shared something – loss. But just as quickly as they connected she grabbed Tuck's hand and walked off. He watched them go.

"Coco's wake's in a few hours." Tequilla said, striding up and breaking the silence, "Ju coming?"

"Huh?"

"Her funeral. Topless cheecken-fights."

He pulled his eyes from Santa and focused on her.

"What?"

"Men. Mira hombre, we're gonna pre-party at Val-val, then music and fuego. Surfer claims he's going to steal alcohol from the Cantina, so we'll see. It's Don Granada's deadline and Coco's funeral. The end of the world, ju know, all that. So fiesta bang-bang."

"Is the boat here?"

"What?"

"Did the boat come?"

"Oh no. Not yet."

"It's not here?"

"No. We don't want it to come until after Coco's party. Mañana."

This is ridiculous, he thought. *The clock's ticking. If the boat isn't here tomorrow, I'm taking Mute through the Interior.*

"When's jur wedding?" Tequila asked. "I mean, your girlfriend's wedding."

"Twenty-seven days." Gunner replied flatly.

"Well, a funeral and a wedding. Bring jur gifiti and be early," she said, patting his chest and parading off, "because this may be the last alcohol for a while. Rumor is, Simian plans to destroy the rest of the liquor."

Chapter 29

Giant puff-clouds drifted across the sky, over the sea. It was a warm, Caribbean night. A full witch-moon painted the clouds and sea silver. Sharp shadows swayed on the ground through the palms, and bongo drums beat around a distant campfire on the beach. Closer, in the brush onshore, grass rustled and—

—SNAP.

Bonesetter stepped on a branch.

He, Awol and Gambler crept through the brush with gas cans.

"When I was free diving," Bonesetter whispered, leaning into Awol as they crept, "I got to two hundred meters. In no limits apnea. I was the first person ever to go two hundred meters. Nobody thought anyone could go that deep and come back. They thought your lungs would collapse. It's dark and cold and lonely and scary down there, that deep. Once, a shark darted out of the black and bit my dive buddy. He dragged him off by the head, back into the black, and we never saw him again. After I broke the record, this guy from Italy, fucken two days later, he dives two hundred and one meters off the continental shelf in Turks and Caicos. Two hundred and one meters! Just like that. I break the lung barrier that stood for ten thousand years and two days later I lose the record. Can you believe that?"

Awol could but didn't care and didn't answer.

"You know what I learned?"

"That I need a blowjob?" Awol asked.

"Do you swallow?" Gambler quipped.

"No," Bonesetter continued. "That there are people out their crazier than you. They'll try harder and go further, and they won't sleep till they beat you. Unless…Unless you go deeper. Unless you're willing to go so deep that you may blackout and never return."

"Christ." Gambler huffed, "Come on! We're on a mission. Quick and quiet."

"Stop mosquitoing me!" Bonesetter snapped back.

They crept on silently for another minute, until Bonesetter pushed through a branch and arrived at the back of a wooden structure. Grey planks rose from some sea grass and blighted out the moon like an eclipse. Bonesetter stopped and grinned. Gambler rolled a match in his teeth and studied the objective.

BOM BOM PA PA, BOM BOM PA PA, BOM BOM…

Bongo drums. They looked right, through the bushes to the beach. There, fifty yards away, the hotties and hippies partied around a bonfire, laughing and dancing like fireflies.

Coco's wake.

Trust Fund and Frat Boy chicken-fought with Tequila and Coco on their shoulders. The hippies hooted and giggled through the music—until Tequila grabbed Coco's bikini top and ripped it off. Coco yelped and her perky tits sprang out. She covered them with one hand and immediately slapped Tequila with the other. Tequila cocked back to swing, so Coco surrendered her tits and grabbed a fistful of Tequila's thick Latina hair with both hands. Trust Fund and Protestor laughed and yelled beneath them, stumbling and struggling to disentangle them as they grappled on their shoulders above.

"Uh oh," Gambler grinned, enjoying the show, "trouble in paradise."

"I'm hungry," Bonesetter mumbled. "You guys hungry?"

CLACK.

Awol popped his gas can.

"Showtime."

Gambler and Bonesetter refocused on the structure in front of them, and Awol splashed gas on the planks. Bonesetter popped his can and followed. He shook a few splashes on the wood, then shook a splash at Awol and laughed. The gas, however, fell short and splashed on his own arm—the good one without the lacerations and baseball stitches.

"Bonehead." Awol whispered. "Pour it on the building. Not yourself."

"There's enough gas here to set the whole world on fire," Bonesetter marveled.

"Quit playing grabass," Gambler scolded.

Gambler took the match from his teeth and struck it against a palm, then lit a small torch and stuck it in the ground. As he did, Bonesetter and Awol continued dousing the footers and dry planks. It wasn't a hard job, but Bonesetter quickly lost focus again and crept up on Awol from behind with his can.

"I swear to God…" Awol scowled, turning on him.

Bonesetter giggled.

Awol stepped at him and he jumped back, spilling more gas on his elbow. It glistened in the moonlight and he tried to flick it off, but as he did he backed towards the torch, inching closer and closer to the burning flame. Gambler opened his mouth to warn him, then stopped. He closed his mouth just as—

—*BUMPH!*

Bonesetter slipped on a coconut and fell into the—

—*WHOOSH!*

The torch touched gas and white light flashed.

"Ah. AHHHH!"

Immediately, fire crawled up Bonesetter's arm.

He stumbled forward and banged into the wooden structure. He bounced off, spun like a flaming windmill and lit the gas-soaked structure like a human match. The planks caught fire fast, and the heat pushed him back towards the fallen torch. He watched the fire grow and burn his arm with shocked eyes and he stumbled.

"Idiot," Awol cursed.

Awol dropped his gas can, grabbed Bonesetter and threw him to the ground.

"Roll!" Awol ordered, kicking him.

"AHH!"

"ROLL!"

Awol kicked him over. Bonesetter rolled on top of his arm and smothered the fire with his body.

"Ughhhhh...."

"Smooth Slick," Gambler observed. "Real smooth."

Awol huffed and shook his head, staring down at Bonesetter. Bonesetter rolled back on his back and groaned again, cradling his arm and looking up at the big moon with big moon eyes. A few patches of burnt flesh bubbled and flaked off his elbow, exposing raw, pink skin. Now he had a burnt arm, a clawed arm, and a stitched hand. Next to him, sparks glowed in the bush and flames crept up the footers as the fire began to light up the night...

...Alive.

"Hell with it," Awol declared, picking his gas can back up. "Burn it all."

Chapter 30

Fifty yards away, the hotties and hippies entwined around the bonfire on the beach. Coco and Tequila had stopped chicken-fight fighting and were now hugging, for some reason. Coco wiped a tear from her eye and smiled, and Tequila helped tie her ripped bikini back on. As she did, Surfer hiked out of the night with three cases of liquor.

"Is this Coco's party or what!?" He clanked the cases down on a large piece of driftwood like a kill. "It's the end of the wooooorlllld!"

"Alright brodie!"

Everyone encircled and big-eyed the precious take. Scotch, vodka, rum… Straight from Simian's stockpile. They knew Simian was starving Don Granada to pressure him or something, and believed they were collateral damage caught in the crossfire, but now they'd taken action and struck back. They'd been pulled into this feud against their will, so they'd risen up and run the blockade. Now, finally, they felt like a political force, which was reason enough to celebrate.

"We did it!" Protestor cheered. "We DID IT!"

Surfer did it, Gunner thought.

Protestor would protest protesting, but this time everyone agreed with him, or he agreed with everyone else, which was rare. They patted each other on the back and passed bottles around, smiling and laughing.

"Nah…" Surfer said over the clamor, "there wasn't even anyone there!"

Then where were they? Gunner wondered.

Gunner lounged further back, away from the crowd in a wooden chair at the edge of the fire's glow. His toes sat on the beach in the light, but the rest of his body flickered just beyond in the dark. He held the gifiti bottle Santa gave him, with the pickled pit viper coiled around the shaman roots inside.

He watched them congratulate each other and celebrate for a minute, then gave up on them. The boat wasn't coming until tomorrow, allegedly, so he had a free night. He uncorked the bottle and smelled. Earth and tannin. The smell of a far-off place he vaguely remembered but couldn't place, like the memory of a memory forgotten, which whispered, *"Come back. It was beautiful here."* And it was, so he nodded and swug.

And the venom entered his veins.

Immediately, a narcotic peace tranquilized him. He leaned back, his muscles relaxed and his tensions faded, until only an underlying hum remained. It buzzed and grew through him like branches, or water filling a void.

His grip on the bottle loosened and he dropped it. It fell from the armrest towards the sand. He instinctively snapped his eyes to watch it, but they screeched into slow motion, and before the bottle had fallen halfway, they glazed over like the snake's eyes. From somewhere far-off he heard a drum beat. He turned to the sound in the darkness and saw the air ripple.

How…?

He squinted, and time and space wavered like a mirage, then collapsed. Space-time imploded on itself from infinity to zero. A beast ripped it apart, violently, like boning a spine from a fish. It tossed the spine to wolves, who devoured it and glared back with green eyes on the flesh that remained. The Monkey Mind crumbled and the Ego died, atomizing construct and judgement with it.

In a flash, he saw himself outside himself, or sensed himself, and only the present remained, simple and clear, without imagined future or remembered past, or the stories men tell themselves. There, space-time froze, like still water on a black pond. There was just the bottle, bonfire and beach, the smell of burnt cedar and sea, laughter, and orange sparks flickering up and out of people's mouths and becoming silver stars flickering up and out of the heavens above, doming beyond the curves of the earth until they touched themselves on the other side, enveloping the earth like a womb. Everything was energy and light, peaceful and perfect, and he could see the cosmos rotating, and sense what space expanded into.

And the world was as it was, at the singularity.

Limitless.

He smiled softly in the zero world.

But it was an event-horizon that couldn't last, like the feeling of weightlessness in a jet before it reaches space at the outer limits of the atmosphere, stalls, and crashes back to earth. There was just a slight, subconscious weight at first, then it felt like someone wrapped their fingers around his ankles and yanked him under, through the surface of the pond and into a black otter hole without form underneath.

He fell fast. Everything accelerated and collapsed past zero into negative integers, until the speed, pressure, density and mathematics were so great that they exploded through a wormhole out the other side, into another world.

Suddenly, he was walking down a passage in a medina. In a maze of narrow alleys and stone that were vaguely familiar and smelled like the gifiti. Flat plaster walls and donkeys, spice cones and hide, sand grains in the cracks and rich red fabrics hanging high on clotheslines in the passage overhead. There were Arabs and Africans and nomads in from the desert, sandaled and hooded in djellabas, almost certainly hiding khoumiyas underneath.

Five quid for a dalla, five quid for a dalla, the oasis, is just a little falla...

Tuareg. He thought, *Fucken traitors. It's five by five nights south by Orion's sword, and the only thing's certain is that you'll drag us into the desert and stab us in the back.*

A Tuareg noticed him like a ghost, through a slit in his indigo turban. The Tuareg pulled back his djellaba and rested his hand on a sword, so Gunner ducked into a setwan. He walked down a long corridor, passed meat hooks and bâyts, and emerged in a hidden riad. A cavity in the world. A world within the world. A bright courtyard of tadelakt plaster and stone. Arches and zillage. Dust drifting through dry light. Yes, this was somewhere he'd been before, before the sickness and sea.

In the middle of the courtyard, an old friend sat at a tiled table under a palm, near a drop pool, drinking qawah and cleaning an M4. His friend didn't see him, or couldn't, but his friend smiled to himself softly, peacefully, like a lion in the afternoon, a big hulking bloke of a man-eating lion, with canines and a gun, as if saying:

I'm good. You can go. Fuck off.

And he was, so Gunner smiled.

Past his friend, in the recesses in the arches, a harem flashed and disappeared in the shadows like a school of silver minnows. He had worried about his friend, but wouldn't anymore, for this was a safe place. A quiet place. A place he must have wanted to be. But it was peaceful like a tomb. It wasn't his place, and he couldn't stay.

So he turned to leave—

"—Heh Bridger."

He stopped, and his friend looked at him, with translucent,

glacial eyes.

"Ya Chekov?"

"We roamed the earth with vengeance. Like fucken reapers."

Gunner grinned. When he did, light flickered in his eye off a khoumiya. He looked up and saw the blue Tuareg squatting on the ledge above, about to spring down. He tensed and the Tuareg jumped, coming down on him with his dagger. A million miles and minutes passed in a heartbeat, and he snapped back. Back to the beach.

Just in time to see the gifiti bottle finish falling and thump-stop in the sand.

He watched it lay there for a few long breaths, and slowly reoriented himself. Some gifiti pumped out the top, into the sand, and the snake's tail flicked out like a tongue. *Nothing,* he realized, *not even light, can travel faster and further than consciousness.*

Time lengthened and space shortened, realigning on the grid. As it did, he saw the hotties converting alcohol to laughter. Coco and Tequila danced barefoot like sirens in the sand to psychedelic trance like before, but now diamonds seemed to sparkle on their lips, their auras glowed amber and their bodies bent the air around them like gravity.

"You're wrong," Protestor argued in front of him. "Violence is never justified."

"Nature is violent," Surfer countered. "Waves. Sharks—"

"—You have to fight violence—"

"—That's violent."

"…With love."

"Jesus."

"War has never solved anything," Protestor concluded.

"Except for slavery. Nazis…"

Gunner shook his head to clear it, then leaned forward and picked up the gifiti bottle. The snake's tail slid back in with a suck like it was still alive, in the way that it was. The psychedelic trance built to a climatic pitch, and Tequila jumped up on the driftwood.

"It's the end of the WOOOOORLLLD!" she yelled, raising a tequila bottle.

YAAAAAA!

"Coco-NUUUUT… Get up here!"

Coco laughed nervously and looked around. Everyone cheered and pushed her forward. Tequila pulled her onto the log, stretching her long legs like a gazelle. As soon as she was on the log, Tequila lashed her arm around her and gave a speech.

"The reason we're all here, tonight, está noche... is to celebrate life, because..."

She sniffled, looked down and covered her lip, just as the trance music transitioned to slow reggae.

"Because this is... Coco's last night."

The party-chatter faded to silence and a weight fell over the scene. Tequila hugged Coco and kissed her temple.

"She's had a good... a good... No puedo... No puedo..."

She wiped her eye.

"Cheese dyeen! OH GOD CHEESE DYEEN! Coco ju sexy bitch I'm sorry! I'm... I'm... Look what juv done to me! I can't! I JUST CAN'T!"

Suddenly, Tequila leapt off the log, skipped a few steps across the beach and swooned into Sail's arms, leaving Coco alone on stage. The crowd quickly pivoted back to her expectantly. She stared wide-eyed and exposed.

They waited.

She fidgeted.

Someone sniffled.

"Oh God, we love you Coco!" Bikini finally broke from the back.

Frat Boy wrapped his arm around Bikini to comfort her.

"I..." Coco trailed off.

"How long, like, do you have?" Bumster asked somberly from the front.

"Well... I..."

"We can cremate her in the ocean," Burner offered.

Frat Boy smacked his arm.

"Ow."

"Do you... I mean..." Yummy Chad said, stepping up next to Barb. "Do you want us to do anything?"

Barb big-eyed Yummy Chad; tall and topless. She threw Pat a clandestine elbow, shook a quick hip and side-shuffled closer to him while Coco fidgeted on the driftwood, struggling to smile.

"I almost feel bad for her," Sail whispered, leaning into Tequila as they watched her squirm. "Maybe making her pay for our trip was enough. She's really suffering."

"Ya," Tequila agreed, "cheese lucky to have friends like us. Who else would do this much to help her?"

Gunner smiled, entertained, watching the drama unfold. His senses had realigned and the visions had faded. Now he simply felt good and drunk.

"What are like, your last wishes?" Coy asked.

"Well I mean, of course," Coco stammered, "that this should be a happy night. Like a celebration. Not about me. No. No! Of life, of our, I mean..."

The crowd waited.

The fire cackled.

"Oh God I'm gonna save her," Sail said.

She reached across Gunner and grabbed his gifiti bottle.

"...of life, and I mean, everyone should just love—"

"—WAIT!" Sail suddenly shouted, springing up. "The Gypsy Witch!"

The crowd spun on her and she raised the gifiti bottle like a severed head.

"The Gypsy Witch made a cure!"

HUUUUU...

The crowd gasped.

"Oh Gawd," Pat gawked.

"She'll be fine! She'll live! She just has to drink this voodoo!"

"People are actually believing this shit?" Barb marveled.

Bikini covered her mouth, amazed, and Frat Boy pulled her closer as Surfer chuckled behind.

"Drink! Drink, Coco!"

"Drink," Bumster pleaded.

"Yah," Burner begged, "drink."

"DRINK... DRINK... DRINK..." the crowd chanted.

Coco held her face and broke down in tears like a beauty queen. Sail rushed forward and passed the bottle up to her like a tiara. Coco grabbed it and hugged her, then grabbed Tequila and pulled her in too.

"I love you!" Coco cried. "I love you guys!"

"Don't cry," Tequila replied. "It makes ju look fat."

"It'll be fine!" Coco shouted to the crowd over the hug. "It'll be fine! DRINK!"

"YAAA!" they cheered.

"To love, life and MONKEY JUNGLE TOWN!"

RAAAAAAAAHGH!!!

Coco chugged from the gifiti and the others followed, toasting and drinking, happy again. Yummy Chad pounded a bottle, growled and turned on Barb like a hunter. She looked up. He looked down. Hungry.

"You're beautiful-ish," he said.

"Oh gawd you're so fucken delicious," Barb huffed and dug her claws into his chest. "I'm gonna pour chocolate syrup all over you and—"

"—WHOOHUUU!" Pat bounced and cheered.

Excitement flashed through Chad's face and they started making out. Inspired, Pat reached for Trust Fund but he saw her coming like a panda and slipped away just as her paw passed.

"WHOOHUUU!" Pat bounced again.

"But!" Sail yelled, jumping back on the driftwood.

The energized crowd turned back to her.

"The only reason the Gypsy Witch made this for Coco… is…"

The crowd quieted, nervous and anxious for the new news.

"Is…"

The fire cackled.

"Because she's pregnant!"

HUUUUUU…

The crowd gasped again and pivoted back on Coco. It was almost too much. Almost.

"I am?" Coco mouthed silently to Sail.

"Yes," Sail mouthed back proudly, patting her heart, "you are."

"Oh thank God," Burner mumbled, amazed at the beauty and bounty of life.

Tequila burst into laughter and covered her mouth. Surfer's smile, however, dropped. He darted a look to Coco, who scanned the crowd. This wasn't funny anymore. Slowly, he shrunk behind Barb and Chad and receded into the shadows just as Coco's eyes fell on the black space he'd filled.

The music thumped back on and the crowd roared.

"MONKEY JUNGLE TOOOOOOWN!"

Everyone cheered and began dancing and drinking again. Tequila sauntered up and handed Gunner a whiskey bottle.

"Come on," she said, "I'm gonna hit ju like a hurricane."

She pulled Gunner to his feet and dragged him away, towards his cabaña. They broke the fire's aura and stepped into the night. The whiskey bottle sloshed as he swayed across the beach, and the party receded behind them. Suddenly, however, Tequila stopped.

"What's that?"

He looked up. His eyes struggled to focus. Something glowed orange ahead.

His cabaña was on fire.

"What the…"

But before he could process the development and it's ramifications, a large shadow darted in front of the flames with a gas can. It stopped and stared at them mid-stride like Bigfoot, with hateful, red eyes.

Awol.

Slowly, Awol's lip curled. He dropped his gas can and strode directly at them. Instinctively, Gunner straightened and his muscles tightened.

"See something you like, Papi?" Awol asked.

Awol got in his face like before.

One second.

Two.

"Fisherman!"

Suddenly, Gambler burst from the dark. He strode up and stepped between them.

"Do you wanna do this?" Gambler asked. "Do you really wanna do this?"

Gunner's eyes stayed locked on Awol.

"What business of this is yours?" Gambler added.

Gunner's eyes shifted to Gambler, and he swayed slightly.

"Jesus," Awol said, "he's lit. Why in hell is anyone worried about this hippie? Why we still fretting this? He's got no skills."

"Heh," Gambler said, stepping closer and lowering his voice, "I'm given you advice here hombre, real advice, from someone who knows what's com'en. Fold. Move on. Leave. Really. Get on that boat tomorrow, because the cards are marked and yours suck." Gambler drew two cards from his back pocket and flashed them. "See? You got a two and a six. I got two aces. You got a losing hand. Don't pay to see the flop. These people, this pueblo… Is it worth it? Is it your problem? The deadline's com'en, but no good's com'en of it."

Gunner squinted, trying to focus.

"Leave. While you still can."

"He's got no heart," Awol stated.

Awol stepped forward and shoved Gunner. Gunner stumbled back and took it—again. Awol laughed and shook his head, then leered at Tequila.

"Follow me," he ordered.

She retracted, but her eyes sparkled.

Awol turned and thundered off, not bothering to see if she'd follow. As he faded out, Tequila turned on Gunner:

"What are ju gonna do?"

He watched Awol disappear, his eyes glossy and indifferent.

"Get on that boat," he slurred. "Sleep. Dream. Go to a wedding."

"Hehzus," she spat, disgusted, "ju really are, just a fisherman."

Mmgh.

She looked back to where Awol went.

"Wait!" She called, and jogged after him.

Gambler studied Gunner once more. Gunner wavered on his feet like the town borracho, with slumped shoulders and glassy eyes, holding a whiskey bottle. Twice. Twice he didn't fight, and he hadn't done a single thing that indicated he was Delta Force, a spy, or even a grunt. Still, Gambler was unsure, unconvinced. He read people, that's what he did, supernaturally-well, and something about the stranger... Something in him reminded Gambler of something. Of himself. Of a dark corner in himself. The stranger had a secret, like everyone, but his felt... Consequential. Maybe they'd know soon enough. After a few seconds, Gambler finally rolled his tongue in his cheek and nodded, then followed Awol into the night.

Gunner grunted and stumbled to the cayuco. He balanced on the gunwale a moment and watched flames slide up the side of his cabaña and begin to tickle the thatched roof. He started to slide back into the boat to pass out, but just before he did, something else caught his eye.

Further down the beach, another flame flickered in the night.

Chapter 31

Blue flames climbed up a counter and over a bar.

Valhalla was on fire.

Tuck streaked in. He darted across the dancefloor, jumped over the bar, climbed a stack of empty beer crates and ripped battle paintings down from the wall.

"Tuuuuuck!" Santa yelled from somewhere outside.

Tuck reached for the amber photograph of his grandpa, grandma, mom, dad and himself as a toddler in the map room in Cartagena des Indies, but a flame snaked through the bamboo slits like a finger, burnt his hand and wrapped itself around the picture.

"AH!"

He shook sparks off his hand, coughed and stretched for the photo again, but a thick roof beam collapsed on his thin arm.

Outside, Santa burst out of the black night and into the orange fire light. She sprinted up the beach, braked in front of Valhalla and shielded her face. It pumped smoke and heat like a lung, catching ablaze perfectly, with its dry palm frond roof, wooden structure and oxygen cavities. It was burning quick, and Tuck was stuck inside.

"TUCK!"

Surfer dragged two splashing pails up the beach. He ran as close as he could to the fire, hurtled one on it and reached for the other. Barboza followed and did the same. The sea water struck it and *hissssed* like a viper.

"Get back!" Don Granada yelled, running up barefoot from Jungle Trail.

"Tuck's in there!" Santa yelled.

Don Granada planted and his eyes widened. He darted in, but heat walled him and singed his beard. The fire hissed and threw flames, dropping him to a knee.

"NO!" Don Granada yelled.

"TUCK!"

Protestor staggered out of the smoky bar, coughing, with two bottles of gifiti in his hands. He stumbled in the sand and face-planted. The bottles tumbled and clanked in front of Santa. He scurried to his feet, scooped them back up and cradled them off to safety.

"BABYYY!" Santa yelled.

Some hippies dickered a safe distance back.

"We should do something," Bikini said.

"What?" Bumster asked.

"Well…"

"If we help," Trust Fund remarked, pointing at the fire, "then we can get sued for that kid's death."

Flames curled out of the bar and onto the palm roof, devouring the dry palms like the Kraken. Don Granada struggled past the hippies with buckets, but quickly dropped them and lunged back. He ripped a beach towel off Bumster's shoulder and threw it over his head.

"Come on man, do something!" he yelled at them.

But Deadbeat just stared back with his mouth agape. As he did, Don Granada grabbed a bucket and dumped it on himself. Bikini picked the other one up to help but was moving too slow, so Granada snatched it from her and dumped it on himself again. He then tossed it at them, pinched the wet towel over his face like a burka and ran straight into the roaring fire.

"Whoaaaa…" Deadbeat finally responded.

HISSSSSS….

"He's right," Bumster replied.

"What?"

"About getting sued."

"Ya but—"

"—BABYYYY!"

Barboza huffed by with two more buckets, sweating profusely from his big round head.

"If we help now," Bikini countered, "maybe we can save the place."

"That's a good point," Bumster agreed.

Burner stood nearby, slightly off to the side, wearing his speedo and his baggy tank top that draped over his thin, bony shoulders. He held a bong, transfixed on the blaze, which reflected orange in his dilated pupils.

"I'm a starburst," he mumbled to himself.

"What!?" Trust Fund yelled over the roar of the fire.

"This is the end of the rainbow!" Burner howled back.

"Or the gates of hell!" Frat Boy laughed.

"TUUUUUCK!"

Suddenly, Tuck helicoptered through the air and out of the fire like the fire spit him out. Flames streaked up the back of his shirt and he torpedoed into the sand, clutching the Odysseus drawing.

Don Granada immediately jumped out the burning bar behind him, through a wall of smoke. The towel burned on his head like a flaming turban. He shucked it off, grabbed Tuck like a sack of sand and hucked him again with old man muscle, ten feet further from the fire.

Santa jumped on Tuck and engulfed him as the fire sucked and whorled behind and above them, trying to pull him back in like it wanted to eat him, needing to burn his carbons to live.

"I couldn't save it. I couldn't save it Mom!"

Barboza ran up from the dark beach with two more buckets of sea water. Don Granada intercepted one, tossed it on Tuck's smoking back and fell to his knees over them, exhausted.

Barboza stumbled on and tossed the other bucket at the fire, still fighting it.

"Come on you BASTARD!" He spat.

The fire sucked a tornado of oxygen around him, and tentacles of flame clutched for him like an octopus. It pulled him to a knee but he rose back up with his ghost dagger, swinging at the flames like a madman, his face pitched and red.

"ARRRGHHH!"

As he attacked, Tuck wormed out of his Mom's grip and ran off, down the beach and into the night, gripping his knife.

"Is this… real?" Burner asked.

Chapter 32

The next morning, Gunner's hand hung over the cayuco's gunwale. His whiskey bottle lay in the sand beneath it, upturned and empty. Sunlight bent and distorted through it, shining on and reflecting off the carapace of a red crab that lay dead on its back next to it.

Inside the cayuco, another crab crab-stepped up Gunner's chest.

Slowly, Gunner's eyes blinked open. They squinted in the bright sun, and through his eyelashes he registered blue sky, hull and mast. A canvas sail flapped gently in the breeze above him, and a black crow circled high overhead, making small, perfect orbits around the tip of the mast. The earth was heating like it did on a slow Caribbean morning.

"Where're we gonna party now?" Someone asked from somewhere nearby.

"How much gifiti did you save?"

"Not enough."

The crab stopped at Gunner's face. It raised its claws and stared at him with antennae eyes. They stared at each other. Suddenly, hands reached down, pinched the crab's claws and snatched it up like an alien abduction.

Padre.

Padre sat on the gunwale above Gunner, holding the crab. Gunner focused and saw Padre's big round face blocking out the sun and grinning down.

"You awake?"

"Urgghhh…" Gunner groaned.

"You know one time, in the hospital, they woke me up to give me a sleeping pill. Can you believe that? They woke me up, to give me a sleeping pill, to fall asleep."

Gunner squinted his eyes shut again and shook his head.

"You woke me up," Gunner replied, "to tell me that one time, someone woke you up, to give you a sleeping pill?"

"No. I woke you up to see if you wanna go to a whore's house."

"A what?"

"A whore's house."

"A padre can't go to a whorehouse."

"Why not?"

"I've never once, in my whole life, seen or heard of a padre, or a priest, or a monk, in a whorehouse."

"That's strange," Padre replied. "Because the closest I've ever been to touching God was in a whorehouse."

"Ya, I bet."

"All those poor, lost souls…" Padre said, looking up to heaven.

"What kind of priest are you anyway?"

But Padre simply smiled angelically, lost in a memory of God knew what. Gunner smacked some spit into his mouth and sat up in the boat.

"Don Granada, that old man, he's supposed to be protecting this place!" Protestor argued nearby under a palm. "He didn't do anything! I have a credit on my bar tab! You think he's gonna honor that now? He owes us! I'm gonna fire-bomb the rest of his cabañas!"

"That was insaaaaane," Bumster awed.

"God loves all his children equally," Padre remarked, watching them, "but I'm not sure why."

Gunner followed Padre's eyes to a topless hippie's round ass, which jiggled in a bikini bottom above smooth, long legs.

"Well, I guess I can think of one reason."

Gunner snickered.

"What? A man of the cloth can't appreciate the Lord's creations?"

Hot Legs turned, and a black, hairy chest stuck out; Burner.

"JEEESSUS!" Padre croaked, coughing on his own spit.

"Hahaha! It's good to see you appreciate ALL the Lord's creations!"

Padre held the crab at him. It snapped and pinched his nipple.

"AHHH!" Gunner jumped.

"Get up," Padre ordered.

Padre yanked the crab off, ripping some skin off in the process. A drop of blood beaded on his nipple.

"Get moving."

"UGH! Alright alright, I'm up! I'm up."

Gunner rolled out of the cayuco and into the sand. He saw the bone dry whiskey bottle and straightened. He rubbed his face and noticed what he hadn't in the dark last night: that the cayuco had been fully repaired and painted, and sat above the sand, looking new and ready to sail. He looked further afield, recapturing more of his surroundings and consciousness, but when he turned inland he froze. His cabaña smoldered in the shade under the palms, razed to the ground. Smoke drifted up from it like a napalm hit.

He stared as he remembered what happened last night. And quickly digested what it meant.

"Hell of a night," Padre remarked, "even for here."

Mghm.

"A night of destiny," Padre replied. "And now a day of... consequences."

Gunner looked up and squinted in the sun.

"So, whatcha gonna do, Gunner? Ya gonna fight? Or flee?"

Gunner stared into the sky.

"I'm going to talk to Don Granada—about that fucken boat."

Chapter 33

Santa stood in the Ranchero's great room, talking to a trap door in the middle of the floor. The trap door opened to black hole under the house, and a rug and a couch lay askew beside it.

"Papa."

Something thumped and banged underfoot, muffled by the floor.

"Papa!"

As Santa peered in the hole, Gunner walked into the house.

"Where were you last night?" she shot, immediately turning on him.

Gunner stopped and surveyed. Don Granada surfaced from the trap door behind her. He clanked a rusty tin box on the floor and climbed into the great room like a bear coming out of hibernation. An old bear.

"You're going to hurt yourself," she said, turning back to her father.

"I told you that quack was going to hurt someone a long time ago," Granada replied, standing up by the trap door and picking up his tin box. "Now he thinks he's a doctor! His brain's more rotten every day."

He walked to the family table and set the tin box on it. Both his hands were burnt and boiled from the fire and covered in pasty white ointment. They looked agonizing, but he didn't seem to notice. He'd stopped whining about scratches years ago. He banged the box open with his raw fist, and a rusty revolver lay inside, wrapped in green felt. He picked it up and blew dust off it.

"Dad!"

Four bullets rolled around loose in the box. He picked them up and chambered them, two rounds short.

"You can't be serious?" she asked.

He set the gun on the table and walked to the kitchen. Santa tracked him, but Gunner's eyes sat on the gun.

THUNK.

Gunner and Santa turned back to the trapdoor. This time, a bandolier thunked down on the floor beside it. A second later, Barboza pulled himself out of the hole. Another old bear. He straightened and cracked his back, then slung the bandolier on over his chest and pulled the old Enfield rifle down from above the fireplace.

"Does that thing even work?" Santa asked.

She turned to Gunner.

"You have to stop them."

In the kitchen, Don Granada rooted through a junk drawer. He fingered through some coins, a medal, an arrow head…

"Where is that thing?" he mumbled to himself.

A second later, he found a rusty bullet. He held it up and assessed it. It had some turquoise oxide on it, which he rubbed off with his thumb.

"You don't even have enough bullets." she said.

He chambered the fifth bullet in the pistol, whipped the cylinder shut and spun it, still missing a round.

"What're you going to do? Shoot five and hit the rest with your gun? You're a… He has an army!"

Behind her, Barboza aimed the Enfield out the window, over the terrace and ocean to Simian's Keep in the distant Castillo, calibrating the sights. He squinted with one eye, then lowered the gun and picked a rusty barnacle off the front sight.

"You'll be slaughtered! That deserter murdered his way out of the army. The hunter kills howlers and that boogie-man knows where all the bodies are buried! Because he buried them!"

She whipped back to Gunner.

"Don't you care? Aren't you going to DO something! This is insane!"

"Alright," Gunner finally huffed. "Goddammit."

They turned to hear what he had to say.

"Listen, she's right. This is exactly what they want. It's a provocation. They'll kill you and claim self-defense if you march in there like that. Heated and armed. It'll be over by lunch. And they'll make themselves sandwiches."

Don Granada buckled the holster, ignoring him.

"Then they'll take the Ranchero and come after Santa and your grandson."

With that, Granada hesitated.

"Can you protect them, if you're dead?"

Granada glanced at Barboza. They eyed each other. Barboza held the Enfield, standing at the ready with his bandolier, dagger, medals and shorts, like a minute-man, buffalo soldier mix from a long forgotten bush war in North Africa, where mercenaries and mondelies fought for countries they didn't even like, just because they liked to fight.

"Look," Gunner continued, "give me an hour. Let me see if there's another way. I'll go talk to them. As a neutral party. I don't have any stake in any of this. Nor do I want to. If that doesn't work, then you can clack off your five rounds and get yourself killed."

Chapter 34

Twenty minutes later, Gunner trekked up to the entrance of the old Spanish fort.

Cazador and his laborers stacked stone on the deteriorated wall, fortifying and rebuilding it. Awol sat in a chair nearby, dry-shaving his neck with an ocelot bone knife, situated under a large kapok that stretched from its buttress roots up a branchless, elephantine trunk to a wide, flat canopy with waxy drip-tip leaves. Tequila sat in a chair next to him, with her bare feet and painted toes in his lap, reading a magazine.

"Come for another beating?" Awol asked as he scraped his neck.

Gunner stopped. Cazador placed a stone on the wall and straightened. He wiped sweat off his forehead, slicked back his hair and watched. Tequila glanced up from her magazine.

"You took a wrong turn, burner," Awol added. "The trail outta town's thata way. And those graves ain't for you. 'Cause when you die on a bullet, you won't deserve to be buried. On account of you being a coward and all. Crows will peck at your eyes."

Awol grinned and—

—*SMACK!*

Slapped Tequila's bare feet. She yelped and smacked his thick, tattooed deltoid with her magazine, but he just laughed cocky, shoved her feet and knocked her backward out of her chair and onto the ground.

"Hahaha…"

Gunner stared silently for a second, then strode past them, through the entrance and into the graveyard.

In the center of the graveyard, near the Keep, Simian and Gambler stood over an unearthed grave, watching two gravediggers extract a coffin.

"Careful." Simian instructed.

Bonesetter sat further back, straddling a new coffin near a shallow, open grave. The veins on his arms throbbed and his traps swelled like Awol's, like he'd just finished working out. Behind him, Undertaker and a soldado stood next to two large cane corsos, leashed to a post.

THUMP.

Something thumped in Bonesetter's coffin. He kicked it, aligned a nail gun along the edge and—

—*WHUMP WHUMP.*

Nailed it shut. As he sealed the top of his coffin, the bottom of the gravedigger's old coffin rotted out and—

—*CRASH!*

A skeleton burst through and splatted on the ground.

"Hell," one of the gravediggers stated.

"Gawdammit!" Simian cursed, shoving the gravedigger in the grave.

Gambler squatted by the skull and studied the scattered bones, like a witch reading prophecies in entrails. After a moment, he wedged a coin in a strange crack in the skull's head, that came from some kind of blunt force trauma, maybe a sword or axe.

WOOF!

One of the cane corsos barked, and everyone looked up.

Gunner.

Gunner stood in front of them, like he'd snuck up on them and had been standing there several minutes. Everyone tensed and stared silently. Gambler rested his hand on the butt of his gun.

"Don Granada," Gunner finally announced, "is… emotional."

"That's been hiz problem from the beginning!" Simian agreed. "Hez too God DAMN EMOTIONAL FOR BIZNEZ!"

Simian kicked the skull like a soccer ball. The coin flew from it and Gambler tossed his hands up in frustration. The gravediggers eyed the coin hungrily, and one stealthily pocketed it.

"Your hairz thicka than I imagined," Simian commented.

"What?"

"No it looks great. Really. Stupendous. I wouldn't dye it. Itz just, the gerls said… Anyway, heh, forgidaboutit huh? Why ya here?"

"To talk."

"No, why ya in this town?"

"I'm not. I'm trying to leave."

"Well great. If there's anything ya need while ya here, lemme know huh? Okay? Some honeys? Huh? Huh?"

Gunner stared.

"Did the old man hiya ya?"

"Like I said, I'm just trying to mind my own business and get out of here. That's all."

"So you're the only one here ain't lookin fwor a fight?"

"Most people here aren't looking for a fight."

"You need to mind your own business out of town," Bonesetter jabbed from his coffin in the back. "You better be gone tomorrow or—"

"—SHUDAAP!" Simian shouted over his shoulder. He took a long, exasperated breath, then continued, "Listen. This whole thingz gotten a bit… outta hand. Willy, itz a simple biznez deal. Hez sittin on all that land like that. Itz undeveloped, unsafe. And now he doesn't even have a bar on it."

"Because you burned it."

"Hiz people are peasants and heh, heh, I'm here, and I can sawlve all that. We can make this place stupendous. Willy stupendous."

Gunner waited.

"Now there's two optionz. The stupendous one and a… less stupendous one. Herez the good one. That prawpatyz actually more valuable now that that ratz nest burned. So I'll, heh, heh, I'll double my awffa. Plus if he sells, I don't needa keep diggen up this shitty townz ghostz."

"What's the bad option?"

Bonesetter grinned.

"Tell him," Simian replied, "that if he comes to the Cantina at noon, at the deadline—"

"—Unarmed— " Gambler added, standing.

"—Then we'll resawlve tis. Peacefully, and prawfitably. Heh, I'm a biznezman, not a tax man, I wanna resawlve this. I'm tryin ta help 'em. But hez gotta help himself too, and this offa expiraz… in one howr."

Chapter 35

Don Granada, Barboza and Santa picked through Valhalla's smoldering ruins. Granada wore a holster with the pistol he'd recovered from the trap door, and Barboza remained ready in full war kit, with his Sahara boots, scarred shines and ghost dagger, shouldering the Enfield from the fireplace, rusty as his medals.

Granada mulled over the ruins, looking down. He kicked a burnt beam aside and exposed a charred picture frame underneath. He brushed some ash off it with his foot and stared at the picture in the ashes. After a moment, he squatted and recovered it. He stood back up and turned it over in his thick grandpa hands, staring at the grainy, amber photograph.

"Papa..." Santa said, walking up.

She saw tears swelling in his light eyes as she approached. She slowed and rested her hand on his forearm. He lowered the picture and smiled softly at her.

"Your mom..."

"She was a princess," Santa said.

"She was a Queen."

Don Granada pursed his lips and stared out, across the beach and over the sea, into the watery ocean of his memories.

"You should have seen her when she was young."

Santa smiled sadly. She wrapped her arms around his hefty belly, and he put his arm over her shoulder and pulled her close.

"Those were good years."

She leaned her head against his shoulder like she did when she was young.

"We lose who we love," he said, "then we lose their memories. I didn't even see them go. They just went out the backdoor, like a dog let out who one day doesn't come home."

He lost himself for a moment in a memory of Santa chasing Tuck around the map drawers in Castillo San Felipe de Baraja, in Cartagena des Indies. Tuck was two then, unsteady on his feet, and he giggled hilarious as his mom chased him. Winter was there, looking for clues in Kidd's journals and Caravaggio's maps. Isadora too, holding Don Granada's bicep.

"Haaaaaa!" Tuck squealed as he fled from his mom,

disappearing around the corner of a map case. His joy echoed loudly off the stone walls in the spartan chamber.

"The soldados will come," Don Granada had admonished.

"Shhh…" Isadora had replied, smiling peacefully, patting her husband's arm and calming him like only she could. "They'll come soon enough. Let them be, for now."

And they were.

And it was infinite.

And ten years passed in the blink of an eye.

"Aghh," Don Granada growled, back on the beach, swaying slightly in Valhalla's ruins, in eight years of work and love, smoldering under his feet. After a moment, he wiped his eye and raised his strong chin.

"This is the jungle. I lived by its law and thrived by its law and ate with its fangs. And we were kings. So I won't cry now that those fangs are turning on me."

"Papa…"

"We think we own things but we don't. Look around. Look at everything I had. This house, this bar, your mother… I had them. I mean I *had* them. How couldn't I? I fought so hard for them. Now they're just gone and going, and soon there'll be nothing left. I'm trying, I'm fighting Sweet-Love, but no matter what I do I can't save them for you anymore. I can't keep them. I'm too old. I'm an old man who's had his day in the sun and they're disintegrating in my grip. Because everything is taken from us, just as it was given to us, to hold but not have, like the fucken ocean in our fingers."

"Papa!"

"AGH!"

He hucked his hands in the air and growled, then waved an angry backhand over Valhalla's ruins, as if dismissing eight years with the wave of his hand.

As he did, Gunner hiked up from the beach.

"What'd he say?" Santa asked, breaking from her father.

"He's giving you one last… peaceful chance."

"Crook," Don Granada spat over his shoulder.

"He's offering you double for your land, and said that if you take the deal, he'll stop digging up the cemetery."

"Puh."

"He wants you to come to the Cantina, unarmed, by noon."

"It's a trap," Barboza concluded, sauntering up and joining

them.

"He can't go," Santa said.

"Ya well… He might have to."

"Why?" Barboza attacked.

Gunner took a deep breath and scanned the area.

"Where's the kid?"

They looked around. Nothing but beach and palms.

"Tuck!?" Santa called.

"He wouldn't," Barboza said under his breath.

"He would," Don Granada replied, jaw-locked.

"Bastard!" Barboza yelled.

"TUCK!"

"The deserter," Gunner explained, "he had the boy's knife. And Bonesetter… Well…"

"Bonesetter what?" Santa darted at him.

"Tuck must have tried something."

"Why?"

They stared at him, waiting for an answer. He took a deep breath and looked them right in the eye.

"They got him."

"NO! No no NO!"

"They've kidnapped him. Holding him somewhere. I don't know."

With that, Don Granada immediately unbuckled his holster and dropped it in the sand. It thumped like a role of rope at his feet.

"DAMMIT!" Barboza yelled.

Santa rushed to sprint down the beach, but Granada grabbed her arm and ripped her back. He held and restrained her, engulfing her in his arms.

"Baby, baby, baby… Calm down, calm down, we'll get him. We'll get him. No way in hell we won't. I'll wipe everything off the face of this fucking earth before I lose him."

He held her until she stopped fighting, but she breathed hard and tears of fear and anger rolled down her cheeks. He put a strand of her hair behind her ear, calming her.

"I know what we gotta do," he reassured her. "I know exactly what to do."

He hugged her once more for a long moment, then nodded at Gunner over her shoulder. He kissed her forehead and handed her the charred picture, then stormed away.

Gunner delayed. He watched Santa and Barboza standing atop what was left of their bar, since he hadn't had a chance to absorb the scene and the magnitude this loss had on them. He'd be upset too if someone kidnapped his family and razed the last eight years of his life. After a thoughtful moment, he turned and followed Don Granada down the beach.

As they marched to the Cantina, Santa looked down at the picture. It was a still shot of her father's memory; the amber picture of her, Tuck, Winter, her father and mother—Isadora—in the old map room in Castillo San Felipe de Baraja, in Cartagena des Indias.

Carefully, she brushed soot off the photo. When she did, she knocked off part of the burnt frame, which fell to the sand. There, at the edge of the photograph, which had been covered by the frame and hadn't been visible, stood Mudo, studying a map. Mudo wore his red felt jacket with gold buttons and lapels. It was buttoned up to the stiff collar, and shined much brighter and more regally than it did now.

After a moment she looked up and, with Barboza, watched her father go. Her father, the man who spoke Garifuna and broken Siwi, and who once placed a radar on the summit of Nandi Devi to monitor Chinese missile launches. The man who crossed the Interior, recruited a Colonel in the Kremlin, sabotaged the Soviet space program at Star City, freed three POWs from a bamboo cage in Laos, and muscled and marched a platoon of Berber insurgents across the Sand Sea like the LRDG to attack Bora Khan, impossibly, from the desert. The man few knew, but everyone claimed to have known. The legend, the shadow, the whisper in rugged men's heads, the carved graffiti in outposts and firebases, and the feeling at the bottom of a gin in a bar in N'djamena, filled with mercenaries and middle-aged men, with African hookers and broken marriages, arms dealers and despots, mad plots and coup d'états, AKs and DGSE, trading security, schemes, pussy and death.

I was there. I was there when he saved Dreadfort Dobbins.

Fuck-you you weren't, but I will be next time.

So will I, so will I…

To Don Granada.

To Don Granada.

To Don Granada… the great explorer, the great soldier, the great no-man… but above all, the great Father, fading in beach haze, like his memories and things.

Chapter 36

Don Granada and Gunner marched down the main road and into town, straight for the Cantina.

They passed Butch, who sat on his butcher shop's porch on a makeshift wooden bench with his clever in his lap. Empty meat hooks hung dead-still on the porch beam in front of him. Butch imagined a skinned cerdo de monte hanging from one, with its muscled sinew and boar's fangs, but the image quickly faded, and he waved his palm in front of his cataract eyes, as if his fading vision, and not Simian's stranglehold on the town, was what was causing him not to see it.

Mudo sat on the edge of Butch's porch, under the meat hooks, wearing his scuffed red coat and shorts. He spotted a rib bone in the road. He got up and grabbed it, dusted it off and tried gnawing on it. After a few chomps, however, he tossed it back in the road, sat back down and rubbed his hands together anxiously.

Next door, Garifuna Mama swept a white-washed porch in a tropical headscarf and colorful apron, while her two toddlers rolled a bent metal bike wheel with a stick nearby. When she saw Don Granada and Gunner approach, she could tell something was wrong. Anybody could. Because nobody moved with that much purpose in this town. There just wasn't anywhere anyone needed to be that fast, that focused, that forcefully. She stopped sweeping and leaned back on her weight and watched.

"Kids…"

In the distance, near the Cantina, the sun shone through the church's bell-tower, casting the shadow of the cross on the dusty road.

"Here," Don Granada said as they strode.

He handed Gunner the oxidized bullet he'd found in his drawer.

"What's this?"

"The second bullet that was in the revolver. When I killed the Mad Czar. In Russian roulette. Near Sáo Gabriel da Cachoeira."

Gunner thumbed it.

"You may need it," Don Granada added.

"For wha—"

"—It was meant for me. I was spying for the British. But

without it, I never would have met Isadora. And without her, we never would have had our daughter. And without Santa, we never would have had Tuck."

"Listen, you're talking—"

"—There still might be one other thing I have to give you."

"What?"

"Anger."

Gunner pulled his focus from the Cantina and eyed him sideways as they trekked.

"Listen," Gunner said, "I'm only helping with this because I promised the boy I'd help him if he ever needed it. This isn't my fight. As soon as that boat gets here this afternoon I'm—"

"—I ain't ever had a problem with killing," Don Granada continued, ignoring him, "but my punch isn't what it used to be."

"We're not punching our way out of this—"

"—And I don't have a good feeling—"

"—You don't need to feel. Just operate."

"That's not true. If you don't feel and live for something, you'll die for nothing."

Gunner frowned and replied, "There isn't any other way."

"That's also not true and you know it."

"No good way."

"Listen, if something happens—"

"—Nothing's gonna—"

"—Lay waste."

"I—"

"—Bullshit. You can fix it. And only you. Or kill a lot of people trying."

Chapter 37

Awol leaned against a stucco wall inside the Cantina, chewing on a toothpick. Bonesetter stood in a nearby side-shadow with half his face obscured, clenching his "family" photo. The veins in his forearms throbbed.

"'Awright 'awright bring it in," Simian said, squaring up in front of them. "Listen up. Don't hurt the 'ol man. Okay? Watever I say and watever I do, DON'T hurt him. Got it? Huh? Huh?"

"Why?" Bonesetter queried.

"Aghhh, Gawd… I'm glad I cawd tis meeting. Listen, if we hurt Don Granada, the town burns. We lose awr integrity, and worse, awr labor force. You know waat that means? Huh? Huh? It means we lose da hearts and da minds of the people. The town turns on us and thinks WE'RE the bad guys, instead of the guys helping them. Killin' howlers, providing security… Once we negotiate down a deal and grant him clemency, then we're the benevolent ones. Wit the land. Gawt it?"

Bonesetter frowned and picked at something in his ear. Awol rolled his tongue over his toothpick, as if considering the logic.

"You know what clemency means?" Simian asked.

"Don't hurt 'em."

"Good. You're learning. Now bow to your saanzay."

Awol looked away, bored. Bonesetter cocked his head sideways and hit it with his hand, trying to knock something loose.

Chapter 38

Don Granada and Gunner walked up to the Cantina and stopped in the street out front, because Gambler leaned against a pole on the porch, in a shadow near some horses and pack mules. He was flicking a deck of cards with one hand, and rested his other hand on the butt of his gun, which was slung low on his hip in his holster. He leaned casually and smiled slightly, but it was clear he'd been watching them come for some time - and nobody breezed by Gambler.

After a long draw, Gambler rolled a card over his knuckles and flipped it over: the three of diamonds.

"The flop," he said.

He flashed the card, stuck it in his back pocket and drew another for himself.

"Nine of diamonds."

Don Granada and Gunner took that for some sort of pass, and stepped onto the porch to enter.

"Wait," Gambler said, sliding the nine in his vest and tapping his pistol.

They stopped. Don Granada clenched his fat fists, ready to fight. Gambler, however, nodded back down the road the way they came.

"That blood-crow."

Surprised, they looked back down the road behind them. In the distance, a crow sat atop a lone electrical wire. It was black as ink, and its ink-shadow painted a white wall behind it like a Rorschach blot, but its eyes were yellow, yellow like two small suns.

"It's been watchen you," Gambler said.

"The crow?"

"It's not a crow."

"Oh ya?" Gunner asked, amused, "What is it?"

"A surveillent."

Gunner thought that Don Granada would have laughed at that, but he didn't. Instead, Granada looked dead serious, and asked:

"For who?"

"I don't know," Gambler replied pensively, narrowing his eyes. "That's what concerns me."

Don Granada and Gunner exchanged a quick look, then Gambler drew his pistol, which WHOOSED when it skinned off the leather.

"Forty, forty-five meters," he calculated to himself with a distant stare, licking his lip and thumbing his front sight tenderly.

Don Granada looked from the pistol to the crow and back, eyeballing the distance himself. It was far. Flat out. Especially for a pistol. In fact, of all the soldiers, spies, traitors, Turkmen, falconers, frauds, highwaymen, hunters, despots and dragoons in all the barracks, bars and brothels he'd ever passed through, he'd only ever met two or three men who could make that shot. Maybe.

He cocked an eyebrow.

Gambler cocked his gun.

When he did, the crow appeared to turn his head and peer directly back at them with its yellow, beady, lifeless eyes. Gunner tried to remember if all crows' eyes were yellow, while Gambler peered back with his slate black eyes through his sights.

CAWWW…

BANG!

A split second passed, then a batch of black feathers burst in the air like splatted ink. The crow's black shadow vaporized from the wall behind it and some feathers fluttered into the road. Its stick-feet, however, remained clutched on the wire; until they simply, slowly, tipped forward and hung upside down, shot off above the knobby knees, still gripping the wire.

"Umgph," Don Granada grunted involuntarily, impressed.

Gambler smirked and holstered, then craned his neck and looked up, out from under the porch's eves, and scanned the blue sky above for more crows.

"Won't matter much though," Gambler said, looking back down at them. "Because you're pot-committed now. We all are."

Chapter 39

Inside the Cantina, Simian sat at the poker table, facing the door. Awol leaned against the wall behind him and Bonesetter lurked further back, in a shadow.

When Simian heard Don Granada's commanding footfalls on the porch, he quickly scooped up a bunch of poker chips from the other empty seats and stacked them in front of him on the table, then touched-up his pompadour with his hands.

Don Granada entered first. He looked around to get his bearings, then spotted Simian and strode directly to him. He stopped in front of him and stared.

SILENCE.

After a long moment, Simian finally spoke.

"Itz good to finally tawk like sensible—"

"—You son of a bitch," Don Granada seethed through his teeth. He spoke with such conviction that Barman slid off his stool and slipped through a kitchen door behind him. He didn't need no part of this.

"Heh, this is a legitimate awffa. This is a good awportunity and I'm only gonna make it once."

Gunner eased up next to Don Granada. Simian got distracted by him for a second and looked him over, then refocused and continued.

"So here it is. I'll double the awffa for ya land. Paid in gold. Right here. Right now. Do ya wanna make this place safe? Help yuwr people?"

"You took—"

"—Ya I heard about the bar. I'm sorry about that. I willy am. And the cabaanya. That too. But I don't think sellen flamen shawts—"

"—YOU TOOK MY GRANDSON!"

Simian froze, eyes wide.

Suddenly, Don Granada lunged for his neck. Simian flinched and Awol drew, but Gunner grabbed Granada's arm and ripped him back before Awol could fire.

"Whoa whoa whoa! Watch da suit! Come on!" Simian said, holding out his hands.

When he did, Bonesetter stepped forward behind him and set a Sig Sauer in his hand, then leaned over and whispered in his ear:

"It's noon."

Simian looked at the unexpected gun in his outstretched hand.

"Wait," Gunner said, pulling Don Granada back and stepping forward, "slow down. Hang on. This isn't necessary. We came in good faith. In peace. To talk this out."

"Too bad we ain't no good at talkin' none," Awol said, scratching his Spartan beard with his gun.

"You think a bullet can stop me?" Granada shot at him sideways, unhelpfully.

"Ya," Awol stated.

"I tried. I willy tried," Simian mumbled to himself, admiring the large gun in his small hand.

"Hang on," Gunner said. "Everyone just calm down."

The conversation was less than a minute old and it'd already disintegrated. Everyone was talking past each other and two guns were drawn.

"Let's focus."

"Why didn't ya just sell the land?" Simian mused, ignoring him.

He shook his head remorsefully and searched for the mag release button on the Sig Sauer, flagging the barrel recklessly in every direction as he did. Bonesetter ducked when the barrel passed over him in one direction, then grimaced when it passed back over him in the other.

"You're not even developing it. And yuwr people, they're hungry. I got a hunter, a dawctor…"

Simian monkeyed with the gun as he spoke. Bonesetter watched impatiently.

"I offered ya a fair price. Mwore than a fair price."

"What," Bonesetter finally asked Simian, "are you do—"

"—I'm raahken it!"

"It doesn't need to be racked. Here."

He reached over Simian's shoulder and tried to take the Sig Sauer and replace it with a small garter pistol.

"Come on!" Simian snapped, shucking off the garter gun and snatching back the Sauer.

"Awright thatz it!" Simian said, jumping to his feet, bumping the table, knocking over the poker chips and waving the gun around recklessly. "New deal abuelo! Hand over the deed, get the boy and leave town. No more money. Nada. Thatz it! Sayonara."

"Go to hell."

Simian leveled the Sig Sauer on him.

"Fine. Everyone saaw me—"

"—Safety," Awol noted.

Simian snorted and looked at the side of the gun for a second, found the safety and flicked it off.

"Okay. Everyone saw me put this old goat down in self-defenze right?"

"And the other one too," Awol added.

Simian turned the gun on its other side, looking for another safety.

"No," Awol said, annoyed, "the other... The fisherman."

"What about him?" Simian asked, still looking for another safety with his finger triggered.

"We saw you shoot them *both of them* in self-defense."

"Let's go," Gunner said, quickly collaring Don Granada and moving him towards the—

—*WHUMP!*

Suddenly, a nail hit the wooden floor near their feet. Bonesetter stepped in front of them and blocked their exit, grinning. He held the nail gun in his bit hand and a pistol in his burnt one.

"You..." Don Granada snarled. "I always knew you—"

—*BANG!*

Gunner instinctively jumped and spun on the surprise gunshot. It echoed loudly, painfully, off the exposed brick in the old Cantina. Another chipped tile fell off the stairs.

CLANK.

Behind him, Simian held the Sig Sauer at an odd angle, mouth agape and eyes wide, silent and shocked. Clearly, he hadn't meant to—

—*THUD.*

Fire.

Don Granada hit the floor like a two-hundred-pound plank. Face first. A small bullet hole bore through his back.

Gunner stared wide-eyed. The bullet hole was smaller than a nickel, but blood already pooled out underneath him on the other side. Simian stared at the gun in his hand, amazed. A smile slowly curled up his lip; power.

Don Granada gargle-coughed, still alive.

Quickly, Gunner grabbed him and flipped him over. The exit wound was considerably bigger and messier than the entry wound, near his sternum. No way the bullet didn't blow out the liver or lung on the way through.

"Welp," Awol said, spitting out the toothpick, "now we gotta kill 'em both. In self-defense."

FSSSST.

A nail whizzed past Gunner's ear. He snapped to the sound and saw Bonesetter pointing a nail-gun at him and Simian pointing a gun-gun at him. He jumped just as—

—BANG FSSST!

A bullet seared past him and an nail drove into his deltoid. He leaped over the top of the bar as they fired again.

BANG FSSST FSSST!

Bonesetter raised his nail-gun and pistol at the bar, then grinned and unloaded.

BANG! BANG! WHUMP! WHUMP! BANG!

Wood chipped and nails stuck.

Awol joined and fired into the bar with him. Glass shattered, splinters whistled and bottles exploded.

BANG! BANG! BANG! WHUMP! BANG! WHUMP!

Gunner ducked behind the bar. He yanked the nail out of the muscle in his shoulder and covered his head. Bullets ripped through the bar above him, punching smoky light holes and shattering bottles on the shelves above and behind it. Glass shards and whiskey rained down, thunking and crashing into him and the floor.

Gambler watched with a sardonic grin off to the side, leaning against a pole with his arms crossed and gun holstered. This wasn't a fight. It was a murder. And they didn't need him for that. Bonesetter noticed Gambler watching, so he pivoted and shot a nail over his head.

WHUMP!

The nail whumped into the pole a few inches above his scalp. Gambler jumped and ducked simultaneously, surprised, and Bonesetter laughed.

While Bonesetter was distracted, Gunner popped back around the bar and grabbed Don Granada's arm. They locked eyes. There was life in them, but they were milky and fading fast.

Gunner quickly heaved and dragged Granada's formidable body towards cover behind the bar, leaving a streak of blood behind him.

Just as he was about to reach the bar, however, Simian aimed his heavy Sauer and yanked the trigger.

BANG! BANG! BANG!

All three shots splayed wildly, but Bonesetter looked back and fired. A nail shot into and through Gunner's hand, breaking his grip. Gunner reached back with the nail still in it, but Don Granada lay like sniper bait, drawing fire. Gunner reached through the fray and grabbed Don Granada again, but Awol unslung an M4 and—

—DA DA DA DA DA DA DA...

Unloaded. Gunner dove back behind the bar as the M4 chipped and thrashed it. He reached around the bar for Don Granada again, but a bullet tore through his forearm, snapping it back. There was nowhere to go. He was trapped.

DA DA DA DA...

BANG!

Miss.

DA DA DA DA...

BANG!

Miss.

DA DA DA DA...

BANG! BANG!

Hit.

One of Simian's bullets finally struck Don Granada again, under his armpit. Simian stared, enthralled and ecstatic, but Awol and Bonesetter keep firing, trying to kill Gunner through the bar with blunt fire and force. There was no grace in it.

BANG BANG BANG! DA DA DA DA DA...WHUMP!

Loud, smoky chaos. Casings PINGED, nails stuck and smoke rose.

"WOOOOH YAAAA!" Bonesetter hollered through the haze.

PING, PING, WHUMP!

CLICK, CLICK, CLICK...

CLACK.

Empty.

Silence.

Like the silence after a stampede passes. They were out of ammo. Cordite smoke filled the Cantina and bullet casings littered the floor. Don Granada lay in the middle of it. Every few seconds, he wheezed horribly for a breath.

Awol clicked in another mag. He and Bonesetter crept forward, flanking the chipped and splintered bar from both sides, guns at the high-ready. They inched in and pied the bar's corners, peering behind it. Smoke, glass, liquor, shards…

"DAM!"

"He's gone!" Bonesetter declared.

Behind the bar, a trail of blood streaked across the floor, through the kitchen door.

"The kitchen."

"Well," Gambler commented from the back, pushing off the wall, "that didn't go according to plan."

He drew a card from his deck and flicked it at Don Granada. It spun across the room and landed on his chest as he wheezed on the floor:

The five of hearts.

"The turn," Gambler said.

He drew another card for himself and flinched slightly when he saw it:

The eight of clubs.

"FIND HIM!" Simian yelled.

Chapter 40

Gunner fled down a trail away from town. It meandered through arid scrub over rocky ground. He moved fast and fluid but cut a blind corner, stumbled on a rock and hand-planted. He rested on his knee in the middle of the trail for a moment to catch his breath, then growled, coughed and spit into the dirt.

Blood.

HOWLLLLL...

He darted a look over his shoulder, back down the trail towards town.

Hounds. The big cane corsos.

Get up. Get moving.

He grunted, rose and kept running.

A minute later, he rounded a bend and the trail opened to an arroyo. It was wide and rocky, but a rivulet trickled through the middle of it like a vein. Without breaking stride, he hip-slid down a bank and reflexively flash-thought something his dad once told him:

You can read the landscape like a book. It tells a story. History. That's what trackers do. See this wadi? You know why it's wide like this? You know where the water went?

No.

It's still here. Just not now. But it'll be back. In August, during the monsoon. It'll come and blow everything back out again. That's why those rocks are there and these igneous ones here. So what's that tell you about these saplings, these cottonwoods?

I dunno.

That they came after the monsoon, and can't be more than a few months old. They've gotta grow fast and strong before the next monsoon. Only some of them will make it. But life fills every gap. Every space. Until it succeeds.

He leapt the rivulet and rushed across the alluvial plain to the other side. He scurried up the other dirt bank and picked the trail back up, following it further out, further from town and its problems.

The trail curved back into thick scrub and gradually rose to a bluff. There, a stone obelisk stood on the rise, under the flat canopy of a large acacia. It was a topographical marker, waist-high. He stopped, rested his hand on it and bent over to breathe.

Blood ran from the bullet hole in his forearm, down his hand and onto the obelisk, which was engraved with the words *Quebrada Quemada*. He tried to wipe it off with his non-bloody hand, but it was wet from sweat, and more blood dripped in the dirt beneath him. He looked back and saw a trail of blood splatter.

Fuck.

There was blood everywhere. On his forearm from the gunshot, on his lower back from the puncture wound, on his hand and delt from the nails... dripping scent and sweat all over the country like a messy murder for the dogs to smell-read like a map. He'd survived the sea just to die in the desert.

Fuck.

ROFF!

Get up. Get moving.

He dragged his hand off the obelisk and staggered forward, streaking more blood across it.

The trail dropped off the bluff and narrowed through a woodland until it hit a thick hedgerow and evaporated altogether, somewhere under it. Suddenly, there was no trail. Just brush and thorn.

RUFF! RUFF!

The dogs were louder and closer, closing on the obelisk, so he lowered his head and plunged into the thicket. It rose over his head on scraggily, crooked branches that scratched his shins and snatched scent on their thorns.

He fast-picked through the branches until he reached a clearing. There, he stopped to reorient himself. The sun burned down high overhead, and he smelled...

Death.

BZZZZZZ...

He followed the sound. His eyes landed on some feet sticking out of some cuttings. Human feet. Toes. Barefoot.

He stepped to them, pulled a cutting off them, batted away some flies and saw that the feet were bound. The ankles were hog-tied behind a man's back to his hands.

With green duct tape.

Intel's duct tape.

He removed more cuttings and saw that the man's neck and head were also lashed with green duct tape. They were pulled back and bound to the hands and feet, so that all the cords met mid-back and were tied together like a bow on a present, bowing the body in a convex, torturous position. Worse, the body had stiffened and swelled from rigamortis, so it strained further and made it look like the duct tape cut deep into fat wrists and ankles.

He shoved the feet and rolled the body on its side.

BZZZZ!

Flies burst out. They swarmed angrily and buzzed in and out of a gaping skull-mouth with shattered teeth. The man's face had been smashed by a large rock that lay nearby, and something had fed on his stomach and gorged out his rib cage like a zebra, postmortem. Maybe a jaguar. The man was no longer recognizable, and too rotten for even coyotes to eat now, but a straw hat was caught on a thorny branch nearby and a pick-axe lay in the dirt.

Prospector's hat and pick-axe.

Prospector.

It was Prospector. The man who got inspired by Gunner and confronted Simian about the cemetery, where his son was buried

A few days dead.

RUFF! RUFF! RUFF!

"He went this way!" Bonesetter cried in the distance, over the hedgerow.

Get moving.

He straightened and quickly nodded to Prospector as a eulogy, then crossed the small clearing in a few steps, covered his face with his forearms and plunged back into the hedgerow.

He drove through thorns that scratched his sides, but the further he fought the more they clawed and slowed him. It was like he was in a dream, unable to run, that became worse the harder he tried. The only advantage was that if it was nearly impassable for a man it would be hard for dogs and impossible for horses. It became a question of who wanted it more. Did he want to live more than they wanted to kill him? Always. Always the prey has the advantage for that.

RUFF! RUFF! RUFF! RUFF!

He grunted and surged harder, straight through the thorns, no longer trying to work around them, reenergized by the thought that they may save him. A thorn, however, sliced his back pocket open, and the makeshift orange plastic envelope that had been tied to his forearm when he washed ashore slid out. It hit the ground behind him, but he didn't notice and pressed on, leaving it behind in the dirt, in the brier in the bush.

Finally, remarkably, he broke through. But insanely, seemingly incredibly, he punched back out at the same arroyo, just further downstream. He either got turned around in the bush and accidently doubled back on himself, or the wash oxbowed like a horseshoe and a cruel joke. Either way, he was exhausted, disoriented and cat-scratched to hell. Worse, if the hunters just stuck to the wash, which they'd probably do because they couldn't get the horses through the thicket, the thicket was not only pointless, but it burnt valuable time. The trackers could halve his lead with half the effort.

One foot in front of the next.

There was nowhere else to go, so he stumbled back into the wash and scrambled to the rivulet. But, this time, instead of jumping it and crossing to the other side, he turned and splashed down the middle of it, trying to dilute his sweaty scent in the water. It was the desperate act of a desperate man, which was never good, but it was still the least terrible option.

He splashed downstream until he came to a pack mule rotting in the middle of the rivulet. It had to be Prospector's. Probably wandered off with a gunshot wound, making it further than its rider. Like Prospector, it was a few days dead. Loud horseflies swarmed it, and sun-burnt ribs clawed out of wilting, dried skin.

BZZZZZZ...

RUFF RUFF RUFF RUFF RUFF!

He squatted and thought. A three to four year old male cane corso, in this heat, could run three to four miles, flat out. He could keep running, but he couldn't outrun horses and dogs in unfamiliar terrain, not in this weakened shape—or maybe any shape. He could turn and fight, but he was unarmed and the cane corsos would maul him. Or he could surrender, like Prospector. Besides these options, there was a dead donkey in front of him and a dark eddy in eroded buttress roots on the right bank, under a large mahogany tree.

RUFF RUFF RUFF RUFF RUFF RUFF!

Quickly, he splashed water on his head and flicked sweat off his hands, then put his forearm in the creek and dug his finger into the bullet hole. It went clean through, but hadn't hit bone.

URGHH...

He gorged the hole and blood pumped out. It poured in the rivulet and floated downstream, hopefully carrying his stink with it.

He scooped some clay mud from the rivulet with his fingers and stuffed it in the bullet hole.

Pinch off veins, plug the holes. Keep the blood in the body.

He ripped off the bottom of his thorn-torn shorts and used the strip as a tourniquet, which he tied above the wound, below the elbow, to pinch the bleeding.

RUFF RUFF RUFF RUFF RUFF RUFF RUFF!

He picked up the donkey carcass, rubbed it on his chest and face and retched.

"HUHHH—"

—BZZZZZZ...

He threw his head inside the carcass like an Indian bearskin, then turned parallel to the stream and bound towards the bank. Halfway, he stopped and looked back. Wet footprints on hot river rock.

ARGH.

No fixing that. A drop of blood dripped down his hand and blotted a rock near his feet. No fixing that now either. He was melting like a bloody ice cream cone in the wash. He grunted and shouldered on.

A few leaps later he reached the eddy and ploughed headfirst into the mahogany roots, crawling through them on his belly with the donkey carcass over him. Under the roots in the bank was an animal den. He squirmed into the hole headfirst and twisted himself around inside it, hoping a snake or leopard wasn't in it. The opening was tall enough that he could sit up, barely, but it narrowed like a cone to a black hole that disappeared into the earth. He quickly pulled the carcass over the entrance and covered it like a teepee.

RUFF RUFF RUFF RUFF RUFF RUFF RUFF RUFF!

CLOP, CLOP, CLOP...

As soon as he covered the hole, Awol, Bonesetter and Cazador trotted down the arroyo on horses. The big cane corsos orbited their heels, sniffing and barking, jacked up on blood and scent. They stopped where the donkey was and sniffed in circles, trapping its putrid death in their floppy jowls.

He peered through the donkey carcass and watched them in the riverbed. Halfway between him and the group, his wet footprints shrank painfully slowly on the rocks in the sun.

"He's still bleeding," Cazador observed.

"Ya."

Cazador tapped Tuck's ocelot bone knife against his thigh, watching the dogs with his dark eyes, thinking. Slowly, his eyes migrated from where the donkey was to the wet footprints that dotted the rocks on the way to the—

"—Gimme THAT!" Bonesetter said, swiping Tuck's knife from him.

Cazador reined back his horse. It neighed and stammered, then he reset it and tracked back on the riverbed to pick up the trail. But the last of the wet footprints faded just before he looked, and he saw nothing but hot river rock.

And something on a rock.

Dark and circular. Nature didn't make perfect circles. Blood? He followed Gunner's route to the bank and his eyes fell on the eddy. He stared at it. Then raised his nose and sniffed the—

—RUFFRUFFRUFF…!

"They got it!" Awol yelled, bumping Cazador's horse.

Cazador's eyes shot downstream to the dogs. They barked and bolted ahead, splashing in the rivulet, chasing Gunner's blood downstream, away from him, skipping into the rocks to hunt faster.

"HI-YA!"

Awol kicked his horse and chased the dogs downstream, but Cazador didn't move. He sat on his horse in the riverbed and looked back at the bank. He stared still, unconvinced. He raised his rifle and peered through the scope, directly at the animal hole. Directly at Gunner.

"What is it?" Bonesetter asked, following Cazador's rifle to the hole. "Is he in there?"

Gunner stared back from the hole, watching Cazador watching him, motionless and breathless through ribs and roots.

One second.

Two.

"No," Cazador concluded, lowering his rifle. "El conejo no está allí."

"What?"

"He's not there."

"Then come on!" Bonesetter yelled, kicking his horse and following Awol and the dogs downstream.

Cazador gazed at Gunner's hole a moment longer, then nodded once at it, at Gunner, then turned his horse and followed the others downstream.

The hunter. The tracker. The tracker let him go.

Why they hell'd he do that?

Gunner exhaled. He dropped his head back against the dirt wall and stared at the other side of the hole. Sweat beaded on his head, his clothes were thrashed, his skin was raked and fresh red blood flowed over dried black blood on his arm, hand, shoulder, and back like lava. Before he could do anything, however, his vision blurred and he blacked out.

Chapter 41

Gunner's eyes crust open and he looked around. Sunlight bore through tears in the donkey carcass, casting grainy rays into the dark hole. Morning. Early morning. A night had passed.

His head rested in the donkey's ribs, which clawed at his face, and he was covered in bug bites, like a living buffet that mosquitos and insects had fed on all night. A thin and industrious line of cutter ants also crawled up his leg and across his stomach, carrying serrated green leaves bigger than they were like a humble offering to something deeper in the hole, to a blackness without form.

He raised his hand and reached into the hole, above the ant line, slowly, carefully, into the black. He felt cold on his fingertips, then bone. Round, smooth knuckles…

Fingers.

"AH!"

He jumped and shoved the donkey carcass off his head and out the hole. Light flooded in and he scurried out the hole and through the roots as fast as he could on all fours. He rolled into the wash and onto his feet, then turned and looked back like something was chasing him.

Stillness.

Silence.

Trogons chirped in the giant mahogany above.

He shook his head, bent over, put his hands on his knees and laughed at himself for freaking out like a kid, but still watching the hole with one eye as he gathered his wits. He straightened, rubbed dirt from his face and picked his way back through the buttress roots to look.

A skeleton lay in the hole. It was partially covered in ragged, weathered clothes and leather boots. It ran through a saddlebag, as if the body had evaporated from within the strap. The saddlebag was empty and the bones were relatively intact. Male. Circa forty years old. Maybe a year dead.

Two corpses in two days. He thought, *Jesus. It's Hades out here.*

He squatted and inspected closer. The wrists were bound by wire and the skull, which was a half-roll from the spine, had three nails spiked through it like a bowling ball. Bonesetter's nails. He removed them and held the skull up to the sun. Light bore through the holes.

He set the skull back respectfully and noticed that a bangle hung loose on the wrist bone—a pit-viper, eating its own tail.

Winter. Winter Lorca.

The Sherriff. The treasure hunter. Santa's husband and Tuck's missing father.

He backed out of the hole and looked around. Nothing but scrub oak and thorn. Quebrada quemada. He squatted by the stream and splashed water over his head and body, trying to wash off ants, dirt and donkey. Trying to raise strength from the dead.

CLOP...

CLOP...

CLOP...

He looked over his shoulder.

Mudo.

Mudo trekked down the arroyo with the two pack mules that had been in front of the Cantina. They were loaded with saddlebags for a long haul.

"Is he alive?" Gunner asked, standing and turning. "Is Don Granada alive?"

But Mudo didn't answer. Instead, he offered Gunner a water bottle and a grin, which Gunner took and chugged. As he did, Mudo reached in his back pocket and pulled out the orange plastic envelope. Gunner looked surprised, like he'd just seen a magic trick, and reflexively patted his own back pocket to confirm his envelope wasn't there. It wasn't, and his pocket was sliced open. He must have lost it in the flight.

"Where..."

But again, Mudo didn't answer and his eyes didn't betray anything. Instead, he pointed his machete upstream, about thirty degrees off center.

"The Interior?" Gunner interpreted.

Mudo nodded.

"The way out?"

Mudo nodded again.

The green mountains rose in the distance, rugged and far. Don Granada had mentioned quicksand and a mire, meaning that a lowland probably also lay on the other side of them. Hell, the mythical Interior may not even start until the other side of them.

He looked back and caught Mudo staring at the cordillera like he was staring into a fire or across an erg. He looked afraid. He shook his head to shake out the fear, then looked back to Gunner and tapped his wrist.

It was time, to go.

Without resting any longer, Mudo turned the pack mules upstream and began trekking. He led them by the reins, and waved the envelope behind him without looking, signaling Gunner to follow.

Gunner looked at the mountains again. Through, up and over that was the out. The solution. The walk-away from all this. The boat wasn't coming, but if he left now he could probably still get back and save Cindy, if he took some pain and they hurried. But he had to decide right then and there, because Mudo was already walking. So this was the choice, follow Mudo through the Interior and out, or turn downstream and go back? To what? A gunfight?

Like he'd said, it wasn't his fight.

He stepped forward and followed Mudo.

CLOP.

CLOP.

CLOP...

But after a few steps, he stopped. Dead in his tracks. He stared at the ground while the mules clopped on in the scree. Prospector rotted dead, nearby. Winter's bones calcified, nearby. Don Granada was probably dead, and the boy was missing, behind. Missing? Hell he was kidnapped, by Bonesetter.

Fuck it isn't my fight. I got another fight, a bigger one, the other way.

CLOP.

CLOP.

CLOP...

Mudo sensed that Gunner had stopped, so he paused and looked back. Gunner was staring at the ground. But after a moment, Gunner sighed, then slowly turned and looked back downstream, towards town.

Chapter 42

Don Granada's ranchero looked peaceful sitting on the hill in the green banana trees, red hibiscus, and white orchids, frozen in time like a Gaugin painting of a lost paradise from another century, when men challenged the world with ship and sword. A cocobolo tree shaded a corner of the house's terracotta roof, short grass sloped down the yard, and a flock of green parrots flew across a simple blue sky.

Inside, the great room sprawled over the stone floor, eerily still, dark and silent.

Inside that room, Don Granada lay atop the family table.

Cold.

And dead.

He lay in state, in a pair of shorts and green socks. His belly extended, his dog tags slumped around his neck and his rusty revolver lay on the table beside him. Two small, clean bullet holes bore through his body; one in his chest and one in his armpit.

Candles glowed around him, hollowing the room like a church. It was vacuous and empty, except for Padre, who stood over him and prayed.

Padre crossed himself and palmed Don Granada's forehead tenderly, then looked up and saw Gunner standing in the door. Gunner's shorts and shirt were shredded, his hair was wild and he was covered in scratches, dirt, bites and blood, like he'd wrestled a mountain lion in its den and lost. His gaze sat on something; Don Granada's gun, which sat on the table next to his corpse.

"Justice…" Padre said, following Gunner's gaze to the gun, "is in heaven."

"Then I won't see it."

"Why not?"

"'Cause I'm not going there."

Padre watched and waited, with his round face and small eyes.

"For the things I've done."

Gunner grimaced, then coughed.

"You're hurt." Padre said, "You're still healing."

UGH…

"Forgive yourself."

"Why?"

"Because God already has."

Undertaker sickled into the great room from the terrace. Barboza followed with his Enfield—somber, stoic and proud. Barboza stood by Don Granada and took his old friend's hand. Santiago, Mulata, Butch, Blacky and other townsfolk trickled in behind him, filling the room to pay their respects.

Santa entered last, with her eyes on her father. The townsfolk parted and she stepped to him. She took his other hand tenderly and gazed at him sadly, then gently wiped some black blood from his white beard, kissed his cheek and whispered something in his ear. After, her sad eyes drifted up to—

"—You."

She dropped her father's hand and charged Gunner.

"You promised! You PROMISED! You promised to protect him!"

She stormed across the room and pounded his chest.

"He believed in you! Where were you!? Where were you COWARD! YOU COWARD! WHERE'S MY SON!?"

He stood and took it, like he'd taken everything else, and the townsfolk glared at him, righteous and betrayed, hurt-angry that he wasn't what they'd believed him to be: a soldier and savior.

Barboza finally stepped over and pulled her off. She crumbled and cried in his arms.

"Where's my boy…?"

But Gunner didn't answer. Instead, his jaw tightened, his pupils narrowed and his nostrils flared; slowly, his eyes gravitated back to Don Granada's revolver, by his corpse.

Gun.

Gun in the Narrows. Gun on the Farm. Gun on the Albatross.

Gun.

Gun had always been there and always would. Even right then, right there, with Don Granada stiffening on the table. Gunner stared and realized that, and finally accepted that, accepted what he always knew, that Gun didn't care and Gun didn't feel, it just was and just sat, for him, like his history and future and fate and the Word of God, waiting to ride out with him to the fight at the end of the world.

It was written.

And it was. Gun was his God.

And eyeing it, he knew why he couldn't stay in the riad, or this place, even if he wanted to. Because peace wasn't his place in the world. Not yet, maybe not ever, not even after all he'd done to get it.

His place was to kill.

To cut down souls and kill for good so evil didn't kill for bad. Maybe. Or maybe not. Maybe that was just some bullshit story they told themselves and killing was just killing and killing was just nature and nobody was going to heaven or hell over any of it because it was just One Big Lie and they just lived or died because nature just survived, that's all. But whatever it was, fuck it, because he accepted what he always knew, that he liked to kill and he was good at it and he didn't care anymore anyway.

"You should've hacked off my wrist when you had the chance."

Suddenly, he lurched forward and grabbed Don Granada's gun, then turned for the door.

"What're ya doing?" Barboza asked.

"Laying waste to this world."

Chapter 43

Onshore, near the cabañas and under the palms, hotties, hippies and surfers packed backpacks and chattered in small groups, scattered like ants with their colony firebombed.

"Did you see the old man?" Frat Boy whispered. "He got blasted, brah."

"He completed his circle," Burner eulogized.

"This is like one of his crazy-ass stories," Bumster commented, "only we're stuck in it."

"Maybe they were true?"

"What, his stories?"

"You know which one this is like?" Trust Fund said.

"What?"

"The one about the howlers."

"Hahahaha..." Bumster laughed.

"How'll they return someday?" Bikini worried.

"And eat the people. To take back the town."

"Bullshit," Trust Fund said. "You don't believe those old geezers' stories do you? Have you ever even seen a howler?"

"I've heard them."

"You know what this is about? It's about that treasure, brah."

"That's the same story!" Barb quipped. "The gold's the sickness, idiot."

Chad nodded obediently in agreement next to her.

"We gotta get out of here," Coco said, looking around and holding her stomach like she was protecting her unborn child.

"And go where?" Tequila asked. "Y como? Without a boat."

"There should've been a boat by now..." Sail whispered, worried, looking to the dock and past it to the ocean, as if she may have overlooked it. They'd all pretended like the missing boat wasn't a problem. Like it'd eventually come and they'd be fine. But now, suddenly, it seemed like a problem. A very big problem. Why wasn't there a boat?

"That means it's real," Trust Fund imagined. "That means the gold's gotta be up there. On the mountain... In the jungle..."

"Biblical..." Burner awed.

Surfer appeared from the trail, cut through the crowd and

grabbed the broken fishing spear that Gunner had driving into the palm after Awol and Bonesetter kicked his ass.

"Listen," Surfer announced, wrenching out the spear, "there's a battle coming. They're going to guns, and you're gonna have to decide what to do. I know you're scared, but—"

—Suddenly, Gunner stormed off Mountain Trail and onto the beach. He blitzed over Valhalla's cinders and hurricaned directly at them, crisp, tense and tactical, gripping Don Granada's revolver.

They ceased talking and watched him, instantly mesmerized, because whatever he was at that moment he was pure. Pure, destructive energy, which was horrifying and beautiful, like a solar storm ripping a planet apart, or the death angel of God.

He popped the cylinder and checked it as he strode. Six chambers. Four bullets. Two empty holes. He rooted through his pocket and extracted the oxidized bullet Don Granada gave him before he was shot. He thumbed it in the fifth hole and offset the empty one, then whipped the cylinder shut and moved.

"Whoa, heh duuuude!" Burner said as he reached them.

But Gunner charged right into and through them, eyes cold and gone, far beyond them.

Further away, up the hill, Santa and Barboza stepped onto the Ranchero's terrace, where, just two weeks ago, Don Granada was drinking café and reading the last newspaper that had arrived in the pueblo in several weeks, when Santa walked out and told him that a body had washed ashore. Now, from their elevated position, they saw that body, that energy, appear and disappear under the palms on the distant beach, growing smaller as it hurtled towards town.

Chapter 44

Town, was eerily quiet.

There wasn't a soul on the street or a twitch in the air. The birds didn't chirp and the clouds didn't drift. The leaves didn't even move. Nothing moved. It was still like a black pond, like everything was stuck in a phase-state. It wasn't a morning-sun or an evening-sun. It was a mid-day sun, a perfect mid-day sun in the middle of the sky that just sat on the whitewashed buildings that lined the deserted road…or the buildings sat in the sun. Without movement and points of reference where there should have been movement and points of reference it was impossible to tell. It was like standing in the middle of a photograph. Something was clearly—

—Suddenly, Gunner burst through the stillness to the Cantina and kicked open the door.

Light flooded in and everyone froze.

Clearly, things must have been moving, because two soldados sat at the poker table holding forks, and Barman stood by the bar holding a broom. The soldados looked like they'd been eating eggs, and Barman looked like he'd been sweeping casings. But now, they looked like statues, frozen by medusa, and everything inside was as shock-still as outside, like time had stopped mid-motion. Or, it was moving slower for him than everything else.

Suddenly, Barman dropped the broom in real-time and bolted for the kitchen.

Gunner broke from the door to the poker table.

"Heh!" one of the soldado's said. "We're unarm—"

—*BAM!*

Gunner shot the man mid-stride and killed him where he sat.

His body SLAPPED back. The other soldado stared big-eyed as the shot reverberated, then popped out of his chair and ran with his fork. Gunner immediately collared him and shoved the gun in his face.

BAM!

His body jumped in Gunner's headlock and Gunner tossed him aside. He thumped the floor like a bloody sack—a pile of messy meat, blood and bones.

The rest of the Cantina was empty. He'd taken the life from it.

So he turned and surged back outside, back through the door and into the road.

Outside, he squared up on the middle of the street and scanned.

Far off, a leg slipped into a door and a shutter clacked. Closer, Butch emerged from a shadow and felt the chopping block in front of his shop for his cleaver. He gripped it, pulled it from the wood and receded back into the shadow. After that, the dead-flat silence and stillness returned. Unreal.

Unholy.

Son, what are you doing here? God has cursed this place.

I know. That's why I'm here.

Gunner raised his revolver and aimed down the road. A hundred yards out, Bonesetter oscillated in his sights.

Bonesetter, Simian, Gambler, Cazador, a few soldados and a handful of laborers stood in the plaza in front of the church. Bonesetter dug at something in his ear, Gambler sat in a sliver of Saint Peter's shade, Cazador leaned against the statue with his bola on his shoulders, and Simian stared at the bell-tower with the oversized Sig Sauer stuffed in his pants. They watched as laborers strung det-cord around the church. Red dynamite sticks plastered the church's white walls like Christmas lights. They were gonna blow the church off the face of the earth.

"Mwore," Simian commanded.

The laborers hesitated and looked at him. A soldado crept back.

"I said mwore! This is my town now. You, heh you, who's the Sheriff?"

"Uh… You?" a laborer replied.

"Wrong! I'm the Mayor. And the Sheriff!"

Simian laughed at himself and grabbed his gun like he was grabbing his cock.

"You!" he said, pointing at Mudo. "Ya you, retaawded. Ya wanna eat? Huh? Mwore dynamite!"

Bonesetter tossed a dynamite stick at Mudo to emphasize the point. Mudo sprang and bobbled it with big eyes, but managed to secure it before it hit the ground. Bonesetter chuckled, but Cazador exhaled nervously.

Gambler tossed a dynamite stick back at Bonesetter. Bonesetter snatched it mid-air. His chuckle-smile dropped and he glared at Gambler. He then reverted to his nature, or his core programing, and escalated. He flashed a lighter and flicked it. Slowly, he moved the flame to the wick as he glared at Gambler through it. Simian watched with a bemused smirk, until the flame got an inch from—

"—Uh, heh…"

POP.

"OW!"

Bonesetter emitted a strange, surprised shriek and crumpled. He hit the ground like a boneless sack and dropped the dynamite stick in the plaza, unlit. He quickly sat up and inspected his leg: blood. A grazing wound, just above the knee, from a…

"I got…"

He and Simian looked at each other, surprised, then simultaneously whipped their heads down the street towards the Cantina. There, a hundred yards out, the fucken fisherman stood in the middle of the road.

"Shot," Simian finished.

"Shit," Gambler mumbled.

Slowly, Gambler looked down at his boots and shook his head. He closed his dark eyes and pinched the bridge of his nose. Time also sped and slowed for him like it did for Gunner. It was an odd trait they shared, like synesthesia or something, another improbable transect in their divergent fates.

After a moment, he took a deep breath and looked back up.

But sure enough, the stranger was still there. Standing at the end of the road. A black, faceless figure, fixed in fate-time like something that had always been there. Only close now, like Barboza had sensed. The River Card. The River Man. The Accountant. Mictlantecuhtli, Anubis, Azrael, Yama, Papa Ghede… Gambler believed that people saw part of themselves in things like a mirror, so that everything was slightly different to everyone. To him, the stranger was Santa Muerte, a reckoning who flickered in the distance like a mirage, with orange flames burning off him, haunting him like his mistakes and loving him like his guilt.

Gambler tore his eyes from the demon and looked up to the stuck sun, like it could tell him something, and it did: the Skull Crusher had come for souls.

"Okay… okay."

And he was almost certain that it would be, Okay, because his son may lie on the other side of that, if there was another side. So he wasn't afraid of death. He welcomed it. Because he hoped to see his son. But what was certain was that it'd hurt like hell to get there, because he'd have to burn himself clean in the journey to do it, and there was a lot to burn. And his son wasn't here now. Only the stranger was.

After a long moment, to Gambler, he ran his hand through his thick, trail-hair, then took one last, long breath in painless peace, and snapped his fingers at a soldado. As soon as he did, time resumed and everyone scattered like rats. The soldado slipped away, Bonesetter limped off and Simian skinned his gun and effortlessly flicked off the safety.

Gambler stepped forward and flanked Simian, and Cazador followed. They formed a line and stared at the stranger down the road. He stared back and they faced off. Dust settled and time slowed, and the black-pond stillness returned.

"Watta ya gonna do?" Simian shouted, "Kill everyone?"

The question rolled down the road like a tumbleweed, then trailed off in the dust and the silence returned, louder than before.

The Stanger didn't reply. He didn't move. He just stood there, flickering in the sun. A gust of heat whistled, and a donkey strolled across the road between them.

Halfway down the road, above the donkey, trepidatious eyes peered through cracks in a shutter. Above them, on the roof, Campasino hid behind a ledge. He set a musket on his crushed arm, which was now an amputated stump covered in a bloody bandage. He leveled the musket at Simian and peered down the sights.

Then, Mudo bolted. He sprinted past Simian, Gambler and Cazador towards Gunner, stealing the dynamite stick that Bonesetter had thrown at him and carrying it like a baton.

"Get 'em," Simian ordered.

Cazador took the bola off his shoulder and stepped forward. He twisted his wrist and swung it above his head, whipping the balls into orbit.

"Come on."

"Tranquilo," Cazador replied calmly.

Mudo was forty yards off.

Cazador planted a foot forward, swung faster and narrowed his eyes.

Fifty.

"Come on!"

Sixty.

He released the bola.

It whipped through the air and closed.

Mudo panted as he ran and glanced over his shoulder like a scared horse, just as the bola struck his legs and snap-wrapped around his ankles. The pelotas tied and locked and he face-planted, laying entangled in the middle of the road.

Cazador grinned. Simian raised his eyebrows and puckered his lips, impressed. Not bad.

Then, Gunner stepped at them.

They countered, walking in a line.

Ninety yards.

Gunner checked his revolver as he moved. Three targets, two rounds. Four empty. One short. He snapped it back shut.

Eighty yards.

Gambler, Simian and Cazador fanned out, spreading the line.

Seventy yards.

Gambler flipped back his leather vest, uncovering his holster.

Sixty yards.

Cazador held his hand over his sidearm. His trigger finger twitched.

Fifty yards.

Mudo stopped squirming, tying to make himself as small as possible before four violent men collided about him.

Forty yards.

From the roof, Campasino slowly squeezed the trigger...

Thirty yards.

...and removed the slack from the—

—Side flash.

BAM-BAM!

Suddenly, Gunner and Gambler skinned simultaneously, but instead of firing at each other they cross-fired towards roofs on the opposite sides of the road.

On the north side, on Big Mama's roof, Gambler sniped Campasino off his musket and blasted him back. Campasino jerked the trigger as he was hit and got the round off, but the ball splayed wide and shot through Simian's silk shirt under his armpit.

On the south side, on the Tack Shop's roof, Gunner hit the soldado Gambler deployed. Gunner hit him square in the chest and he fell forward, into the bullet and off the roof.

Before he fell all the way to the ground and thumped the road, everything burst. Gunner bolted for him and—

—BAM!

slung his last round sideways on the run at—

—UMPH!

Gambler. Gambler was spinning back and adjusting off his shot at Campasino to kill Gunner, but Mudo grabbed his ankle from the ground and entangled it in the bola. Gambler swung down to shoot Mudo instead of Gunner, but Gunner's final slug struck him in the side and he UMPHED back.

BAM BAM BAM!

THUMP.

Gunner reached the soldado who fell from the roof just as he pounded the earth. He grabbed the Glock out of the soldado's dead hand on the run and leapt into the alley behind the Tack Shop as bullets chewed up the dirt and walls around him.

Simian was the only one not firing. He stood shock-frozen in the middle of the crossfire, over Mudo, still sticking a finger though the musket hole in his shirt, under his arm.

Gunner quickly racked the soldado's Glock and stepped back out of the alley. He walked smoothly, deliberately, directly at them, directly into the fire, firing the Glock methodically with a steady, straight arm, advancing through the hailstorm.

BAM!

BAM!

BAM!

BAM!

A side-arm fire-fight in open terrain.

Mudo tried to crawl away, entangled in the bola in the road between and beneath them as they fired above him. Targets moved and spread. Gambler rose and fired, but stumbled back and gripped his stomach. Gunner shot Cazador in the quad. He fell to a knee, then onto his side.

VVVVVVRRRRROOOOOM...

Suddenly, a rusty Willys careened into the road and hurtled at them. It skidded and Awol leapt out, blasting his M4 and hitting the ground on the run.

DA DA DA DA DA DA...!

Awol sprayed recklessly, firing at Gunner through Simian and Gambler, and over Cazador and Mudo, danger-close. Walls and wood lit up.

DA DA DA DA!

Simian covered his head, turned and fled on his short donkey legs, past Awol and back up the road. Gunner dove back into the alley.

"Get up!" Awol yelled.

Gunner popped out from behind the building to fire, but—

—*DA DA DA!*

M4 rounds chipped the wall around him, driving him back to cover.

"GET UP!"

Awol kicked Cazador and yanked Gambler to his feet. Gambler shoved him but stumbled. He held his stomach and his hand was bloody, and Awol noticed that he was hit. Above the hip, off-center, in the gut. Awol broke his inertia and stalled and stared at the wound a second, realizing what happened, and realizing it was bad. He looked up from the wound and into Gambler's eyes to assess the severity of the gunshot another way, like he'd done on the battlefield, by measuring the life left in his soul. Gambler held his stare, defiant and pissed.

Good.

Then Gambler's cheek twitched.

"You're fucked," Awol diagnosed.

Gambler spat at him.

Awol turned his back on Gambler and raised his M4 at the building that Gunner dove behind. He quick-stepped on it and closed the distance fast, then pied the corner and looked into the—

"—GOD DAMMIT!"

Empty.

The alley was empty.

Chapter 45

Tuck woke slowly in a warm, cozy space, rested and peaceful. He blinked his eyes open and gathered himself, slowly hauling in his senses like he was hauling in a fishing net. It was completely black, except for a few rays of dusty light. He couldn't see much, so he decided to get up and turn on the light. As soon as he did, he hit his head on a plank right in front of his face. It knocked him back. Surprised, he lifted his hands, but they were stuck—glued to his waist. He could barely move.

He woke faster.

A lot faster.

He couldn't see, but could feel. His hands were bound in hemp rope and his mouth was gagged with a handkerchief like the bit on an oxen. The light bore through perfectly circular, drilled holes in front of his face, like air holes.

Outside, of whatever he was inside, he heard distant, muffled shots. Gunshots. A firefight. A sudden fear flashed through him; everyone was going to kill each other and nobody would remember to come get him. He'd die here. Slowly. Painfully. Trapped. He kicked hard, but his feet thumped wood.

A coffin. He was in a coffin.

He remembered now. His pupils went big and wild, and it was suddenly hard to breath. He worked the gag out with his tongue and yelled.

"AHHHHHH!"

He screamed, but wood and dirt swallowed the noise. He craned his neck and reached for a hole to suck air, but dirt streamed through it and into his mouth.

"HEEELP!"

Chapter 46

Gunner crept through a room with his gun at the low-ready, through light rays made from bullet holes in the wall, like the light that bore through the air-holes in Tuck's coffin. Big Mama sat in a corner, holding her scared toddlers close. She held her hands over their mouths and watched Gunner with quiet, steady strength, like she'd hunkered through a thousand battles. Somewhere on the other side of the wall outside, Awol yelled muffled orders and jackboots scurried in response.

Gunner put his finger to his lips.

Shhh...

Mama nodded and pointed to a back door, then up to the roof. Gunner exited and found a long wooden ladder leaning against the wall. He stuffed his gun in his belt and climbed it.

He climbed over the gutter, which had some weeds growing in it, and stepped onto a flat roof. There, Campasino slumped dead near the edge on the other side, with Gambler's bullet hole drilled over his eyebrow. A quick, clean death.

He scrambled across the roof to Campasino's body and peered over the other edge and into the road. Soldados scampered below. In the plaza ahead, he saw Simian flee down a passageway between two buildings.

"He didn't get far!" Awol barked below. "Isolate the block! Clear house to house! Find the bastard!"

Gunner pivoted and looked around. Campasino had two bottles next to him, filled with gas and stuffed with rags: Molotov cocktails. Beneath him, a door splintered open and boots stomped.

"Where is he?"

SLAP.

"Der children!"

He fleeced Campasino's pockets and found a lighter. He grabbed one of the bottles and lit the rag, which sparked and burned blue from chemicals.

"WHERE IS HE?"

SLAP!

He lobbed the Molotov cocktail over the edge and into a group of soldados in the road.

BOOM!

A flame burst and debris rained down.

He grabbed the second bottle and lit it, then looked across the roof at the next building as the fuse burned. It was fifteen feet from the edge with an alley in-between. Its roof was about five feet higher than the roof he was on and was Spanish colonial; so it was slanted and covered in terracotta tile. A few feet below eyelevel, however, was a large window.

He stood and calculated, then backed up a few steps, crouched and sprinted across the roof as fast as he could. When he reached the edge he hucked the bottle and…

Leapt.

DA DA DA DA DA…

Gunfire ripped through the sky like bullets through water.

BOOM!

The second Molotov cocktail exploded next to the shooting soldados in the road below as he soared between bullets in the sky above. He descended across the gap towards the second story window and—

—CRASH!

Crashed through it with his arms shielding his face. He broke an end table, rolled into a hallway and somersaulted onto his feet in a single fluid motion, but—

—HUUUURAAA!

A soldado immediately grabbed and hucked him into a wall in the hall with his forward momentum. Planks bumphed. The soldado swung but Gunner ducked and the soldado's fist blasted through the wall. Gunner recoiled off the duck and headbutted him in the nose. They locked, grappled and smacked each other into the walls in the narrow—

—BOOM!

Surfer suddenly burst through a door and into the hall, eyes wild and hands bloody. He gripped the fishing spear and shived it violently into the soldado's ribs, gritting his teeth and driving it home.

BUMPH!

Another soldado, however, immediately ran up some stairs and tackled Surfer from behind. The four grappled, punched and hurled each other in the confined space. Pictures crashed and walls dented, reconfiguring the linear hall.

Gunner headlocked his soldado, smashed his face into the wall and tossed him out the broken window that he'd just crashed through. Then he ran at Surfer's soldado, who had pinned Surfer down, and tackled him off Surfer and down the stairs behind him.

They rolled and thunked down the stairs and smacked into an oven in a kitchen at the bottom. The soldado came up with a hot iron and they squared off like wrestlers.

Outside, black burn marks streaked the road. A disfigured soldado lay contorted in the blast radius and a few soldados stared like zombies nearby, shell-shocked and bleeding from the concussion.

"Get up!" Awol yelled. "Go! He's running, damn it!"

The dazed soldados shambled forward.

"MOVE!" Awol yelled, kicking one. "Remember the bounty! Remember your brothers! He killed them! Unarmed!"

Cazador tied a tourniquet over his bloody quad and clicked in a mag.

"VAMOS!"

A minute later, Gunner jogged down a quiet alley littered with old tires. He held his Glock at the high-ready, and a linear burn ran up his arm from the hot iron. He passed a window and flinched, because Mudo and Blacky stood in it. Mudo grinned and waved the red dynamite stick he stole just as—

—a soldado popped into the—

—*BAM!*

Gunner dropped him.

"He's over chair!" Cazador yelled from somewhere nearby.

Gunner dashed to the soldado, fleeced two mags off him and did a combat reload as he peered around the corner. The church rose like a bulwark in the plaza ahead.

DA DA DA DA!

Bullets blasted around him. Awol fired at him from near the Cantina down the road. Gunner dropped to a knee and fired back.

BAM! BAM! BAM!

A bullet sailed across the divide and split Awol's tattooed trapezoid, knocking him back into the Cantina's porch. Just then, smoke wafted by Gunner. He turned and saw Blacky flaming a burning tire behind him. Mudo stood by and flashed a thumbs up, then put the dynamite against the burning tire and lit the fuse.

"Take it!" Blacky yelled.

Gunner quickly grabbed the dynamite, turned and hucked it at Awol's position. It somersaulted through the air to the Cantina and—

—*BOOM!*

Bodies flew and the Cantina's terrace and front wall collapsed and crumbled over Awol. A few seconds later, however, Awol burst from the rubble like a jumping shark. Bricks shrugged off his shoulders and he spit dust.

"God!" Awol yelled.

"Damn," Blacky cursed.

Mudo rolled the flaming tire past Gunner and into the plaza.

BAM! DA DA DA!

The tire drew fire and toppled at Saint Peter's statue. Black smoke swirled and billowed around it, making a smokescreen.

"Scan your sectors," Awol commanded, already back in the fight. "Shoot anything that moves."

"Run," Blacky suggested, "now!"

Gunner took one last look into the street, then bolted from cover and sprinted towards the church. As he did, a murky figure streaked through the smoke and—

—*UMPH!*

—Tackled him like a linebacker.

Intel.

Big, solid Intel. Intel hit him with the full force of his bull body and bear-hug death-gripped him in his thick arms. They smacked ground and rolled over the burning tire and into the statue. Gunner's head smacked to a stop against its base, which caused his head to instantly start bleeding and made his eyes roll. Stunned, Intel quick-ripped two feet of green duct tape from his roll and hogtied Gunner's ankles like a rodeo calf. As Gunner regained his senses, Intel boar up on his chest and straddled it, pinning his arms to the ground with his knees.

Intel grabbed a chunk of stone that had blasted off Saint Peter's ribs and raised the rock above his head with both hands. Gunner's eyes focused through the smoke, light and confusion from the impact, and he saw the large stone hovering above him, about to crash into his face like it'd crashed into Prospector's.

Intel grinned, almost as if he was sorry, but wasn't, ultimately.

He heaved the chunk up a few more inches, drew breath and—

—CRACK!

A bullet skimmed off his skull. His head ricocheted left and his neck went limp. He fell forward and dropped the chunk. It crashed onto his own head, then fell for Gunner's face. Gunner bucked and turned just as the stone whisked by and exploded against the cobblestone.

"You didn't think I was going to let you have all the fun, did you?"

Gunner looked past Intel, laying on him like a dead bear, and saw Barboza peering down from high in the bell-tower above, waving his old Enfield against the sky and grinning like a crazed fool.

DA DA DA!

Bullets splayed Saint Peter and stone chunks from his head and ear rained down on Gunner. He twisted and looked back over his shoulder the best he could and spied more soldados running up the road and through the smoke at him.

"Hurry!" Barboza yelled, jumping back on his sights in the tower above.

Gunner heaved Intel off, grabbed a flint of Saint Peter's ear and sliced the duct tape off his ankles, then scrambled to his feet and sprinted for the sanctuary.

Chapter 47

Tuck sucked air through a hole in the coffin, nearly hyperventilating.

HA HUH HA HUH HA HUH...

He dropped his head back and tried to calm himself like his Grandpa had taught him.

Relax, breath, he heard his Grandpa say. *One step at a time, there's only so much you can do...*

He closed his eyes and slowed his breath. A few seconds later, he reopened them to reassess his surroundings, calmer. He pivoted his head in the cramped space and saw a rusty nail bending through the wood near his waist. He pushed his body against the coffin and caught his tiny hemp-bound wrists on the nail. He rocked against it as best he could to try to slice the rope. Instead of cutting it, however, the hemp twanged like a guitar cord.

He took another deep breath and reset. With forced patience, he closed his eyes and tried again. He caught the hemp on the nail again and began to rock against it. A strand of hemp cut, then the nail slipped and punctured his wrist.

"AGH!"

Blood spurted from his wrist and he panicked:

"AHHH!"

Chapter 48

Gunner broke through the thick wooden doors of La Iglesia de los Caídos.

Dust kicked into the air, into stained glass window light, drifting towards the ceiling, to a mural that spread across the dome and depicted a great battle between Conquistadors and Aztecs, half real and half imagined. On the floor below, bibles scattered and pages fluttered. Pews lay askew, and det-cord and dynamite ran around the cavernous vestibule, strung from the swords and shields of stone statues that stood in recesses along the walls. Statues of strong and stoic holy warriors standing eternal watch; San Jorge, San Miguel, Joan of Arc, Lancelot du Lac, Roland with Durandal, Sigurd killing the dragon...

"Up here."

Barboza peered through a hatch in the roof that lead to the bell-tower. Gunner quickly braced the door behind him with a beam and ran to a ladder that ran to the hatch.

A minute later, he pulled himself through the hatch and into the cupola.

"Glad to see you got your balls back." Barboza greeted.

Barboza sat against a column, next to his Enfield, quick-tying canvas gaiters to the front of his scarred shins. He wore his tunic, medals and short Afrikaner shorts like always, and for once they, combined with his thick handlebar mustache, somehow looked completely appropriate to the circumstances.

"Nice shot," Gunner said, scrambling up alongside him.

"I was aiming for you."

"Tell me that wasn't the first shot you've fired since World War Two."

"World War One."

Gunner chuckled.

"Relax gringo. I've fought in every war that ever was. Once, Don Granada and I had these Sandinistas and a belly dancer in a helicopter—"

"A belly—"

"—two hundred meters up. You know what happens when you shoot someone in a helicopter?"

"Ya, you have to—"

"—There!"

Suddenly, Barboza pointed over the ledge. From this height in the bell-tower, Gunner had a panoramic view of the battlefield. Beneath him, Mudo and Blackys' tire burned in the square, creating a thick billow of dark, clumpy smoke. Intel lay beside it, near Saint Peter's feet. Beyond the plaza sat the main road and buildings, which clumped into a puzzle of alleys and mazes that opened to a field and the shore. There, he saw what Barboza was pointing to; Simian ran across the field like a jockey, between the town and shore, towards the Castillo and cemetery on the coast.

Barboza snatched his Enfield and aimed.

"Crap. Too far. Even for me."

He came off his sights.

"Go! Find the boy and save him, you hear?"

WHIZ!

"Blasted HUNS!"

DA DA DA DA!

Bullets chipped up the bell-tower and plaster fell on them. They peered back over the ledge and saw Awol firing up at them from the other side of the plaza.

"He's a goddamn mosquito!"

DA DA DA!

Silence.

Then, a low RUMBLE.

MMMMMMMRRRHHH...

The cupola's wooden floor vibrated. A lorry stopped at the edge of the plaza and twenty more soldados dismounted.

"Curses," Barboza mumbled—happy. Almost rapturous.

He raised his Enfield and aimed at the Commandante, who was gesturing to the soldados as they leapt from the lorry and their boots hit the cobblestone plaza. He centered the sights on the Commandante's chest and squeezed the—

—CRACK!

The rifle jumped loose off his shoulder and kicked into his chin. The bullet pinged a chicken coup ten feet from the Commandante. Feathers poofed and chickens boked.

The Commandante looked at the chickens, then up to the bell-tower. He saw the sun splash off the tip of Barboza's rifle, and a slow smile crept on his face. Gunner glanced at Barboza sideways.

"I told you I was aiming for you," Barboza grumbled.

Barboza slid another round in the chamber and actioned the bolt. *CLICK.* He wrapped the leather strap firmly around his forearm, tightened the rifle into his shoulder and re-aligned. He lined the Commandante back up in his iron sights and slowed his breath just as the Commandante pointed to the bell-tower and—

—*CRACK!*

The Commandante stepped back and looked at his chest. He touched it, then looked up at the bell-tower, surprised. He stared a second, then collapsed.

"HOT DAMN I'm back boy!"

Gunner patted him on the shoulder encouragingly as a volley of return fire sprayed down.

DA DA DA PING CHIP WHIZ!

"GO!" Barboza shouted through the crossfire. "I'll hold 'em off!"

"They'll light this church up!"

"Ha! This old war horse? Nobody's used it since the padre was murdered here twenty years ago! And look how strong it stands."

They clasped forearms like Romans.

"Pop smoke! Get outta the plaza before the Japs surround it!"

"What Japs?"

"GO!"

Gunner nodded and swung back into the hatch as the last of the soldados leapt from the lorry and fanned out across the plaza.

Chapter 49

Tuck heard something scrape against the outside of the coffin.
SHICK, GRRT, SHICK…
Inside the coffin, the sides shook and light filtered in through the cracks.
THUNK. THUNK.
"I'm here!" Tuck yelled, wide-eyed. "In here!"
Dirt fell through the cracks and air holes. Tuck coughed and spit it out.
"Help! I'm alive! I'm alive!"
THUNK.
Something heavy hit the coffin, then the lid creaked open and light flooded in. Tuck shielded his eyes and gulped fresh air. A shadow stepped over him and blotted out the sun, allowing his eyes to focus and see…
The Bonesetter.
"NO!"
"Heh boy!"
Bonesetter reached down and yanked him out.
Bonesetter shook dirt off him like a dusty pillow and tossed him harder than he intended against a headstone, knocking Tuck's knife off the top of it, which Bonesetter had set there. Bonesetter grinned at him like a hyena, holding his gun in one burnt hand and his wounded leg in the other.
"Watta ya doing?" Simian ventured.
Bonesetter whipped around and saw Simian standing a safe distance back, watching.
Bonesetter's smile faded and his pupils sharpened.
"Mind your own business."
Bonesetter's eyes burned hate, and Simian stepped back. Bonesetter turned back to Tuck and smiled again, but Tuck brandished his knife at him.
"Whoa," Bonesetter purred, "easy there…"
Tuck's nostrils flared.
"…son."
Tuck's hand trembled.
"What're ya gonna do? Hurt your own dad?"

Tuck stared strong, but Bonesetter's words cut worse than a weapon. Bonesetter straightened, then smiled warmly and stepped at him with open palms.

"That's right son. I'm ya daddy."

Chapter 50

Gunner exited the back door to the church and darted to a mango tree behind it. As he did, foot soldiers moved further across the plaza, starting to surround the church and strangle his escape. He hid behind the mango tree and looked for an out. There wasn't one. Worse, a soldado in a shop's doorway across the plaza behind him spotted him. The soldado grinned and raised a rifle at his back.

As the soldado aimed, a cleaver glistened out of a shadow behind the soldado. The soldado aligned Gunner's back square in his sights, and a hand aligned the soldado's collarbone beneath the cleaver. The soldado squeezed the trigger just as—

—the cleaver swooped down.

THUMP BANG!

The cleaver thumped into the soldado's neck bone. His shot jumped and splatted the trunk above Gunner's head, bursting bark. Gunner duck-spun, surprised, and saw the soldado fall to his knees behind him with the cleaver in his neck and his eyes and mouth shock-stuck open.

The blind Butcher.

Butch stepped out of the shadow and felt for his cleaver. He patted the soldado's head and shoulders until he zeroed in on the handle, then wrenched it out of the soldado's neck like a hambone. The soldado slumped forward and fell on his face. Butch wiped his bloody hands on his smock, then back-stepped, feeling for the sides of the doorway. He found them and disappeared back into the shadows from which he came.

Gunner whistled a sigh of relief, then turned back ahead and saw more soldados securing more positions. He wasn't gaining anything by waiting, and planning was pointless, so he sprung from the tree and bolted across the plaza for the passage that Simian ducked into. As he ran, a soldado popped out of the passage directly in front of him and raised his rifle. Gunner sprinted to try to tackle him before he—

—*CRACK!*

Sniper shot. The soldado spun back on his shoulder like a top and hit the ground. Gunner leapt over the body and glanced over his shoulder as he ducked into the passage.

Barboza.

Barboza watched from the bell-tower like a guardian angel. As soon as Gunner slipped through the perimeter and escaped into the passage, he grinned and got back on his sights.

Less than a minute later, Gunner was out of the plaza and inside town. He quick-stepped down a crooked corridor, Glock raised and finger triggered, advancing deeper into and through the narrow space. Shots echoed and receded in the plaza behind him. He could tell them apart; the soldado's new M16s banged forcefully while Barboza's old Enfield cracked tiredly.

BANG! BANG!

CRACK...

BANG! BANG!

CRACK...

He took a corner and turned down another passage, moving deeper into a dream-like maze of semi-illogical back alleys. As he did, the shots faded and the distances closed around him.

Just then, he spotted blood splatter on the ground. He followed it up to the wall and saw a bloody handprint. The handprint was clear, like the handprint on an Apache horse, but someone had dragged it along the wall, using the wall to prop themselves up. He followed the smear around the corner and saw...

Gambler.

He flinched to fire, then caught himself and slowed.

Gambler sat in the alley, in the dirt against a wall with his legs splayed in front of him. An M4, poker chips and a few gold coins lay scattered around him like a crash site. He held a whiskey bottle with one hand and playing cards over his ribs with the other where Gunner had shot him at first contact. Blood stained the cards and his stomach.

It was a losing hand.

"I fold," Gambler said, looking up at Gunner and smiling weakly.

Gunner lowered his gun.

"I've been waiting for you," Gambler added.

"What?"

"The Reckoning."

Gunner peaked back around the corner and cleared his six.

"Hell," Gambler said, "I wasn't even 'spose to be here. Got sidetracked. Lost my way. I don't know."

Gambler shook his head and ticked.

"We thought we were here for the treasure, but weren't. Simian was here for the power. Awol for death, and Bonesetter, well... Me, I was here for the time. Father Time, the hermit, was trading memories for time, and everyone here was running short of that... So we were betten memories for time. For days, minutes even... Father Time's a bastard, so ante was a song, and all the memories that went with it."

Gambler closed his eyes and sung:

"Shoooould oooooold acquaintance beee forgot, and neeeever brought tooo mind... *UGH UGH UGH*. God. Damn. I won that."

"You're delirious," Gunner said.

"Ya. I'm bleeding out."

"Ya. A gutshot kills painful."

Gambler grinned knowingly, then held up the stone he took from Bonesetter's bag.

"Ya see this? It's a rock. Just a rock. That's all. Grey. Plain. A rock. I picked it up in front of our house the day my son died."

That stopped Gunner. He stared cold and waited.

"Father Time wanted it. Bonesetter tried to steal it. But they never got it. Neither of 'em."

Gambler wrapped the stone in his fist and gripped it tight, and his eyes, which could see things other men's couldn't, drifted back to Gunner, watery like his memory.

"You know, there's a day in your life, when you pick your son up and carry him for a while. Then you set him down, and never pick him up again."

Gunner had seen a lot of men die in a lot of places for a lot of reasons and never felt nothing. If anything, he'd felt a sense of relief and accomplishment, like he'd split firewood or planted a row of corn. The first person he'd killed had fallen in a dirty street in Congo, with his head cranked up on a curb at an odd angle and his shoes off, wearing red socks. Even then, the only thing he'd felt or thought was that just a few hours ago that guy was alive and pulling on those red socks. Did he ever think that'd be the last time he'd put on socks? Did he ever imagine he'd die in red socks? Would he have chosen red socks that morning if he knew that he'd be dead by lunch? Red socks... seemed like a strange choice. But that's just how it goes, he'd thought, one day you put on your socks and that day you're dead.

A few years and a hundred or so deaths later, he'd be surprised by how many people died without shoes on. It was strange. It seemed statistically improbable. But it happened. Over and over again. As if Death just blasted their shoes off their feet. And if he felt or thought hardly anything after the first death, he felt and thought even less by the hundredth. If anything, he thought he should feel more. Once, he summed all that experience up for a first-tour by advising him, "Ain't much good come thinking about it, once you done it, killin'."

And it was true. But strangely, standing there and looking at Gambler like this in this place where he'd put him, with Don Granada's oxidized, Russian roulette bullet from Sáo Gabriel de Cachoeira finally coming to a stop many years later in the side of Gambler's gut in a lost and forgotten outpost, he felt something. Not regret or remorse, or moral confusion, but instead, understanding, and with understanding was almost, empathy.

"Then you came," the gambler continued, "from the bygone... with salt in your beard. And the wind howled through cracks in the planks..."

"I never meant to come here," Gunner stated.

"Ya, but you were meant to be here."

"Maybe. Ya. Maybe."

"In the end, would you trade all the memories in your life but one, to live a month longer?" Gambler asked.

"I'd give 'em away for free."

"But if you had to keep one, what memory would it be?"

Gunner didn't respond. Gambler looked at his stone and said:

"I'm keeping this."

"The memory of your son's death?"

"That pain... It's all I have left of him. I can't let that go."

He squeezed the stone, staring at Gunner, and silent tears streamed down his cheek. He kicked his boot pointlessly in the dirt, as if angry at God himself. Maybe that was it, Gunner thought, maybe that's how a decent man ends up on the wrong side of things, if there is a wrong side, fighting God and all his creation, because God had given and taken his.

"The treasure, though..." Gambler said, tossing his bottle at the gold coins scattered in the dirt around him, "it's real."

Gambler kicked his M4 towards him with a loose boot.

"Gun up. Bonesetter will go for the boy. They're in the

graveyard."

Gunner tossed his Glock and grabbed the M4.

"And kill that fucken crossroader for me. Badly."

Gunner slung the M4 over his chest and prepared to move.

"Wait."

Gunner paused.

"The river."

Gambler reached in his back pocket, pulled out some cards and tossed them on the ground; the two of hearts, the six of clubs, the three of diamonds and the five of hearts. The hand he'd been drawing whenever he saw Gunner.

"You got shit," Gambler said, nodding to the cards. "A two, three, five, six. Off-suit. Six high. I got two aces, an eight and a nine. So only two cards left in the deck that can beat me. The fours. You're on a gutshot draw. Gotta hit that middle four to win. Unlikely, but I got that nine, the curse of Scotland, and all the rest of course. Ya... you already got it. No matter what you do you'll hit it. You'll pull the four. I don't even have to look. It's like that sometimes, Fate. Unruly. Screwing that bitch Statistics like a dog any chance he gets. It's statistically proven."

Gambler removed his hand from his stomach and fanned out the bloody cards he'd been pressing over his stomach. With the compress off, blood pumped slowly from the wound, in time with his fading heartbeat.

"Pick a card."

Gunner took the least bloody one.

"You don't have to show me. Like I said, you pulled the four."

Gunner stuck the card in his back pocket without looking at it. Gambler flipped his cards over and looked at them.

"Shit," he grumbled.

There were his two black aces, his black eight of clubs, his nine of diamonds and his final card, the river card; the eight of spades.

"Black aces and eights," he chuckled, "dead man's hand."

He grinned ironically and tossed the cards in the dirt with his bottle and bullion, then leaned his head back against the wall.

"Where's Mulata?"

"Why?" Gunner asked.

"Only she can save me now."

Gunner eyed him for a long second.

"Maybe I shouldn't have shot you." Gunner wondered.

"I would have shot you."

"Ya well, I'm sorry, about your son."

Gambler frowned sadly, then nodded back respectfully. They were soldiers. Warriors. They'd kill each other, but they understood each other.

And with that, Gunner stepped over Gambler's limp legs and continued on, leaving him to bleed-out and die in the alley.

Chapter 51

Barboza fought furiously in the bell-tower, cocking and sniping.
CLICK CLICK…
CRACK!
CLICK CLICK...
A soldado ran across the courtyard.
CRACK!
He dropped.
CLICK CLICK...
A soldado peeked out from the statue.
CRACK!
He dropped.
CLICK CLICK...
A soldado sprinted to the church.
CRACK!
The bullet plowed dirt and the soldado disappeared under the bell-tower beneath him.
CLICK CLICK...
"I am besieged by a thousand or more Mexicans under Santa Ana..." Barboza mumbled aloud to himself as he tracked another runner in his sights.
CRACK!
The runner dropped.
CLICK CLICK...
Another runner made it across the plaza and disappeared under the bell-tower.
"You will be needlessly slaughtered," he continued.
"ARGHHHH!"
Suddenly, a soldado burst through the hatch in the cupola behind him with his knife raised. Barboza spun and—
—*CRACK!*
The soldado folded over the bullet and collapsed beside him. Barboza flipped the wood hatch back shut and pressed his boot on it as he spun back to cover the plaza. Bullets pinged and ricocheted in the cupola above and around him.
"We have had a shower of cannonballs continually falling on us..." he whispered as he aimed.

CLICK CLICK...
BOOM!

The tower rumbled and shook. He peered over the ledge and saw the backhoe ram into it.

BOOOOM!

Another soldado climbed a ladder against the tower. Barboza grabbed the soldado he'd just shot dead, dragged him to the edge and heaved him over like a sack. The body fell down the tower and ploughed into the soldado on the ladder, knocking him off. The soldados and ladder fell together and thumped the courtyard, but as soon as they hit, another soldado sprinted by Saint Peter for the ladder.

"Not a step backward."

DA DA DA DA DA!

From across the plaza, Awol blasted rage against the tower.

DA DA DA DA DA...

"AGHHHH!" Barboza yelled.

Concrete chipped and the bell pinged. Barboza pulled back and took cover behind the pillar. Suddenly, the bell fell and thunked against his head like a cantaloupe. Blood streamed down his skull and his eyes rolled.

"Ughhh..."

DA DA DA DA DA!

Slowly, he regained himself. His head, face and mustache were covered in red blood and caked in white dust, like a crazed tribesman. He couldn't kill them all like this, so he slung his Enfield on his back and crawled for the hatch. He slid into it and descended the ladder into the belly of the church. As he did, a soldado ascended the ladder from below and raised a Lugar up at him.

"Once more unto the breach."

He loosened his grip and slid down the ladder like a fireman. He landed on the soldado's face with his heels just as he fired, knocking him off and riding him in a semi-controlled free fall to the ground. The soldado thumped ground under his boots. His face absorbed most of the fall, knocking him unconscious or dead, and Barboza's old but hardened bones collapsed in a tired heap on top of him.

Barboza stumbled up, grunted and scanned the church, studying the det-cord and dynamite that ran around it, hanging from the stone knights.

THUMP...

A foot kicked the main door and a soldado squirreled through a side window. Barboza aimed at the window and—

—*CRACK!*

Killed the soldado dead in it.

THUMP…

Another blow to the door.

"Our supply of ammunition is limited," he huffed.

He whipped the Enfield on his back and grabbed the baling twine. He pulled it off the stone knights and piled a messy heap of det-cord and dynamite on top of the collapsed soldado at the foot of the ladder.

THUMP…

"Marche ou crève."

He created an entangled pile of wires and dynamite and slogged back up the ladder.

THUMP!

The soldado finally breached the front door. He looked around, saw Barboza ascending the ladder and ran at him with a knife. He jumped the dynamite pile and sliced his shin. The knife, however, cut harmlessly off his gaiters. Barboza looked down and grinned proudly, but the soldado simply jumped back up and stabbed him square in the back of the calf.

"AHHH CURSES!"

Barboza kicked the soldado off and continued climbing with the knife sticking out his calf.

He pulled himself back into the cupola, dragging his leg. The soldado's hand immediately reached through the hatch behind him and grabbed his ankle. Barboza yanked the knife from his calf and stabbed the clawing zombie arm with it.

"AHHHHHH!"

The hand released and disappeared back down the hatch. Barboza twisted and threw his Enfield back over the lip to fire at the soldados securing the plaza.

CLICK, CLICK…

CRACK!

"Hold until relieved," he mumbled, weaker than before.

CLICK, CLICK…

CRACK!

DA DA DA DA DA… BOOOOOM…

The tower swayed.

DA DA DA DA DA...
CLICK, CLICK...
THOT.

A blank. A misfire. A gut-sinking sound. He speed-checked the chamber: empty. The mag: empty. He looked back up and over the lip and spot-checked the battlefield: overrun.

A seemingly endless number of soldier-clones swarmed the church from all directions. They ran across the plaza like ants and scaled ladders up the tower like crabs. They breached the church's heavy front door, bored through its windows and yelled muffled commands underfoot, assaulting the church like a hive. He was alone and out of ammo, surrounded and trapped.

There was no escape now and he knew it.

"Fix bayonets," he ordered.

But there were no bayonets to fix. And nobody to fix them.

So he exhaled deeply, and after a long moment, set his trusty Enfield down, turned his back on the soldados, and slumped against an arch, realizing for the first time how exhausted he was. Blood-crows circled above him, Japs yapped below, blood stained his medals, and the soldier-clones closed.

He knew that warriors for millennia over had experienced this moment. The moment when they realized they were outnumbered and defeated and going to die. Soon. And painfully. General Custer at the Little Big Horn, Captain Danjou at Camarón, Davey Crockett at the Alamo, Matthieu de Clermont at the Siege of Acre... It was a calm moment, the last moment, before a very violent death. Improbably, Barboza had already experienced and cheated it once before, when he'd sat much like this against a wimba tree with an arrow sticking out his sternum, in a place so deep in the jungle that it had never been written in any language by any discovered tribe so he wrote it on a matchbook in blood and named it into the world himself like a thing born: El Pozo–The Well. Then, there, at El Pozo, he had accepted death like a brother, and a strange, zen-like peace came over him. But by the grace of God, Don Granada had crossed the Tanarú Gap on foot and saved him by slaughtering the cannibals with a Winchester repeating rifle.

But Don Granada couldn't save him this time. Unless he could cross the threshold of Death itself; and even that, Barboza thought, may be too much for the Great Don Granada.

"My enemies have always been the authors of their own

calamity," he mumbled.

He reached in his tunic and extracted his pineapple grenade. He inhaled, bit the pin and yanked it out defiantly with his teeth. Then, in one last heroic act in a lifetime of unsung ones, he released the safety lever and counted...

Nine.

Eight.

Seven.

Six.

Five.

Four...

At three, a soldado surmounted the ledge into the bell-tower and charged him with a knife. As the tip neared his chest, Barboza dropped the pineapple grenade down the hatch like a depth charge, to the pile of det-cord and dynamite in the belly below.

"Take care of the little boy."

Chapter 52

Gunner jogged across the open field that Simian ran across earlier, from town to the Castillo. He carried Gambler's M4, and the town receded behind him. Tin and tile roofs crested the trees, and the bell-tower rose above the canopy, painting a deceptively picturesque and peaceful landscape.

BOOOOOOOOOM!

Suddenly, a gigantic concussion rippled the air. He stopped, spun, and saw the bell-tower explode.

A fireball burst and the ground rumbled like an earthquake; then a shock-wave gusted by like a nuclear blast. He winced and squinted at the force and the dust, feeling the air suck out of the space around him; then the energy recoiled and blasted back through him, shaking his skeleton in his body.

A moment later, he regained his sight through the dust, and saw the bell-tower crumble under its own weight, with men and souls aboard. It disappeared under the canopy, and a dust cloud rose above it. When the dust settled, he knew there'd only be blue sky where the bell-tower had been.

He knew what that meant, and dropped his head.

He stole a second, then looked back up.

"What a magnificent old bastard," he said.

Get up. Get moving.

Then he turned and continued jogging for the graveyard.

Chapter 53

Bonesetter dragged Tuck down the beach. He clutched Tuck's collar with the skeletal fingers on his monkey-bit hand and held his pistol in his burnt hand. His muscles gorged, his veins throbbed and he limped on his gunshot leg like a hunchback. The once handsome man now looked monstrous.

"Come on!" he snarled.

Tuck, however, jerked free and escaped. He ran back down the beach for town. Bonesetter started to chase him but saw Awol galloping down the beach towards them on a big black horse, like one of the four horsemen of the apocalypse. Unable to outrun the horse, and unwilling to turn back on Bonesetter, Tuck turned and ran into the ocean.

"What the hell are you doing?" Awol yelled at Bonesetter as he galloped up, reigned back on the horse's powerful neck and drove its hooves into the sand.

"You spooked him." Bonesetter replied, tossing his hands up and watching Tuck splash into the sea.

"Where's Simian?"

"I don't know."

"Whatta ya mean you don't know? Did you leave him?"

"He can't swim."

"Screw him! Come on, we gotta find the fisherman before he escapes."

"We gotta get the boy."

"No we don't! Simian ordered you not to touch him."

"I'm not going till we get him. Besides, if we have him, the fisherman will come to us."

Bonesetter nodded at his own plan and strode into the ocean after Tuck. Awol watched him for a moment, then cursed:

"Damn!"

He was right.

Awol dismounted onto the beach, skinned his M4 from the saddle and slung it over his tattooed, bloody shoulder. The M4's strap, however, dug into his bullet wound and he grimaced. It was too heavy with that wound in the water. He unslung it and re-holstered it in the saddle, then stepped for the sea as Bonesetter waded in.

Thirty yards from shore, Tuck struggled to keep his chin above water. His mouth was agape, saltwater splashed in and his big eyes glanced back. Bonesetter and Awol surged through the waves and closed on him from opposite sides. A wave hit his face, so he gurgled and dove under.

He flattened and opened his eyes underwater. Bright coral reef fish swam by. He stroked and kicked to escape, but a hand broke the surface and latched his ankle. It yanked him back like a snare and pulled him out; splashing, gasping, slapping and struggling like a fish on a hook.

"Come on kid," Awol said.

Tuck fidgeted and fought in Awol's strong grip.

"Where ya gonna swim to, huh?"

"Far from you."

"Don't worry, I won't let him hurt you."

"See that?" Bonesetter gloated, wading up, "I just taught him to swim!"

"I know how to swim Bone-sucker," Tuck shot.

"Just like your old man," Bonesetter smiled proudly.

"I'm not retarded," Tuck added.

"We'll take him to the Keep," Awol stated, stepping towards shore.

"Eh eh, no dice, soldga' boy." Bonesetter replied.

"What?"

"Ya, no way, we're going the other way," Bonesetter said, nodding up-coast to the Ranchero.

"We're finishing this job," Awol stated. "Getting the gold. And letting the boy go."

"Nope," Bonesetter said, "that was never the plan."

"What?"

Awol froze, trying to understand what Bonesetter meant. Never the plan? That didn't make sense. Kill the old man, take the town and get the gold. That's the plan. Simply. Why mess with the kid, unless...

Suddenly, Awol got it.

Datapoints connected and his eyebrows rose. Bonsetter came into focus. Now, now it all made sense.

Bonesetter tilted his head and dug a finger into his ear, then pulled something out and looked at it—a larva. Fat, round and wet.

A larva, out of his ear.

"You're sick…" Awol realized.

Bonesetter held his hand up in front of him and inspected the wounds on it.

"You got bit," Awol continued, "in the jungle. The howlers… That day with the machete… You got Monkey Jungle Worm. And the kid…."

"I'm taking my son," Bonesetter quipped, flicking the larva at him, "and getting my wife."

"Your son? What, who, him?"

Bonesetter stared crazed. A wave lapped against his hip.

"I'm hungry," he commented.

"You are a freak."

"RAGH!"

Suddenly, Bonesetter whipped a pistol up from underwater and—

—*BANG!*

Awol thudded back. The bullet hit him square in the chest. His thick muscle took it well, but still, it was a bullet. Blood poured out of a small entry wound, and ran down his abs.

He released Tuck and stumbled back, looking down at the wound, shocked. He patted his shoulder to unsling his M4, but it was lost, gone. He searched the shore with panicked eyes. They settled on his gun on his horse on the beach, across the water, too far away. He reached back for Tuck, but grasped a fistful of empty air and stumbled back, splashing into the sea.

Bonesetter thrashed forward and grabbed him. Bonesetter picked up his big body and tossed him, monster strong. Stronger than he was. Stronger than he should have been.

Awol splashed, rolled and struggled for shore, but black blood squirted out of a larger exit wound in his back. It stained the turquoise sea black, like octopus ink.

"AGH!" Awol groaned.

Bonesetter sprung up from behind, grabbed Awol's ankle and plunged Tuck's knife ruthlessly into his kidney. Awol cried and arched back as the blade cut it, but Bonesetter crashed down and stabbed him again. He tried to spin over, but Bonesetter grabbed his fancy fútbolista hair, shoved his head underwater and stabbed him again and again in the back, punching through the water and growling madly through his teeth, stabbing and drowning him simultaneously.

Awol's arms lashed behind him, trying to grab Bonesetter, anything, life. Sea splashed through his Spartan beard and his body fought and convulsed, but he grabbed only air, because it was too late, life had simply, quickly, somehow got away from him, then just quietly stepped to the side.

He fought and lived longer than he should have, like a snake with its head cut off, but eventually he couldn't keep his head up, and it stayed underwater. Slowly, his arms stopped flailing and his body went limp.

Bonesetter straightened. He stepped back, caught his breath and watched him, floating face down in black blood, rocking in the swells, drifting away in the sea.

Tuck jumped to run for it again - but Bonesetter snatched him.

Chapter 54

Gunner jogged to the mahogany tree at the graveyard's entrance and slowed by its big trunk. Strangely, the tree's green leaves had fallen off and bare branches scratched the sky like skeleton fingers. He passed under the branches like a shadow and entered the Castillo, grasping Gambler's M4.

Inside the old walls, headstones tilted over mounds and more graves had been dug up and tossed. The Keep rose above them in the middle, and its door swayed open. He crept through it, into the room. Simian squatted inside, scooping handfuls of gold coins out of the safe with his small hands.

"Where's the boy?"

Simian whipped around, surprised. He spotted Gunner and lunged for his big Sig Sauer on the table, but Gunner butted him savagely in the face with his rifle, blasting him back into the wall.

"AHH!"

"WHERE'S TUCK!?"

"Hell that HURT!" Simian yelled, "I don't know! Freakshow took him! Jesuz!"

"WHERE?"

"I don't know! Who knowz watz in hiz head! Hiz brainz rhatting out. Fracking guy thinks hez a self-taught doctawr! I ordered him not ta touch da kid in the first place, let alone bury him!"

Simian wiped his bloody nose and inspected the blood on his fingers.

"Crap, I'm helping this town! And nobody cairs! I'm building it, given security. Cazador's out there killen howlaz every day! And rebuilding the fort. You know wat would haapen witout me? You know wat haapens ina ecosystem witout predators, huh? Huh? Disease and disorda! If we're not the predators den we're da prey and this place tears itself apart from the inside. And nooboody caaaairs! They didn't even have fresh watta until—"

"—You..."

"Waaat!?"

"Forget it."

BAM!

Gunner fired.

His bullet pierced Simian's throat. Blood pumped out his neck. He gargled and choked, wide-eyed and scared.

"I… I… Huh, huh…"

He slumped, and a handful of gold coins spilled onto the floor at his side.

"I…"

But Gunner turned and left before he finished dying.

Chapter 55

Bonesetter rode Awol's black war horse up the trail to Don Granada's Ranchero. Tuck sat in front in the saddle, trapped between Bonesetter's muscled but burnt and dog-torn forearms.

They reached the Ranchero's yard, and Bonesetter dismounted in the grass. He pulled Tuck down and collared him up to the front door. There, he paused and removed his *Family* photograph from his breast pocket.

Tuck wrenched out of his grip and watched him. The photo took him back to a happier time and place, which calmed him.

"You see son, we're a family."

Tuck eyed him suspiciously, so he handed him the photo. He flipped it over. In it, Bonesetter was young and un-burnt and un-bit and un-deformed and un-shot and handsome. His face was infused with youth, instead of weathered by time, and his arm was wrapped around Santa, who was smiling and pregnant.

"That was Macapa. You were born two days later. In a cyclone."

Bonesetter smiled proudly.

"That was the happiest day of my life."

Tuck eyed him like he was an idiot-madman, so Bonesetter snatched the photo back jealously and pocketed it. He grunted, then wiped dried spit from the corners of his mouth and tried to style his ocean-matted hair with his hands. He tucked in his shirt, tried to dust some dirt off it, and brushed some blood off his teeth and gums with his finger. He then grinned at Tuck and nodded, and pulled out a key, unlocked the door and stepped inside.

Chapter 56

Gunner jogged down the beach with the M4 heavy on his back. A body lay ahead in the sand like a Normandy soldier, near where Gunner had washed ashore. But Tuck's knife stuck out of it, and it wasn't rising. A wave washed against it, and black blood-crows pecked at it with yellow eyes and bloody beaks.

Gunner slowed and eased up on it like Cadejo had sniffed up on him. The crows cawked angrily, like they were guarding it, so he fired a round and they scattered into the sky. He squatted and deadlifted it over. It sucked sand and suction from the water.

Awol.

A gunshot and multiple stab wounds. His face was sandy and his tongue was fat. A crab crawled up from inside his throat and into his mouth. The decapod reached its legs out and pulled itself past Awol's white teeth and over his lips, then segmented across his beard and down the beach.

Gunner looked up and around, up the beach and over Valhalla's ruins to Don Granada's Ranchero on the mountain. He caught his breath and struggled to find strength.

Get up. Get moving.

He unslung the M4 and used it as a crutch to stand, then jogged on towards the Ranchero.

Chapter 57

When Gunner neared the end of the beach he angled off the wet, hard sand on the foreshore through the soft, dry sand mid-beach and slogged towards Shore Trail, on the clay earth under the palms. He was tired and moved slow. He passed the cayuco and neared his whiskey chair under the uvero tree, then suddenly raised his M4 in a burst of energy and leaned forward to fire.

Cazador was there, another straggler from the battle, splattered across town like shrapnel from a grenade.

He trained his gun on the threat, but Cazador wasn't a threat. Cazador bent over and held his hand on a palm to hold himself up. He coughed painfully and stumbled aimlessly a few steps to another palm, then caught himself on it and held himself there a second. He finally managed to straighten and stabilize himself by leaning his forehead against the pulpy trunk. He had a bloody tourniquet wrapped around his shot quad, his bola was twisted around his ankle and his pistol lay a few meters away in the sand, which was tossed in odd directions.

There'd been some kind of scuffle—recently.

Cazador rolled on the trunk and faced him, leaning back against it, huffing and holding a bloody hand against the side of his neck. As he did, one of the cane corso puppies, the big silver one who wasn't much of a puppy anymore, wiggled up and licked salty blood off his ankle.

"Shoot me," Cazador said.

"No," Gunner replied, lowering the M4, "I owe you. For the wash. You knew I was there. You let me live."

"If chew owe me, shoot me."

Cazador removed his hand from his neck, as if to explain things. Underneath was a bite mark, from a human, oval and fleshy and gorged. The teeth had broken skin and it was bruised purple. Cazador covered it back up to reapply pressure, then thumbed over his shoulder with his free hand, up the trail, towards the Ranchero.

"He's strong now."

Bonesetter. Bonesetter had done this.

"No boats. No radio. Bonesetta's sick like the monkeys, and chew, chew wash ashore…"

Gunner waited.

"What's wrong?" Cazador asked.

"Did he have Tuck?"

"Take the dog," Cazador replied, ignoring his question and nodding down to the dog, "for Cadejo. I felt bad when I heard that. I really did. He's a good one. Strong. I named him War Dog. I replaced his front canines with titanium teeth. They'll pierce metal and kevlar. He'll protect chew."

"Did he have Tuck?"

Cazador grimaced and rubbed his eyes, then looked up and off, out to sea.

"I need to go home now."

"Did he... CAZ! Did he have Tuck!?"

Cazador refocused, then closed his eyes and nodded.

"Ya, he has him. Bonesetter has him. That way."

Gunner started to run, but the M4 was heavy as an anchor by now. He could move faster without it, and may not get there in time with it, so he stripped it and hucked the magazine and stock in the bushes in different directions. He then continued on, running past Cazador and up the steep trail to the Ranchero.

Chapter 58

Inside the Ranchero, Bonesetter and Tuck sat on the couch in the great room, in front of Don Granada's body, which still lay on the family table behind them. Bonesetter's M4 lay atop Granada's cold corpse, so that he looked like one of the entombed knights in the church, holding their swords on their chests, taking them into death for whatever lay beyond. It was quiet and peaceful but oddly cold, and the air was hollow like a crypt. Still, Bonesetter's muscles swelled hot, his veins throbbed and his heart pumped strong—too strong—yet he sat still, staring catatonic.

He blinked back, looked at Tuck and smiled tenderly. He handed him a water bottle. Tuck eyed him suspiciously, but snatched it and chugged. He then dug in his pocket and extracted a bag of plantain chips, dry and salty. He ate one and offered Tuck the bag. Tuck grabbed one and popped it in his mouth, then grabbed a handful more as he chewed, ravenous. Bonesetter chuckled like a proud father.

"You see, this is how it should be." Bonesetter said, "Sitting on the couch. At home. Doing a simple thing with my son. That's all I ever wanted, you know? To eat chips with you. Things like that. That's all."

He watched Tuck and enjoyed the moment, wanting to keep it forever like the stone in Gambler's pocket. But the moment didn't even last a minute. Footsteps bumped on the terrace outside. They barged into his awareness and broke the spell, dragging the outside world in like a dead iguana. He tensed and groaned slightly, because the stone wasn't in his pocket, it was in the pit of his stomach, and no matter what he did, he couldn't claw it out without killing himself in the process.

He handed Tuck the plantains and stood. When he did, Tuck noticed a red dynamite stick in his waistband.

"Honey…" Bonesetter said. "Honey, we're home!"

The front door burst open and Santa blew through it, gripping her boning knife at her side, the thin blade covered in blood. Soldado blood. She stopped flat when she saw Bonesetter, and a confused look froze on her face.

"Honey," Bonesetter repeated, smiling warmly.

He spread his arms and stepped towards her for a hug. As he did, Tuck ran past him and into her arms.

"Baby!" she cried, squatting, "are you all right? Oh my God, I was so worried about you. Thank God you're here. I love you. I love you so much!"

"I love you, Mom. I love you. I'm sorry, I—"

"—Shhh…"

"I—"

"—It's okay now. It's okay…"

She brushed dirt from his face and stroked his hair. Bonesetter reached to stroke hers from above with his monkey-bit hand.

"How was your day?" Bonesetter asked.

"What?" She said, recoiling.

"What?" he asked back from above, surprised, his smile stuck on his face.

She grabbed Tuck and stood to run, but Bonesetter kicked the door shut behind her.

CLAP.

"What have you done?" she asked, spinning back on him.

"What? I told you I'd fix everything. I brought our son ba—"

"—He isn't *our* son!"

She stepped in front of Tuck to shield him.

"Don't say that."

"I know, I just… brought him back."

"You took him!"

"You took him!" Bonesetter snapped. "No wait, I mean…"

He took a deep breath, clenched and unclenched his fists, and exhaled slowly to calm himself. With concentrated effort, he refocused and redirected.

"Look." He said kindly, "Look around. We're all together again. At home. We're a family."

"You never should have dove a hundred and twenty meters."

"No, I know. I made a mistake, you're right but I…"

"It destroyed part of your brain. Changed you. Leave us alone."

"…I never stopped loving you. That's why I found you, and came back. He's my son too."

He handed her his photo, desperate to remind her of what she'd once seen in him. As she looked at it, he got down on one knee and opened the red felt ring box he'd hidden under the sink. A five caret, princess-cut, diamond wedding ring sparkled out. She stood stunned.

"Santa Lucia Granada Braganza, as God is my witness…"

Before he could finish, however, she ripped his photo in half and threw it in his face.

"NO!"

"Freak."

SLAP!

He sprung from his knee and backhanded her.

"Why'd you make me do that!?"

Tuck jumped in front of his mom.

"LEAVE US ALONE!" she shouted, ricocheting back with her knife.

He charged her. Tuck punched him in the stomach but he blew right over and through him. She swung her knife and stabbed him square in the deltoid but he shrugged through it, grabbed her hair and—

—SMACK!

Tossed her to the floor.

Tuck punched him again from behind, but he backhanded Tuck to the ground like King Kong swatting a Japanese Zero. He stomped over him, collared him, and dragged him across the room and onto the terrace like a sack of laundry.

"What are you doing!?" she shouted after him.

"If we can't have him together," He declared, "we won't have him at all."

He heaved Tuck up and hammer threw him over the edge.

"NO!"

Tuck flew horizontally through the air like a ragdoll, as if sailing to the distant beach beyond, then quickly dropped over the lip like a rock and crashed through the canopy below.

"NOOOO…!" she yelled, running at Bonesetter.

Bonesetter thundered back into the house with the boning knife still stuck in his shoulder. He intercepted her halfway and smacked her with an arm bar. He grabbed her by the shoulder, trying to hold her steady, but she thrashed and her hair flew as she tried to escape.

"You're a MONST—"

—CRACK!

He punched her in the face to calm her, but her head whipped back and she spit in his eye.

"One hundred and twenty-THREE meters!" he yelled.

CRACK!

"I was the world champion!"

"Your brain bent!"

"I did it for YOU!"

CRACK!

She fell and her head thudded against the floor.

"WHY DO YOU DO THAT!?" he barked over her, yanking the knife from his shoulder and tossing it behind him. "WHY DO YOU MAKE ME DO THAT? I LOVE YOU!"

"Why'd you kill Winter!?" she lashed back from the floor. "Why'd you kill him!? He was a good man!"

"The howlers got him."

"Bullshit! What'd you do? What'd you do with my HUSBAND!?"

"I put a nail in his head."

Suddenly, the anger left all at once in a rush, like a burst damn that had only been plugged by the small hope that until that moment, while Winter was almost certainly dead, nobody had ever confirmed it, and the possibility remained that he may still walk through the front door one day. But he hadn't. Bonesetter had. And, once his death was confirmed, her spine collapsed from the inside, as if hope had been holding it up, and only the deep underlying exhaustion remained.

"Why..." she groaned painfully. "Why...?"

"I put him out of his misery and his miserable love for you."

"No... No..."

He lorded over her, both furious and loving, convinced and confused, like two people were trapped inside him at the same time. She mumbled beneath him, his words more hurtful than his fists, then rose for Tuck.

"Baby..."

He ripped the dynamite stick from his waistband and held it with bloody knuckles, then extracted a lighter from his pocket and reached for—

—*BOOM!*

A force smacked him like a plank.

Gunner tackled him to the floor.

Gunner scrambled to maintain momentum, but Bonesetter shucked him off and instantly hulked over him. Bonesetter took a second to realize what happened – Gunner had run into the house and tackled him. He picked Gunner up and hucked him into a wall.

SMASH!

Gunner hit the wall and crashed to the floor. He would have dented it, but it was coral stone, so it dented him. Virus blitzed through Bonesetter's veins.

"That feels GOOD!"

He charged back to Santa.

Gunner struggled to his feet, grabbed Bonesetter's M4 from atop Don Granada's corpse and leveled it at him. Bonesetter twisted on his spine and eyed him like a beast: hunched, bloody and crazed. What remained of the handsome young man he once was almost all but gone now. Gunner coughed and his legs buckled. He aligned the sights, but his vision blurred and the barrel twitched.

"You're weak," Bonesetter grinned.

The barrel slumped. He looked up at Bonesetter from under his brow.

"But you don't matter. None of you matters," Bonesetter waved a hand over and beyond the room and town. "Why were you even here anyway, huh? Where'd you come from? Jacking up our life? MESSING UP OUR FAMILY!"

Gunner's stomach cramped and he keeled forward, holding it with one arm.

"LEAVE US ALONE!" Bonesetter grunted and waved his hand.

He turned back and snatched Santa up. He choked her and held her like a human shield, gripping the dynamite in one hand and waving the lighter across her face in the other.

"I love you," he whispered in her ear, panting in her neck, drooling from his lip. He stroked her hair from her face with the dynamite stick. "I always loved you."

"I... I..."

"What? What baby?"

"I..."

"What?"

"I never loved you."

He continued smiling slightly for a second, then a twitch ran up the side of his face and over his eye like a scar. His smile fell and faded to sadness. His Adam's apple knotted and tears swelled in his eyes. Real sadness and real pain. Old pain from old memories that slipped out like a prison break. Suddenly, he was back in Sao Paulo, twenty-two years old, with a bright future and a hot pregnant girl, watching himself make the exact wrong decision at the exact wrong time. Over the years that pain and regret rotted to self-hate, which rooted in such a deep and dark stone-knot in his stomach that only one thing could suppress it when it surfaced: Anger. But the stone-knot denigrated his stomach lining more every day, becoming harder and harder to suppress.

He swallowed his Adam's apple and his jaw tightened, then he flicked the lighter and held it near the dynamite's fuse.

"You'll love me. In our next life. This one got all fucked up."

He lit the fuse. It sparkled in front of their faces like the stars had once sparkled for them.

"We have five seconds now. Just us. Together. Like before. Like always. Forever."

FZZZZZZZZZ...

"Five."

Gunner struggled to level the gun, focus and aim. He aimed at the thin fuse in front of Bonesetter's face, but it was mostly hidden behind her head.

"Four," he whispered, his lips nudging her ear lobe.

Gunner's sights bobbed and swayed on and off the fuse, on and off Santa and Bonesetter behind it.

FZZZZZZ...

"Three."

Bonesetter rocked her tenderly, blocking, exposing and re-blocking his head with her body, planning to carry her like a child outside of their bodies and into the next life, because after all these years the pain in the pit of his stomach had finally grown stronger than the anger, and he couldn't keep it caged. Now, only death could destroy it, but to do that, it had to destroy everything else with it.

Suddenly, a crack appeared in the floor near his feet.

The trapdoor.

It widened and small eyes peered through it.

FZZZ...

"Two."

Tuck reached through the trapdoor and grabbed the boning knife on the floor near Bonesetter's foot.

Gunner's sights bobbed off the fuse, Santa and Bonesetter.

FZ...

"ONE..."

Tuck drove the knife down like Gunner had shown him—

"—YAHH! —"

— into Bonesetter's foot.

"AHH!"

Bonesetter yelled and jerked back, surprised, exposing and aligning the fuse—

—*BAM!*

Gunner fired.

The bullet shot across the room, cut through the fuse and drove into Bonesetter's eye socket behind it. His head snapped back on the spine and his body punched into Don Granada's corpse. It slumped to the floor beneath Don Granada, streaking blood on the table. His mangled head came to rest against the table's leg, twisted at the odd angles that people die in.

Dead.

The Bonesetter was dead.

And the dynamite stick lay on the floor, inert.

A long moment passed, forming a line between the world that was and the world that is. As the line cemented in time, Santa dragged herself and Tuck across it. She collapsed to her knees on the other side, in the safety of that new space.

Gunner saw the line and glimpsed the peace on the other side, but when he leaned towards it he stumbled to a knee and caught himself with his hand. It wasn't his peace. Maybe, like Bonesetter, he could only find peace in death. He propped himself back up on his M4 and looked ahead.

As long as there is breath in your lungs…

Get up.

Get moving.

Chapter 59

A little while later, Gunner walked Awol's horse down the road by the reins and into town.

CLOP,

CLOP,

CLOP…

The pueblo was destroyed. Bullet holes splatted buildings, soot stained walls, horse-flies buzzed bodies, blood-crows circled overhead and corpses twisted and drowned in debris with feet and arms grasping out, like the devil was pulling them through the earth and into hell.

In the street in front of Big Mama's house, Mudo kneeled by a half-burnt body.

Butch.

Butch's arms flopped above his head and his cleaver stuck out of his chest, in his heart. His ribs were cooked and burnt like a pig on a spit and his eyes were open, but his blue cataracts were milky white.

In the plaza, the townsfolk rooted through rubble. Intel lay near a smoldering tire. Undertaker slunk up to him, grabbed him under the armpits and dragged him away like a vulture. His heels left drag marks in the dust and he groaned to life.

"Shhhhh…" Undertaker whispered, glancing up to see if anyone noticed, and dragging him into a dark alley like a den.

In the center of the plaza, Saint Peter's statue toppled over a pile of bricks, and a dusty, limp arm dangled out.

"He's here!" Santiago del Toro yelled, running up.

Santiago kneeled over the arm and heaved a brick off the man's face. Townsfolk hustled over and circled around, staring with silent reverence.

CLOP,

CLOP…

Gunner approached slowly from behind the crowd.

Mulata saw Gunner first and stepped back. His skin was tan, which brightened his sea eyes, and his muscles had already started to recover from the shipwreck to meaten his tall, athletic frame, but he was blown-out and run ragged from the battle and before. He was covered in blood, dirt and dust, and his hair was thick with salt and sweat. To her, he was a ghost-soldier. A mirage in human form who drifted into this world like a sleepwalker. Given this, she didn't believe he was bound by physics the same way as most men, by space and time and pain and averages. To her, he was Fate itself, who knew God-men and could raise the Army of the Black Hand.

He dropped the reins and stopped.

CLOP.

He stood and stared. After a moment, he left the horse outside the crowd and trudged in. Blacky, Surfer, Big Mama and others parted, clearing a path for him to the body like they'd done for Don Granada just a few weeks, but a lifetime, ago. When he reached the epicenter, Santiago retreated. Gunner squatted by the body everyone encircled.

Barboza.

Buried in blocks. His face ashen and eyes open. His faithful Enfield locked in his grip, but splintered in half. The grenade pin was hooked in a dislocated knuckle in his other hand, and a crazed smile stuck on his face.

After a long moment, Gunner nodded respectfully and closed Barboza's eyes. Barboza. The great Barboza. The old soul, taking his seat at the table of kings.

"So this is it," Gunner said, "Sergeant Barboza…"

The townsfolk circled closer to hear his battlefield ode, but he paused and looked up.

"What was his last name?"

Nobody replied. A few people looked at each other. Big Mama shrugged.

"Nobody knows his last name?"

"I'm not sure he was a Sergeant," Santiago offered, correcting Gunner's speech already.

"He was a Corporal," Blacky injected, "when he fought for the forty-forth Gurka Brigade."

"No, no, no…" Santiago corrected. "That's when he fought the Barbary Pirates, in the Gulf of Aden."

"Barbary Pirates? There aren't Barbary Pirates in the—"

"—He was a Colonel in Saigon, when Don Granada— "

"—Alright!" Gunner said.

The townsfolk stopped abruptly. They stared and waited. After a long moment, Gunner took a deep breath, looked back down at Barboza and continued.

"Anyway… Barboza, you—"

—Barboza's eyes sprung open.

Gunner flinched and froze, his eyes as big as Barboza's. Gunner stared. Barboza stared. Gunner stared some more, until Barboza blinked.

HUUU!

The townsfolk gasped.

"Grghgh…" Barboza gargled rocks.

"He's ALIVE!"

Quickly, they surged forward and tossed bricks and blocks off him.

"Hurry!"

"How…" Gunner awed.

"God damn," Barboza grumbled, spitting out rocks and struggling to sit up in the rubble, "I'm even tougher than I thought."

Gunner grinned.

The townsfolk threw blocks off him and helped him sit up. After a moment, he brushed dust and debris out of his handlebar mustache and looked around to reorient himself. It reminded him of Saigon after the Vietcong shelled it.

"You know what this means?" he asked.

"What?" Gunner replied, smiling amazed.

"That another war's comin'."

"Why?"

"Cause God's not done with me here."

"LOOK!"

Everyone looked where a man pointed.

Behind Barboza, at the base of the toppled Saint Peter statue, a hole punched into the ground, exposing a cavern. Santiago shined a light in. At the bottom, sparks reflected back like water.

Gold sparks.

"What is it?" Blacky asked, picking his way forward.

"Gold."

"Gold?"

"The treasure?"

"Captain Kidd's gold!"

"In Saint Peter's tomb!"

The crowd awed and pressed forward to peer inside.

"Argh!" Barboza groaned as they climbed over him and smashed the bricks on top of his legs to get to the hole.

In the hole, a vacuous cavern stretched underground into negative space. In the middle stood a pedestal. On top of that sat a sarcophagus. The sarcophagus was simple solid stone, heavy and eternal. A tomb. The tomb of an ascetic who believed that the goal wasn't to collect things, but to cut them to the bone.

But the rest of the tomb wasn't simple or Spartan. Oddly, on the back wall behind the sarcophagus stood a statue of the Monkey Jungle God, which watched over the stone coffin with its wrists crossed over its chest, holding daggers in each hand. A howler with knives. The tomb also had a dark underground entrance, or escape tunnel, on the back wall. The tunnel ran towards the Castillo and was tall enough for a short man to walk through standing up. Given this, the tomb looked like it had been discovered and lost and repurposed several times, and was a strange mix of Christian and animistic religions, like something had gone terribly wrong—more than once.

Despite this, the first and only thing anyone other than Gunner noticed was the floor, because it was covered in gold. Aztec gold. In the same gold coins Bonesetter had taken from Winter, and the ones scattered around Gambler's legs in the alley, only a lot more. They spilled over the cavern like water, and sparkled in the light like minnows. But the gold had always attracted sloth and greed like gravity, and was never alone, not in legend, and not now. Slumped on top of the gold against the back wall, under the Monkey Jungle God, was a human skeleton, wearing the same clothes he wore three hundred years ago when he died.

"Caravaggio…"

The Pirate, Caravaggio.

The Watchman.

Watching over Captain Kidd's gold.

Caravaggio's mandible hung agape by a thread of calcified tendon. His knuckle-fingers still clutched his cutlass, and his hollow black skull-eyes were just hollow black skull-eyes, but for some reason they looked mad, for he was surrounded by howler bones, like he was retreating and killing when the howlers finally pushed him up against the wall and overran him. He sat but didn't rest, still guarding the gold three hundred years later.

Back above ground, Gunner pulled himself off the hole. He stood and cut back through the surging crowd, away from the treasure and towards the Cantina.

Chapter 60

Gunner limped into the Cantina.

It was burnt and blasted. Half the front was dynamited off and its red plaster bricks tumbled into the street, exposing it to open air. Dust settled in war light, a cow ate some mangos by the stairs and a crow cawked and fluttered out of a deep shadow and into the day. A surveillant. Animals were inside and entails were out, because the world had been tossed inside out.

Two legs of the poker table had been cut out beneath it, and the first two soldados Gunner shot lay dead in poker chips by it. One was still holding his fork. Nearby, Don Granada's dried blood streaked across the floor.

Gunner followed the blood streak to the bar.

The bar that he had hid behind when Don Granada got shot was splintered and riddled like chopped kindling. The glass backstop on the wall behind it was shattered in ice-burg chunks, reflecting a fragmented but accurate image of Gunner and the rubble-world behind him.

The liquor shelves in front of the glass were either missing or seesawed. Only one remained straight, and on this, only one bottle still stood, alone and un-shot; a Red Sea Whiskey bottle.

He strode forward and grabbed it by the neck.

Chapter 61

Gunner trudged down Shore Trail to the uvero tree, strangling the whiskey by the neck. He stepped under the tree's craggy canopy and thick, waxy leaves, and saw that his whiskey chair and glasses lay tumbled in the sand beneath it. Cazador was gone—God knows where—maybe dragged off by a howler. The only thing that remained was the scuffed sand, his blood streaks on the palm and his cane corso tied to it. War Dog growled at him.

He growled back.

He set the chair back up and put the whiskey on the table, then skinned his Glock and eyed the heavy metal in his hand.

Gun.

Gun in the Narrows. Gun on the Farm. Gun on the Albatross.

And now, Gun in Monkey Jungle Town.

Gun had always been there for him and always would be, waiting to ride out with him to the fight at the end of the world. So he reared back and hucked it as far as he could. It rose into the sun like a cosmonaut and fell back to earth like a meteor, crashing silently in the sand.

Vaya con dios.

It could rust there. He was done with it. He was done with violence. With killing.

No más.

He fetched the two whiskey glasses from the sand, blew them out and set them on the table. He sat in the chair and filled them with whiskey, then dropped a rattlesnake rattle in one and watched it twist slowly in the woody liquid. After a moment, he picked it up and toasted the other one.

"Well John… finally. To the best of man, and the… Mudo?"

Suddenly, Mudo stood in front of him, grinning like an idiot.

"Ahhhh… Jesus."

He lowered his glass from his parched, cracked lips and stared, waiting, but Mudo just stared back.

"What?" he finally asked.

Mudo pointed to his wrist, then to the cayuco on the backshore down-beach.

"Nahuh, no way, hell no. I'm staying here now hermano. I'm

done killing. Gonna have some whiskey and relax. Decompress like everyone said. Then I'll rebuild the cabanas. Maybe take up surfing… Always wanted to run a bar. I mean, who hasn't? Don Granada and everyone were right. I shouldn't have been trying to leave. I should've just been accepting and enjoying what is. Because everything I need is right here. This is it. This is the place. The last paradise on earth."

Mudo tapped his ring finger.

"Cindy? Screw her. She's gonna marry someone else. Besides, no boat in almost three weeks now? It's too late. She's probably dead. They all are. I'm not going back. None of us are. Ever."

Mudo pulled a newspaper clipping from his pocket and scribbled on it.

"I didn't know you could write," Gunner commented, slightly concerned that his speech to conclude the conversation hadn't concluded the conversation.

Mudo handed him the clipping. Reluctantly, he grunted and set his whiskey back on the table, then snatched the clipping and read it.

"I pulled Don Granada from the Cantina. He was still alive, then. He told me to give this to you."

Gunner looked back to Mudo, waiting to see what it was that Don Granada told Mudo to give him, but Mudo just stood there.

"What?" Gunner finally asked.

Mudo pointed at the clipping and spun his finger. Gunner looked back down and flipped it over. It was the newspaper article Don Granada was reading two weeks ago, when he first heard that Gunner had washed ashore.

Castaway Rescued

Department of Defense officials confirmed that Mexican fisherman rescued a U.S. Army officer off the coast of Tulum Monday. The officer, First Lieutenant Casey "Jinx" Luck, had been adrift in a battered dingy for 87 days. Luck, who was dehydrated but in otherwise sound form, said that his helicopter crashed during a routine training exercise off the coast of Brazil, and everyone else in his platoon burnt to death. They have been categorized; 'Lost at Sea.'

Gunner read it silently, then leaned back in his chair, shocked. His shoulders slumped and his mouth slacked.

"He's alive? Jinx, is alive?"

Mudo didn't reply, but looked worried. Gunner stared, amazed. Palms rustled overhead.

"Holy shit…"

Gunner lurched up and knocked the table over. The whiskey glasses and bottle crashed to the ground.

"Do you know what this means? Do you know what this MEANS?!"

Gunner's eyes darted from side to side and he began pacing between the uvero and Cazador's palm, cracking his knuckles as his mind raced. The whiskey bottle pumped dry in the sand, and he suddenly stopped and turned.

"I have to go," he said excitedly. "I can still save some."

Mudo waited.

"I have to find Jinx." Gunner explained, "And kill him."

Mudo nodded and held out Gunner's Glock—the one he'd just hucked and swore he'd never touch again. Gunner stared at it a second and frowned, then growled and swiped it back.

Gun.

Gun in the Narrows. Gun on the Farm. Gun on the Albatross.

Gun in Monkey Jungle Town.

Chapter 62

For the first time in as long as any of the locals could remember, the cayuco had moved. It wasn't warping and wilting in the sun on the backshore. Instead, it sat at the shoreline, half on the beach and half in the surf, refurbished and ready to launch. It was more like a dhow now than a cayuco, because Mudo had painstakingly shaved, sanded and sealed her weathered but sound hull, reset her mast, stitched her sail, replaced her rigging and painted her cobalt with a white trim, resurrecting and reinventing her like a middle-aged divorcee, with her experience and sightlines, exquisitely flawed.

Gunner and Mudo stood shirtless in the ocean and loaded her with supplies; water, food, tackle, jerry cans, chilies to combat scurvy... As they did, the townsfolk and tourists watched from the beach like shell-shocked tsunami survivors, marooned and oddly paired in a New World. A world without their geographic and social landmarks and anchors, like Valhalla and Don Granada, or even their houses. In just a few weeks, ever since Gunner washed ashore, the town had significantly and alarmingly degenerated towards its base state. It was once again a lost and severed outpost in the jungle, but this time, it was stalked by a feeling that something had gone even worse—Out There.

"Stay," Santa said.

She stood near the waterline, with an arm wrapped over Tuck's shoulder and chest.

"Ya," Santiago concurred, "we can rebuild my store."

"Or the cabañas," Trust Fund countered.

"Or the bar," Bumster contributed. "I've always wanted to own a bar. I mean, who hasn't?"

Gunner frowned and kept loading. Not that it mattered, but nobody was rebuilding the bar or stores anytime soon.

"Where's the card Gambler gave you, in the alley?" Mulata asked.

She knew things she shouldn't, but Gunner didn't have time to ask why. Maybe she'd been there, maybe Gambler was still alive, maybe she sensed it... Without looking, he pulled the card from his back pocket and handed it to her. She flipped it over and looked at it.

"He can't stay," She prognosed.

Santa eyed her sideways.

"Ya, he has to go," Frat Boy confirmed. "If he doesn't, he can't come back with help."

"Cheese not going for help," Tequila quipped.

Coco held her belly and looked around nervously. As she did, Surfer strode up with two M4s. He handed them to Gunner, who set one near each bench in the boat.

"I'll start on the fort," Surfer said, nodding to the Castillo down-coast, "pick up where Cazador left off. Reinforce the ramparts on the inland side first and map the tunnels. Looks like they run everywhere, with some bunkers in-between, like people were living in them, underground, like animals."

"Strange," Gunner replied.

"Ya. There's more town below ground than above it."

"Maybe Polito's down there."

"Ya, maybe."

"How 'bout Cazador?"

"Nothing. He's still missing. But Barboza and I are going to look for him after this."

"Good, we may need him."

Gunner patted Surfer on the shoulder, then sloshed back to the beach. He cut through the crowd and strode away from the boat, up the beach to the razed cabañas on shore. As soon as he left, the townsfolk and tourists condensed near the boat and chattered amongst themselves.

"How much booze do we have now?" Frat Boy asked.

"Are you serious?" Blacky replied.

Frat Boy looked at him like he was an idiot. Yes, he was serious.

"Booze isn't the problem Candypants," Barboza said, striding up to join the group.

Barboza was caked in dust from the collapsed church and looked like a ghost. Pebbles were still entrapped in his mustache and teeth, and a small dust cloud hovered around his short Afrikaner shorts. Blood blotched his medals and he only had one boot on, like he was half-dead, or had come back from the dead, both of which seemed equally possible.

"Well, maybe it is," Barboza continued. "See, you got all the booze Simian stole. Cases. The problem's the food."

"Why?" Coco asked.

"You don't got any of that."

"How much food ju got?" Tequila immediately asked the merchant, Santiago.

"Enough for myself."

"See," Barboza said, shaking his crooked, dislocated finger at Frat Boy, "better learn to fish."

"Huh huh huh huh…" Burner laughed.

"What?" Frat Boy shot to Burner.

"Candypants." Burner repeated, a few beats behind.

"Oh ya, hippie?" Blacky shot. "Where you sleeping tonight?"

Burner's smile stuck stupid on his face as the thought hit him.

"Congratulations," Barboza said to Burner, "looks like you got your first job."

"Vacation's over," Santiago piled on.

"We're all on permanent vacation now," Trust Fund countered. "We don't have to work, with all this gold."

"It's not your gold," Santiago said, "and even if it was, where'd you spend it now anyway, huh? What're you gonna buy, coconuts?"

As the townsfolk and tourists talked, in what was, basically, the early stages of forming a new society with new rules to govern the new distribution of scattered resources, Santa cut through them to Mulata.

"What do you mean he can't stay?"

Mulata eyed her, then flashed her Gunner's card: the four of clubs. That gave him the two, three, four, five and six. He drew the gutshot straight with the Devil's Bedpost, just like Gambler foresaw.

"What's that mean?" Santa asked.

"A lot of things." Mulata replied. "And none of them good."

"Where's Padre?" Gunner asked, suddenly walking back from the shore and cutting back through the crowd to the boat, carrying his whale-bone oar with him. He tossed the oar in the boat and turned on them, waiting for an answer. They stared back, waiting for more.

"What?" Santiago finally ventured.

"Where's Padre?"

"Who?" Barboza asked.

"The Padre."

They looked around, confused.

"You know, big guy, Franciscan, jolly…"

The stared blankly, like they'd never seen or heard of Padre before, because they hadn't.

"Come on."

Big Mama raised her eyebrows. Blacky looked at Santiago to see if he knew what Gunner was talking about, but Santiago simply shrugged.

"Ha. Funny." Gunner replied flatly, "Well... Tell him I tried my best."

"Tried your best what?" Mulata asked. She cared, because she sensed that Gunner was talking about a spirit or spectre, or something he'd brought back with him from death, something only he could see.

"What?" She repeated, "Tried your best what?"

"To be a good man."

THUNK!

Mudo thunked Butch's clever into the gunwale like a gavel. Gunner looked at him across the bow and saw that, with that, he was done. The boat was packed. All the food and water and weapons were in all the right food and water and weapons places. It was time. Time to go.

He nodded at Mudo and turned back to the crowd.

"Well... This is it."

They stared, shell-shocked and unsure what to say. They looked like war-torn refugees on the beach. He measured them one last time, calculating their odds. Barboza, Surfer, Santa and Tuck were wolves, but the others looked like they didn't have any idea what they planned to do when he left, let alone how they'd feed themselves tomorrow, or next month. When he arrived, there was Valhalla, the church and the great Don Granada. Now, there were none of these things. Only survivors. Before, he was the castaway. Now, they were. Mulata would be fine. She could live like a leopard and probably transform into one. Santiago, Blacky and Big Mama, with her toddlers, would probably manage, along with some other indig he didn't recognize, but it'd be tough for the tourists. Sail, Tequila and Coco huddled close and looked completely inappropriate to the situation, but spectacularly glamorous all the same. Sail was nearly out of lip shimmer, Coco knew she really wasn't pregnant, probably, but remained concerned about the baby, just in case. Frat Boy was still calculating booze. Trust Fund had moved on; to scheming for the gold, which was probably totally useless now for a few hundred years. Coy and Bikini were unknowns, so they were doomed, and Bumster and Burner were along for the ride, which was going to be a bad trip. Fat Barb was the smartest and strongest and would probably do the best, forming a tribal alliance with short Pat and man-meat Chad. But still, the community's structure, security and father were gone, along with other heroes of the revolution, like Prospector, Campasino and Butch, and they still hadn't processed that. Polito and Cazador could help them survive, but they were probably dead, while Intel and Undertaker would kill them and were probably alive. Worse, the howlers were orbiting close and the soldado's corpses littered the town, rotting it sick from the inside like tapeworms. Still, as bad as it was in town and as bad as it was going to get, it was worse out there, and although they couldn't completely understand why he had to leave to save them, he figured he should at least say something meaningful and profound to sustain them.

"Thanks for everything," he said.

They stared. They looked at him like he was fucking mad. Like he was an alien speaking alien, about to re-board his spaceship and abandon them after visiting and unknowingly torching their planet.

Nobody said anything. Coco's mouth slacked open and a few pillars of smoke billowed from the distant plaza behind them. Sail blew him a kiss, across the apocalypse divide.

He nodded firmly, then turned back to the cayuco. He and Mudo quickly shoved it off the beach and into the sea with the tide, easing it into waist-deep water.

"Wait," Santa said, wading in after him and touching his bicep from behind.

"Come back," she said, "seriously."

"I will. That's the plan."

"You will, or that's the plan?"

He smiled tenderly.

"Heh Mister," Tuck said, sploshing up. "When are you coming back?"

Gunner pulled Don Granada's revolver from his waistband and handed it to him.

"You did good, kid. You're strong. Take care of your mom, alright?"

Tuck took his Grandpa's gun and nodded, two years more mature than he was two weeks ago. Gunner looked at Santa one last time and memorized her face—her arched eyebrows, high cheekbones and sleek chin. Her smooth skin and amber eyes. The Nordic winter warrior.

WHOOF!

Suddenly, War Dog ran clumsily down the beach on his big paws and splashed in the water with his big ears. He dog-paddled out to them and Mudo grabbed him, struggling to lift him over the gunwale and into the boat, where he shook and splashed them with water.

"Agh," Gunner grumbled. "What's he gonna eat?"

But Mudo just scratched War Dog's head and smiled deaf and dumb.

"Well, we can always eat him if we have to," Gunner concluded, and conceded.

Gunner shook his head and turned back to Santa. There was nothing left to say, so he simply tucked a strand of her sun-streaked hair behind her ear, then turned and pulled himself into the cayuco. Mudo pointed it towards blue-water and began to paddle.

Like the others, Barboza watched them go from the beach. His hand rested on his ghost dagger, tucked in his waistband, and he had a proud grin on his face and a spark in his eye. The same boyhood spark he and Don Granada had had many times before, when setting out on great adventures.

"Give 'em hell," Barboza blessed. "and Godspeed."

Chapter 63

He left like he came, by sea.

They paddled out, with Mudo in the stern and Gunner in the bow.

They thrust their oars in water and sculled. Two strokes on the right and one on the left, digging and driving through the surf in a cyclic power cadence like Polynesian outriggers. The tropical sun burned and blazed in the blue sky overhead, and the townsfolk watched and shrank on the white sand behind.

A few minutes later, they breached the reef-break, reached still-water and coasted. Gunner set his oar in his lap and caught his breath while Mudo ruddered the cayuco in a current so they drifted up-coast, paralleling the shore on a north-west bearing.

Behind them, from this distance, they could see the entire arc of the beach in the bay. The Spanish Castillo crumbled on the rocky isthmus to the east, and Jungle Mountain rose into a cloud to the west. The green palms backstopped the space between, and the beach bridged them like a giant whale bone. Strangely, the townsfolk seemed to have become small, humanoid-like figures, with slouched shoulders and long, black arms, slowly turning, dispersing and sludging back up the beach and into the palms.

When the last of the humanoids evaporated, only three grainy survivors remained, watching them. It was impossible to tell who they were through the haze and heat, but Gunner knew it was Santa, Tuck and Barboza. They stood steadfast, but looked small and vulnerable, abandoned and alone.

Slowly, the current pushed them west around Jungle Mountain, and with that, the last vapors of them, and civilization, disappeared. They broke the gravitational pull of Monkey Jungle Town, snapped the invisible tether that tied them to it like a sutratma, and crossed an invisible frontier into an unchartered quarter.

Then, there was jungle.

Only jungle.

And sea.

Gunner pulled his eyes from the jungle and looked down at the sea. It was darker past the reef, bluer and colder from upwelling, and it lapped so hypnotically and peacefully against the hull that a shiver ran up his spine and into his brain stem, because he knew how dark and deceptive it could be.

Uneased, he looked up and out to the horizon to calm himself, away from the coast to blue-water, but there, a cumulonimbus cloud crumbled up, coming over the curve of the earth like an army over a hill. It was wedding-white above and funeral-black below, and a bolt of lightning cracked silently across it in the upper troposphere.

A little squall was coming.

Some weather.

Reflexively, his pupils dilated, his jaw knotted and his knuckles squeezed white on his oar. The last time he was out, before he washed ashore, he swore he'd never go back to sea. He'd never float again. But here he was. Floating.

TAP.

TAP.

TAP…

Mudo tapped him from behind. He turned on his bench and faced him, and saw that he held his orange plastic envelope. The envelope was still sealed and waterproof. He'd rigged it from an thick biohazard bag, but the sun had faded the plastic so the contents were roughly visible.

"You wanna know what's inside?" Gunner asked.

Mudo nodded.

"Go on then."

Mudo sliced the envelope open like he was gutting a fish and extracted the contents like they were encrypted intel smuggled in its stomach.

A dog tag.

A letter.

A picture.

The dogtag was matte black instead of silver. Mudo flipped it over and read it:

Bridger, Ben C.

2292955

O+

Christian

"That's me," Gunner admitted. "Task Force Green. First Special Forces Operational Detachment Delta. Delta Force. Eat a bullet. Fuck off."

"Hahahaaaa…" Mudo laughed, because the crazy townsfolk

were right. He was a soldier, and not only that, but Delta Force, just like they crazily imagined.

Gunner grinned guilty.

Still smiling, Mudo set the dog tag on the bench next to him and opened the letter. It was written on a piece of scrap paper that had chemical equations and DNA string-codes etched by a precise and serious hand on the outside. The handwriting on the letter itself, however, was jagged and unsteady, like a child's or an old man's. As Mudo read it, Gunner recited it aloud from memory:

"Dear Mom, Forgive Ben. He had to do it. Man, I could really go for a pint right now."

Mudo looked up and shrugged, wondering what the letter meant, expecting more. Gunner, after all, had washed ashore with it and carried it all over hell.

"John wrote it," Gunner explained. "Father John Cook. My friend."

Mudo looked down and read it again like he missed something, but he hadn't. That was it. That was all the letter said. He pointed to the '*He had to do it*' part. What did he have to do?

"I had to kill him."

Mudo's eyes widened. A Father, a Priest. Gunner *had* to kill a priest. Why?

"That's him," Gunner said, pointing to the picture in Mudo's lap. "That's John."

Mudo set the letter down and flipped the picture over.

Padre smiled back.

Padre's small, circular eyes beamed between his rosy cheeks on his round face, sweat beaded on his brow, and his smile slanted in one direction while his homemade haircut plastered against his forehead and slanted in the other. His brown friar's frock draped over his shoulders and rotund belly, and he stood in a fertile green valley in some kind of mission-like field setting. He looked friendly and completely defenseless, like a pale, hairless, farm hog snorting and smiling in the predatory wild. His happy-go-lucky blind-faith goofiness contrasted so sharply with his surroundings that Mudo thought of all the camouflaged carnivores that were almost certainly stalking him from the jungle around him: snakes, jaguars, chiggers, mosquitos, spiders, pit vipers, ants, bullet ants, flies, bot flies, teste flies, narcos, guerrillas, narco-guerrillas…

A padre. Gunner had to kill a padre. And the padre knew it

beforehand, so he wrote a letter to his mom, asking her to forgive Gunner for what was about to happen, because it had to be done. And Gunner was what, carrying the letter around to deliver it to the padre's mom, to clear his conscience?

Mudo stared at the letter, trying to untangle it like a fly stuck in a spider's web. Why did he have to kill him? Why did the padre forgive him? And where the hell did he even wash ashore from to begin with?

He knew the explanation had to be somewhat rational and linear, but the more he tried to figure it out, the more irrational and non-linear it became, entangling him further.

He looked at Gunner with a confused, knotted face, but Gunner gazed out to sea, drifting away in his memories. The rocking, sun and salty smell of the sea made the memories swim back harder and more powerfully than he liked, stalker-angry he'd neglected them.

"It was the twenty-second of December," Gunner said, "when I first heard about it."

He sounded like he was talking to himself, or the squall, like he was negotiating with something. Or confessing. Slowly, he shook his head and fell back in time.

"Four months ago. I was in Dahuk. We worked nights in Mosul. We roamed with vengeance and came like reapers, snatching terrorists in their sleep.

"One day, I'd just woken up and was sitting by the fire pit, having a green tea from the DFAC. We had to double stack the paper cups because they leaked. I'd just pulled the cups apart to see if the honey was leaking through the seam when my friend, Chekov, walked up and said, 'Something strange is happening.'"

Gunner's eyes narrowed and his jaw tensed, as if the story skipped ahead in his head to a painful place.

"Islamic Front did it."

His face tensed.

"We hit the ship. The Albatross. Off the continental shelf of Brazil. We had to go, we were out of time. We were lucky to get the intel we got, but it was a shit-show from the start, the whole op. The ship was crawling with IF. Like all the jihadis we'd killed had come back from the dead to meet us on a ghost ship for revenge. And they were angry. Like wasps. We got in the guts of the hull, in their hive, and got the virologist and his monkey, but Chekov got shot through the thigh and bled out. Everyone got shot. Terrorists, the virologist… everyone. Then the monkey got hit in the crossfire. I slipped on Chekov's blood and brass trying to get to the monkey but couldn't. I couldn't save that fucken monkey. Neither could Jinx. The monkey's body parts were everywhere. And you can't put something like that back together again. So Jinx dropped down and slurped the monkey's blood up off the deck. Right off the deck. He ate one of the monkey's hairy fingers too. Like a chicken wing. It was smart. To get the only known anti-virus in his body. But as soon as he did, there was a huge concussion. Our Blackhawk got hit and crashed into the ship. You don't hear a concussion that loud, just feel it. The next thing I knew I was flying through the air, then drowning in the water."

Gunner's pupils were dilated and glassy, staring ahead but looking behind. He was completely gone now, talking to himself and wading carefully through his memories like he was wading through a swamp, like he was trying to find something, or avoid it.

"The water was on fire. It was cold and dark. Like Death was touching me, all over me, with little kid fingers, like I was trying to breathe through an octopus. I couldn't see. I couldn't breathe. Padre pulled me into the raft. He saved my life. We were the only survivors. Me, Padre, Jinx and a terrorist; a skinny Maldivian named Atoll.

"My whole platoon got wiped out. Except Wahwoke and Kam Fong. Before any of this started, before we knew what was happening, Wahwoke and Fong parachuted into Agadez, in the Sahara. We were supposed to pick them up at a rally point a month later, after they killed a terrorist. Obviously, we didn't make it. After the Albatross. We abandoned them there. They probably wondered what they hell happened to us. I guess they could still be alive, but doubt it. They'd have to cross the Sahara, on foot.

"We floated, for a long time. Then the sharks came. They took Atoll. Took him overnight. Gone in the morning. And the sun came up and the sun set, like it didn't even give a shit Atoll was gone, because it didn't. That's how life is. That's how death is. We think it cares about us, but it doesn't. We just are, until we're are not.

"There was no food. We were starving. But Jinx had to stay alive. He had the monkey's blood in him. He was the only one. The only one who could save the world. And that was our mission, to save the world. What were we supposed to do?"

Mudo didn't know what he was supposed to do, and didn't dare ask.

"We didn't even draw straws. Padre died smiling. I swear to God. But God already knows. He said something from the Bible about bread and his body, then just smiled goofy again like he always did. And I cut his throat from ear to ear. As fast as I could."

Gunner stared quiet for a moment.

"I've sliced a man's throat before. Actually, I haven't. I've only ever killed terrorists. And some others. I tried to imagine that I was killing a terrorist, but couldn't. Then I tried to imagine he was just a goat. I was just slicing a goat's throat. But I couldn't. He was as real to me as a rock. Still is."

Mudo's eyes widened. The cayuco felt even smaller than it already was.

"Calories... It doesn't bother me anymore. I'm not a saint. I told you that. I told everyone that. I tried to be a good man. Padre was, but I'm not.

"I'm the devil."

A cramp ran up the side of Gunner's face and over his eye, like a spirit corked up inside him and a slow bolt of pain shot through him. He grimaced and took it, because pain was progress, always was.

"Padre saved my life. Twice. And I took his. Once. After that, I swore I'd never pick up a gun again. Never kill again...

"A week later, Jinx stabbed me in the liver when I was sleeping. He said he just wanted to eat my liver, and we could share it. Like I was going to eat my own liver. We weren't right. We weren't in a good place. I mean how the fuck are you going to eat your own liver to survive? And that made some sense at the time.

"We fought and fell out of the raft and went into the water. The last I saw of him he was swimming after the raft, which was outpacing him in the current. I thought he was dead, I really did. I thought he never reached it. I thought he died out there and the cure died with him.

"I was so tired. I was so fucken tired. All those days, on the water. Floating. Before that, in the worst selection course I'd ever had, I thought I was near Death. I wasn't even halfway there. That's what makes Death so scary. You can't see him. Sometimes you think you're standing right next to him but you're not even close, then you're giggling with a girl and he's reaching for the back of your neck. I couldn't catch the raft, starving and stabbed like that, and I didn't even want to. I just wanted it to end. So I let go. Finally. I just stopped fighting. Gave up. I knew I was going to die, and as soon as I did, an incredible peace came over me. It was like I didn't have to worry anymore about anything. I didn't have to fight or survive or save the world, or carry anything; my beliefs, ego, guilt, hunger, nothing... All that subconscious construct and tension collapsed like a building that I'd been building, that'd I'd been holding up, on my shoulders, like a weight, and this stillness... There was this incredible stillness, under it. The sky was so blue, and I could feel... energy. Connected. Everyone is trying to connect with someone. I felt connected to humanity. Not just to myself, or a woman, but to everyone. Maybe more than that. More... universal. And I just lay there, in the middle of the ocean, a speck in the middle of the ocean, floating in the current, in weightless nirvana.

"Next thing I knew I came-to, in Monkey Jungle Town."

He shook his head and closed his eyes, then put his face in his palm and rubbed his head with his strong fingers.

"Gunner," Mudo said.

"I don't know. Maybe I'm wrong. Maybe it's fine out there, now. Maybe everything's normal. Maybe they found a cure. Maybe there's water in the faucets and cars in the street, football on TV... Maybe we're having babies again."

"Gunner."

Gunner shook his head.

"Gunner. Ben."

Gunner-Ben looked up and turned back to Mudo. Slowly, he returned to the present and his pupils sharpened. He looked slightly confused, like he'd just woken from a dream and wasn't sure if he was still in it—or if the dream was reality or reality was the dream.

"What?"

"What did Islamic F-f-front do?"

"What?"

"What'd they do? Why'd you h-h-hit the boat? Why'd you need the monkey?"

Gunner looked around and gathered his senses, fixing himself back in the boat, back in the present. He locked back on the ocean, and Mudo, and War Dog smiling in the bow.

"They made a virus," he stated.

"A v-v-v-virus?"

"Yes. That makes you sterile. If you survive. By now, every single... Wait."

Suddenly, he turned on Mudo.

"Wait, what'd you say?"

"Wh-wh-what'd Islamic Front do?"

"You can... talk?"

Slowly, Mudo grinned like a thief.

"I can... s-s-stutter."

"Wha... Whoa, hang on. How..." Gunner stared, amazed, then tilted his head back and laughed. "Hahahahaa... Jesus! You can talk? And hear?"

"How am I supposed ta t-t-talk if I can't hear?"

"Hahaha! This whole time, you could talk?"

"And hear."

"But... why?"

"I never said I couldn't t-t-talk."

Gunner stared stuck, suddenly speechless, completely yanked from his memories and anchored back in the present, in the revelation that Mudo could talk. And hear.

"It's dangerous to... talk."

"What?"

"It's one of our greatest threats. And they say you shouldn't... Talk, unless you can improve on the silence. But you know what happens then, if you don't... Talk? Everyone talks to you. Nobody shuts up. You know how much stuff p-p-people tell you when they think you can't... Hear, and you can't interrupt them to shut them up? Even when you're talking, people aren't listening. They're just waiting for you to stop talking so they can start talking again. I heard that somewhere. Because I was listening."

Gunner's jaw slacked and mouth parted, dumbfounded.

"It's dangerous to hear, too. I've heard too much. I'm the spy who knows too much. I'm tired of hearing everyone's... Secrets. You'd think it'd be fun but it's not. They're secrets for a reason. It's like watching people shit. Really. I'm sorry but it is. It's like watching them shit out all the crap they're trying to hide and pretend they don't have jammed up in them, stuffed in their... Bowels before they shit it out to the world. You know Blacky likes to draw pictures of women's feet? And Santiago is almost convinced he'd sleep with his m-m-mom if he had to ta save her life, although I don't know why he even debates that, since she's dead. Cazador sleep with that fat girl, Barb. So did A-awol. Awol deserted the Army because he went to war for so long that his wife left him for another man. These are deeply flawed people… Humans. We're crazy. The only ones who aren't are the ones you don't know well enough. Some other guy said that. Undertaker, he was spying for S-simian and knew B-bonesetter murdered Winter but didn't tell Santa, because Intel gave him a gold coin so he could buy some porcelain dolls he collects. Porcelain dolls. All that time, Tuck was marking off places on his map and making notes in his journal, looking for his… Dad, and Undertaker didn't say anything so he could get a… Doll? Cazador fears La S-s-sucia, and Gambler fears La LLorona, like… Goddesses. Dark ones. Don Granada said a man wants to worship a w-w-woman like a Goddess because we want to worship what gave us life. But Gambler's wife drowned his son in a river that was two feet deep because Gambler slept with a younger… Woman. Bonesetter hacked Polito in the achilles with a machete when they were chased so he'd fall and the howlers would eat him. But he didn't die. No, not Polito. He's survived worse. But that's my point, it's shit. All the way through. And when you play with shit you get shit on you. I said that. So your… Problems, with the padre, don't worry about it, because it's just shit. That's just how it is. God tells us to be pure, then throws that at us? What the hell were you supposed to do? What kind of choice is that? Save your conscience or the world? You know, you actually sacrificed yourself for the world. I mean, God'll never forgive you for what you d-d-did for sure, and your conscience is shattered, so you actually sacrificed your a-a-afterlife for everyone else. God, and the world, didn't need an angel there to make that decision. They needed the devil. Don Granada told me something like that once, in Cartagena, when I was his bellhop, at the Royal Canadian Hotel, after he saved my life when I was sh-sh-shived by a c-c-choir boy. Then we left to escape Bonesetter and start a new life for his family. He used to be a good man, you know… Bonesetter. We all start off that way, good, Don Granada said. Some last longer than others and others lie to themselves that's all, but if you're around long enough at the end it's just fucking and blood and shit and shit and fucking… except Isadora. She was special. She floated a half inch above the earth, you know? He played Russian roulette to save her. She was his Goddess. And they're together in heaven now, laughing. That makes me happy. She died when we crossed the Interior. We lost her there. Put her in a hole. I stopped t-t-talking after that. Just didn't have anything to say for a while, I guess. One day turned into the next, and the next turned into a year. Then we got to town and people told me things, which was useful to Don Granada. So I became his spy. You can never have too many spies. Spies are one of our greatest threats. And women. Women and spies. But Don Granada wanted what was best for his family, that's all, but that was too hard, the In-interior. To survive something like that. Some days, we didn't go more than a kilometer the whole day, in there. It wasn't the ja-ja-jaguars or jungle or being lost that got me the most. Not even the snakes or sleeping on the ground. Actually, the snakes were horrible. And the jaguars. They followed us. Tracked us. It was the insects. They were the worst. After the jaguars. The little things, eating you alive slowly from the outside, burrowing in. Mosquitos, ants, scabies, stomach parasites, sand fleas, k-k-kissing bugs... You know why're they're called k-kissing bugs? Because they bite your face. I'm never going back in there. The Interior. And even after all that, B-bonesetter ended up finding us anyway, eight years later. But he loved Santa and his son in his own way, not to free them, but to possess them. Maybe that's not love, I don't know. But Don Granada didn't talk about losing Isadora. Even though we used to sit by his fire in the Ranchero at night and drink dark Caribbean rum with brown sugar and tell stories. All those stories. And all those stories about him and Barboza were true. The Mad Czar, Marrakech, the minefield near Siwa... Talk about risky. But the greatest one to me, Barboza once told me, and Barboza was with him for ages, in other lives, ask Mulata, Barboza said that in London once he spied Don Granada put money in Barboza's parking meter when Don Granada happened to walk by and see it'd expired. That's all. Simple like that. That's how he was. There for ya, you know? It's not shit, man. It's really not. I lied. I'm sorry, but I lied. It's beautiful. The struggle and pain and ravages of time, even the loss in some sad way, and the people you freed and the ones who freed you. It's beautiful. Too beautiful for words I guess. My words anyway."

Gunner stared. He'd never, in his whole life, heard anything like that.

"I'll shut up now."

"No no, go on. You got a few things rattling around in your coconut up there. All that input without enough output, it's gotta be... unhealthy."

"I have... nerves."

"Nerves? You're scared of your own fucken shadow! But you're here aren't you? You said you wouldn't go back in the Interior but you got the burros and were gonna take me. You got the dynamite and tripped Gambler, pulled Don Granada out of the Cantina... That's grit man. More grit than most men got. Going when you're scared. Every time."

Mudo smiled slightly at the thought.

"A choir boy?"

"There were four of them."

"Hahahahaaa..."

Mudo said people confessed to him because they didn't think he could hear. Gunner had done just that. They'd confessed to each other and felt better, because it externalized the past into stories they told themselves. The past was just a story. The present was beautiful and light. And the future...

"So," Mudo said, after the moment had trailed off, "this virus..."

"You're sterile."

"What?"

"So am I. We all are. Every single male on the planet is sterile now. Except Islamic Front fighters. And Jinx."

"Sterile?"

"Ya, but the women are fine. Every women who could have babies before still can. Your sister, your girlfriend, your wife... But now, only terrorists can impregnate them. And Jinx."

Mudo stared.

"It's called milk, the virus, after milk al-yamin, the idea they have that they're allowed to rape kafirs. To cleanse them. Convert infidels with their cocks. It's biologic jihad. Rape. And they weaponized it, chemically. By now, it's probably killed about eighty percent of the men on earth and sterilized the rest. They're going to breed us off the face of the earth. If you're childless, you'll never be a father. If you're a father, you'll never be a grandparent. But your wife might. Every single ancestor you've had for millions of years has reproduced, except you. You and your bloodline will die—unless we get the anti-virus. That's nature. That's how it is. Survival of the fittest, and they out-fitted us."

Mudo looked petrified.

"Jinx's got the anti-virus in him, from the monkey, that's why we needed the monkey, and hit the ship, but he's not a good man. He'll use the anti-virus to raise an army and a harem of Amazon women. They own the surface now, IF and Jinx. You know what kind of power he has? The power to give babies. To give life, like a God."

Mudo stared shell shocked.

It was the most stunned look Gunner had ever seen, so he chuckled. He laughed slowly at first, then harder when Mudo stayed stuck and didn't blink. It was a slow, churning, volcanic laugh from the pit of his stomach, because Mudo's reaction was right; it was too much. It was all too much. Iraq, string codes, the Albatross and sea. The beach, palms, jungle and town. A winter warrior and starship son. Butcher and Bumster. Don Granada and Bar-bozo, stationed at a lost outpost for the end of days. Three salt water tides washing over Captain Kidd's broken neck, the slave mines of Hanuman, and that son of a bitch Jan Jeffers. The eel whores in the swamp shanties speaking bastardized swamp slang to shrink Blacky's head while it was still in his skull, and Mulata in her leopard den, smelling like creosote before the monsoon. Sun and moon. Glossy lips and sixties hips. Paradise and peace. Until the dog. Cadejo. Peace be upon him. And skull-fuck his enemies with the death angel of God. Castaways all, washed ashore. The deserter and doctor, self-taught. The scout and hunter, hunted by La Sucia's horse's head. The gambler gambling memories of memories forgotten for fate-time. Lost memories to find and ghosts to forget. Blood crows and blue crabs. Harpía eagles and trogons riding thermals. Howlers of unusual size. And fire. Fire in the wild like fire on the water, in the chase through the thicket with the wicked to the hole. To murder. To deceit and defeat and the death of Don Granada, taking his seat at the table of kings, in a room hollow like a tomb, with stone soldiers standing eternal watch. But gun. There was gun, like always, to lay waste to the world and wash it clean with blood, with Papa Ghede and Santa Muerte, and shadows without eyes in El Pozo. And then Barboza's battle and Gambler's goodbye, while the wind howled through cracks in the planks, until everything was reduced to rubble to regenerate, and only shell-shocked tsunami survivors remained, stranded on the beach, watching them paddle out, towards sterile womb death across the apocalypse divide.

Ya, it was too much. So much that Gunner's eyes filled with tears as he laughed. A man could only take so much, and he'd taken it all.

Mudo watched worried at first, but Gunner's laugh was so genuine, contagious and cathartic that a smile crept up Mudo's face and he began chuckle-laughing too. What else could they do? It was so bad they might as well smile, because they were doomed. Everyone was doomed. Death loomed and they couldn't stop it, so why worry about it? For now, they had a bellhop and boat and air in their lungs—and a fight—and that was enough.

So they floated in the cayuco, in the current off-coast, laughing at life as it shredded its own flesh, wrecking the weak to grow stronger from within. Savage and relentless. Catastrophic and total. And beautiful, in a way.

Eventually, Mudo's laugh tapered to a long, cathartic sigh, and he smiled up coast, to the fight at the end of the world.

"So, where're we going?" He asked.

Gunner caught his breath and pinched the bridge of his nose, then he sighed too, and nodded. Ya, maybe Mudo was right. Maybe an angel couldn't save this world. Maybe God needed the Devil to do it.

"To find Jinx.

"To get his blood.

"And save the world."

Copyright

FIRST EDITION
Updated January 2019

Kendle E-Pub Edition:
ISBN: **978-0-9961147-3-8**

CreateSpace Paperback Edition:
ISBN: **978-0-9961147-2-1**

Monkey Jungle Town

Also by Dug Popovich:

Dad School

Also by Roland Minez:

At the Limit of Complexity – British Military Operations in North Persia and the Caucasus 1918

pop@firebasez.com

Firebase Z
Instagram - firebasez
www.firebasez.com